Praise for the million-copy selling

Sophie McKenzie

'Brilliant . . . you can't stop reading' Robert Muchamore

'Will have you gripped for hours' *Sunday Express*

'Sophie McKenzie is the queen of nail-biting, page-turning and addictive reads' Amy Alward

'Please read this book: it is brilliant!' *Guardian*

'Whenever I hear the phrase "YA thriller" I only ever think of one name – Sophie McKenzie. Why? Because nobody does it better' Phil Earle

'Brilliantly described, scary and touching' *The Daily Mirror*

'Page-turning' *Independent*

BY SOPHIE MCKENZIE

THE MISSING SERIES
Girl, Missing
Sister, Missing
Missing Me

THE MEDUSA PROJECT
The Set-Up
The Hostage
The Rescue
Hunted
Double-Cross
Hit Squad

LUKE AND EVE SERIES
Six Steps to a Girl
Three's a Crowd
The One and Only

FLYNN SERIES
Falling Fast
Burning Bright
Casting Shadows
Defy the Stars

Blood Ties
Blood Ransom

Split Second
Every Second Counts

Sophie McKenzie
HIDE AND SECRETS
SIMON & SCHUSTER

First published in Great Britain in 2021
by Simon & Schuster UK Ltd

3 5 7 9 10 8 6 4 2

Simon & Schuster UK Ltd
1st Floor, 222 Gray's Inn Road, London
WC1X 8HB

www.simonandschuster.co.uk
www.simonandschuster.com.au
www.simonandschuster.co.in

Simon & Schuster Australia, Sydney
Simon & Schuster India, New Delhi

A CIP catalogue record for this book is available from
the British Library.

PB ISBN 978-1-4711-9910-3
eBook ISBN 978-1-4711-9911-0
eAudio ISBN 978-1-4711-9912-7

Typeset in the UK by Sorrel Packham
Printed and bound by CPI Group (UK) Ltd, Croydon, CR0 4YY

To Daniel, Thomas and Jack McCarthy

1

Until the message arrived, there was no doubt in my mind: my dad was dead.

This wasn't the only thing I was certain about.

Back then, on that sunny morning in late July, I was also sure that the summer would end without me having a single friend, and that nothing exciting was ever going to happen to me while I lived in boring Brockledore.

As it turned out, on all those counts I was wrong . . .

Bess and I are sitting on a rug in the back garden, under the shade of the oak tree. I'm about to stroll over to the Barn. My head is already there, imagining the dress I've just pinned out, ready to cut. But Bess is finishing a drawing, and I know she'll want to show it to me when she's done. Her tongue peeks out from between her lips as she concentrates on the last few strokes of her colouring pen. We don't look anything alike, Bess and I. She's got Dad's brown eyes and a heart-shaped face, framed by long, fine blonde hair that's always escaping the bands Mum plaits it into.

I'm fairer-skinned with blue eyes. And my hair is short and spiky – like me.

'Cat! *Cat!*' Mum is calling from the house. I can just see her pink rope sandals out of the corner of my eye. I don't look up. Everything about her is Just. So. Irritating.

'What does she want now?' I mutter.

'*Cat!*' The pink sandals stomp across the grass.

Bess stiffens. She hates it when Mum and I get mad with each other.

'Why didn't you answer?' Mum demands, arriving at the edge of the rug. She waves her arms in the air so violently that her bangles collide in a clash of tinkles. 'I was calling for ages.'

'Sorry,' I say, trying to keep the fact that I'm not at all sorry out of my voice. 'I was *miles* away.' I'm deliberately using one of Mum's favourite phrases. She tends to flutter her hands when she uses it, presumably to indicate how easily distracted she gets by alternate spiritual planes.

Mum glares at me, clearly picking up on my sarcastic undertones. She has clients today, so she's wearing one of her waftier outfits: a crimson sundress with rainbow chiffon frills under a fringed pink shawl that's pinned to the straps of her dress with several of her astrological sign brooches.

Mum's a celebrity astrologer who used to be famous. Not movie-star-level famous, but well-known enough that people would stare when she took me to primary school. I *loved* that when I was little. Back then she had a weekly slot on a morning TV show to run through 'what the stars have in store this weekend'. She denies it if anyone asks, but I reckon she'd give anything to be back there on the nation's screens every week. She certainly laps it up when anyone recognizes her now.

'There's something I need you to do this morning, Cat,' she says, brushing a stray red curl off her face. I know for a fact Mum's hair is really as straight and dark as my own, but she seems to think her clients prefer wild red curls washed through with hot-pink streaks.

'What?' I gaze up at her warily.

'Darling, don't look at me like that.' She sighs. 'You need to clear all your . . . your *scraps* out of the barn this morning.'

My jaw drops. '*What?*'

'And once you've done that, a quick dust and vacuum. Right now, Cat, please?'

'But that's so unfair!' I blurt out, my voice rising to a shout.

I can't believe it. The Barn is a cottage on the other side of our back garden. Mum has plans to use it next year as a guest house for her wealthy clients, but right now it's empty. The attic room there, with its wall of glass windows, is the perfect place for me to spread out my designs and store all the fabrics I've accumulated since I started dress-making earlier this year.

'Why do I have to clear my stuff out?' I protest. Beside me, Bess tenses with anxiety. I try to swallow down my temper. 'I've pinned a dress with a skirt I'm going to cut on the bias. It's all laid out like I want it.'

Mum frowns. 'Mrs Trimble's already picked your bits and pieces off the floor. They're in boxes by the Barn front door.'

'What?' I leap to my feet, my fury surging uncontrollably. 'But I'm in the middle of making my dress. Why did she do that?'

'Because I asked her to,' Mum snaps. 'But it left her short on time, which is why you need to run the vacuum cleaner round to make the place—'

'No! *Please*, Mum, I *need* the Barn. I'm *using* it.'

Mum glares at me. 'Well, you can't use it any more,' she snaps. 'Now hurry up – the Tuesdays will be here in a couple of hours.'

What is she talking about?

'Who are the Tuesdays?' I demand.

Mum rolls her eyes. 'The mosaic specialist who's going

to renovate the courtyard, and his son. They'll be staying in the Barn for a few weeks. I'm sure I told you about them the other day, Cat.'

My jaw drops. This is typical Mum, ruining my life in order to spend money on stuff we don't need. It's ironic: she's always making out how spiritual she is, but the truth is she's been super-materialistic ever since Dad died.

Bess tugs at the hem of my shorts. I glance down at her. She stamps her foot; it's her signal that I should stop arguing.

I ignore it.

'So you're saying that not only do I have to give up all my plans to make dresses in the Barn, but a random man and his random son are moving into it? For the whole summer?'

'Stop making such a ridiculous fuss.' Mum's bangles clink loudly again as she points in the direction of the barn. 'Fetch your boxes so the poor Tuesdays don't trip over them, then dust and vacuum. *Now.*'

She stomps off, leaving me open-mouthed. Bess tugs at my shorts again. I glance down. She makes a goofy face, sticking out her tongue and crossing her eyes. She can see I'm upset and is trying to make me laugh.

Something twists in my stomach. 'I'm fine,' I say.

Bess raises her eyebrows as if to ask: *really*?

I nod. 'Really.'

She goes back to her drawing: a puppy with dark splodges on its white fur and a dark brown patch over one eye. Bess has been obsessed with puppies ever since our dog, Pirate, was run over the week before Dad died. Because she's mean, Mum refuses to let us have another pet, so Bess draws one new 'Pirate' after another. Her pictures are amazing. Way better than you'd expect from an average almost-seven-year-old. We both get our creative talent from Dad. He worked in a fancy jewellery shop, but he always said he was really a frustrated designer.

He died on his boat, in a storm out at sea almost eighteen months ago. I still miss him every day: the way he let me put golden syrup on my toast when Mum wasn't looking; how he took me and Bess out sailing every weekend, always happy, even when it poured with rain. And his huge goodnight hugs that smelled of soap and sawdust, that made me feel like I was totally safe and that nothing bad could ever happen.

'I'd better go to the Barn.' I force a smile for Bess's sake. Before we lost Dad, she used to irritate me. I was mean to her, always telling her off for following me around or teasing her for playing with stupid dolls even though she was only little. She used to say stuff like, 'please let me play, Cat, please'. And I'd always run off too fast for her to follow, her wails echoing in my ears.

I hate how I acted then.

She's almost seven now, and I'd give anything to have her ask me to let her play.

But she doesn't ask. In fact, she doesn't say anything at all.

Bess hasn't said a word – to anyone – since Dad died. For the first few months, Mum kept saying we just needed to give her time. But it's been well over a year now and Bess has got into the habit of not saying anything at all.

Worse, we've all got into the habit of not expecting her to.

The cardboard boxes full of my sewing stuff are just inside the front door of the Barn. The fabric for the dress I've been pinning is in a jumbled heap in the top box, the pattern fluttering loose and to the side. Pinning anything cut on the bias is really tricky. It took me ages to get the pattern in exactly the right place and now I'll have to start all over again.

The vacuum cleaner stands expectantly next to the stack of boxes. I glare at it. This is so unfair. There's nowhere in the house with enough space and light for me to do my dressmaking and Mum knows it. My bedroom is small and gloomy. I've been wanting to move into the spare room for ages – it's huge with lots of space and big windows that let in loads of natural light, perfect for dressmaking. But Mum keeps it cluttered to bursting point with crystals and astrological ornaments and all the old designer outfits she doesn't have room for in her wardrobe.

I pick up the boxes, anger still hot in my chest. No way am I doing the stupid dusting and vacuum-cleaning. I stomp off across the courtyard then around the side of our house. I dump the boxes in the front porch. I'll pick them up later; right now I have to get away from Mum. From all of it.

I hurry along the drive and into the woods. I pick my way along the winding path down through the trees to the road, then stroll the fifty metres or so into the village. Brockledore is tiny: there's a pub, a grocery store with a post office, a cafe that sells chips and sandwiches and an antique showroom, as well as a handful of pottery shops and boutiques selling old-fashioned clothes.

I stand at the war memorial opposite the bus stop and gaze along the familiar high street, resentment burning inside me. I used to walk down here with Dad sometimes. He'd always give me some cash to spend on sweets in the grocery store and everyone we passed on the way would say 'hello'. Dad would never have let Mum take the Barn attic away from me. He'd understand why I needed it. Yes, if he was still here, he wouldn't let Mum be so greedy, basing all her decisions on how much money she can either spend or make. He'd let Bess have another dog and he *definitely* wouldn't allow a couple of strangers to live in the Barn over the summer to make a stupid mosaic in the stupid courtyard.

But Dad is gone.

And Mum is determined to make my life miserable.

Learning to pin and sew designs is basically all I've wanted to do for the past six months. Mum just doesn't understand. I've found something for myself that's a million miles away from the way she uses astrology to manipulate money out of people. Dressmaking is creative, like Dad was – I can lose myself in it. Now I don't know what I'm going to do for the rest of the summer holidays. It's not like I've got any friends I can hang out with.

Feeling sulky and cross, I wander back through the woods that lead home. The sun is shining and the birds are singing, but with every step I feel more depressed. I emerge from the trees on to the lane that leads up to our house. My phone rings and I glance down. I don't recognize the number.

I've been told a million times to be wary of random callers. But that isn't why I reject this call – I just don't feel like talking to anyone. The sun beats down on my head, the only sound the crunch of the gravel under my feet and the soft sway of the trees in the breeze. My phone rings again.

Man, they're persistent.

I close the call again and am just about to block the number, when my phone pings with a text. I gaze down. It's the same caller.

Hello, Cat. I'm Rik. A friend of your dad's. I'd like to talk to you.

My stomach contracts with shock. A creeping anxiety twists through me. Dad's been dead for a year and a half. How would a friend of his have my number? And why would they be calling me and not Mum?

This feels wrong. Another message:

Please call me, Cat. I need to tell you something. It's important.

Why doesn't he text whatever it is? Whoever this Rik is, he's doing all the wrong things to get me to speak to him.

Irritated, I text back:

What's so important?

I wait for a second, my finger hovering over the block icon. And then a third message comes through. An answer to my question that makes so little sense it feels like my brain is crashing.

Your dad is alive.

2

My legs give way.

I sink to the ground, the earth warm and rough against my skin.

Your dad is alive.

I stare at the message, my head spinning. Images from the one-year memorial service we had for Dad back in February flash through my mind: Bess pale, clutching a doll. Mum's eyes hidden behind dark glasses. Everyone watching us. A glimpse of white flowers. Then my shoes, as I look down, only seeing my feet walking over the wooden floor.

That day I ached with the pain of missing Dad, my head full of the crazy fantasy that any second he might somehow walk in and grin at me and say: *Let's get out of here!*

Is it possible he could still be alive? For a split second, a tidal wavc of hope surges through me.

Then common sense washes it away.

No. Not after the police investigation and the coroner's report and all the time that has passed. There's *no way*.

Another message pings through.

Please call me. We need to talk.

Who is this Rik? Why is he sending me this lie? Why does he want to talk to me?

The answer shoots into my head: it's a wind-up. *Has* to be.

I gasp, sick to my stomach. Who would do such a mean, horrible thing?

That's easy. There are plenty of girls at school who don't like me.

It wasn't always like that. Up to my second term in Year Eight I got on with almost everyone. And my best friend, Cindy, and I hung out all the time. But, after Dad died that winter, everything changed. Cindy and some of the other girls kept asking if I was all right, and I just kept saying I was fine. Not because I was – obviously – but because I didn't know what else to say. Anyway, eventually everyone except Cindy stopped asking, and by the summer term my status had slid from averagely popular to total outcast. Which was when Delilah Jenkins decided to glue my cardigan to the table in art, then make out it was my fault for leaving the top off the glue pot.

From then on I was an easy target: the year group weirdo who barely said a word outside of lessons. Even Cindy backed off, leaving me, officially, as the friendless freak they'd all decided I was anyway.

But why would any of those girls wind me up during the holidays? It's not like I'm on any of their social media. The clothes I make get some likes on Instagram, but none of those come from people I know. In fact, I've heard from literally nobody since school ended. Why would they contact me now, pretending to be a friend of my dad's?

Another message from 'Rik' pings on to my phone. I snatch it up.

Cat, are you there? What's the problem? Are you alone?

Fear crawls over me like a spider. Never mind the mean girls at school, maybe this is some weird internet stalker?

Anger rises like bile, overpowering the fear. I'm not going to let some crazy stranger intimidate me.

I stab at the open screen.

How did you know my dad?

I press send and wait. My heart thuds furiously against my ribs, drowning out the birds and the breeze that ruffles the leaves over my head.

A minute later and there's a reply:

We worked together at Ballena Jewellery. Please, Cat. I'm going to try calling you again in one minute. Please answer.

I hesitate, more confused than ever. Dad *did* work at Ballena jewellery. He got a job there a couple of years before he died. Is it possible this Rik person is genuine?

I quickly type another message:

How do I know you were really friends?

A short pause and then an even shorter message.

Kitterbug.

I gasp, my whole body trembling. Kitterbug was my dad's nickname for me when I was little. Nobody else has ever called me that.

Cat, are you alone yet?

My head spins. I type quickly:

No

It's a lie, of course, but I need time to think. Another short pause, then Rik writes again.

Okay. Call me when you're alone. Tell no one. I'll explain everything.

I can't stay on this number for long. Call me by 1pm.

A shiver snakes down my spine. I check the time: 12.28 p.m. I set down my phone, trying to let what has just happened sink in.

What if this Rik guy is telling the truth?

What if Dad really is still alive?

My heart hammers against my ribs as I stumble along the lane. Around the corner and our house comes into view. A battered estate laden with cases and bags is parked alongside Mum's gleaming pink car. I don't give it a second thought.

The sky overhead is clear and blue. The air is hot and still. But there's a storm in my head. Rik's words crash against my skull.

Your dad is alive.

It can't be true. I crunch over the gravel of our driveway. Past the cars. I'm at the front door now. I take a deep breath and let it out slowly.

Except . . . what if it *is* true?

Suddenly I know that I need to speak to Rik. Hear what he has to say.

I hurry inside, letting the front door slam shut behind me.

'Cat! Where on earth have you been?' Mum's sharp voice cuts through my thoughts.

I spin round. She's just emerged from the kitchen, arms spread out so that the pink fringe of her shawl flutters like the wings of an exotic bird.

'Mum, I—'

'At least you're here now.' She cuts me off, glaring as if to indicate I need to watch what I say. A second later I realize why, as a man steps out from behind her. He's tall and black, with closely cropped hair and a warm, kind smile.

'Hi, there,' he says, stepping forward with his hand outstretched.

'This is Mr Tuesday, the mosaic restoration specialist,' Mum says primly. 'My daughter Cat.'

I shake his hand awkwardly, my eyes on the stairs. It's 12.32. I have just half an hour to make the call to Rik. I need to get up to the privacy of my room as soon as possible.

'And this is my son, Tyler.' The man steps aside.

I wait, impatiently, expecting a little boy to emerge from the kitchen. But it's a teenager who appears. Fairer than his dad, his skin the colour of almond butter, and tall. Not just tall, I realize, but upright and straight-backed. A faded T-shirt hangs perfectly from his broad shoulders. My stomach drops away inside me. He looks like a model. His brown eyes fix, unsmiling, on mine.

'Hi,' he says, holding up his hand.

'Hi.' It's like there's sandpaper in my throat.

Mum gazes at me, a slight frown creasing the centre of her forehead. 'Tyler's the same age as you, Cat,' she says. 'Isn't that nice?'

I stare at her, blankly. Mum's eyes flare with exasperation, then she spins towards Tyler, placing her hand on his arm and half closing her eyes. It's a gesture I've seen her make a million times with her clients. Usually they gaze eagerly at her, desperate for her spiritual insights, but Tyler just watches, a wary expression on his face.

'Ah,' Mum breathes softly. 'I sense the pain. The last thief is death and he always leaves a mark.'

How embarrassing. Tyler and his dad are both looking at her like she's mad. I shove my hand in my pocket. My fingertips find the warm plastic of my phone. Another minute has ticked by while I'm standing here, doing nothing.

Your dad is alive.

I take a sideways step towards the stairs.

Mum's hand flicks up, the tiny stars on her nail varnish catching the light. 'I thought so,' she says with a gentle sigh. 'You're radiating a very high empathic frequency, Tyler.'

I wince. It's bad enough her going on about stupid

astrology all the time but I really hate it when she gets all 'fake psychic', especially in front of complete strangers. The hall clock is now saying 12.35.

'Am I?' Tyler sounds baffled.

'Um . . .' Mr Tuesday is clearly lost for words.

I turn away and hurry to the stairs.

'Cat!' Mum snaps.

I freeze, then turn to face her. Her eyes flash a warning at me. I grip the bannisters. Surely I'm free to go now?

'Cat, show the Tuesdays around the Barn, please,' Mum orders.

What? My heart thuds against my ribs. *No.* I need to call Rik.

'Me?' I stare at her. 'No . . . Mum, I can't.'

'Of course you can,' Mum insists, steel in her voice.

I glare at her. How dare she order me about?

Ignoring my stare, Mum turns to Mr Tuesday. 'I'm afraid I have a client in a few minutes. Please spend the rest of the day settling in. I'll pop over later when you've had a chance to look at the mosaic. I can't wait to get your expert guidance on the renovations. Just a quick question . . . is it likely to be noisy?'

Mr Tuesday frowns, clearly confused.

'It's just . . .' Mum laughs. 'Well, as a fellow artist I am sure you'll understand. I do highly sensitive work with my clients, so my appointments have to take precedence if any of the renovations are likely to *disturb*.'

I grit my teeth, embarrassed now as well as furious. Typical Mum to assume her needs are more important than everyone else's.

'Mosaic work doesn't usually involve too much noise,' Mr Tuesday says with a gentle smile. 'But I'll let you know when I've taken a look.' His voice is deep and dignified. Unlike Mum, fluttering about with her constant hand gestures, he moves slowly and calmly.

'Right, then.' Mum sounds flustered.

I glance at Tyler. Heat creeps up my cheeks as he meets my gaze and raises an eyebrow. He must be able to see how embarrassed Mum makes me, how desperate I am to get away.

Mum turns back to me, lowering her voice so that only I can hear her. 'Now, Cat, please,' she hisses, 'or you'll be grounded for the rest of the week.'

3

I think quickly. So long as there's no more standing about and talking, twenty-five minutes is more than enough time to walk the Tuesdays to the Barn, show them around quickly and get back to my room to call Rik.

'Fine,' I say reluctantly. 'I'll take them to the Barn.'

Mum glares at me, clearly appalled by how sulky she thinks I'm being, then flits away.

'This way.' I lead the Tuesdays outside. As I cross the uneven patio I wonder if I should warn Mr Tuesday to watch his step – Mum always does when clients come out here. But when I look around, he's already striding purposefully on to our lawn, looking around at the trees and flowers round the sides and the high brick wall behind. I sneak a sideways glance at Tyler. He's also gazing around, his jaw hanging open.

'What pretty delphiniums,' Mr Tuesday says approvingly. 'And just look at those roses.'

'It's so big,' Tyler adds. 'Nobody's garden is this big in London.'

I fidget from foot to foot. Inside my pocket, my hand curls around my phone.

'The Barn's this way,' I say, impatiently.

'After you, Cat,' Mr Tuesday says.

I lead the two of them across the grass and around the wall to the courtyard. The Barn stands opposite us, with the apple orchard beyond to the right.

'What a lovely old building,' Mr Tuesday says. He has a soft, calm way of speaking. I can't imagine him ever getting angry. I follow his gaze to the Barn. I guess it is old, though I've never thought about it before. It's made of pale stone and is much smaller than the main house.

'Ah, here's the mosaic . . .' Mr Tuesday gazes down at the courtyard, his eyes gleaming with interest.

I haven't looked at the courtyard mosaic in ages. Set around an old stone sundial, it's supposed to be a horoscope showing the signs of the zodiac, but at least half the tiles are damaged, with weeds poking up all over the place. The inner circle of star-shaped tiles around the sundial is still intact, but the outer rim is almost completely gone, while three of the twelve huge star signs in between are completely missing.

'Oh, dear, this is a mess,' says Mr Tuesday with feeling. He crouches down to take a closer look. 'We'll have our work cut out for us here, Ty.'

Tyler leans against the wall, watching him. My fingers feel sweaty on my phone.

'Er, sorry to rush you,' I say, 'but I really need to show you inside now.'

'All right, then.' Mr Tuesday straightens up. 'Now who's this?' He smiles, as Bess tiptoes around the corner of the Barn, her drawing book tucked under one arm.

'That's my sister,' I say, immediately feeling defensive. Strangers always expect Bess to speak. I can't bear the look of pity on their faces when you tell them she can't. 'Her name's Bess, but she doesn't like to talk.'

'Well, hello, Bess,' Mr Tuesday says kindly.

Bess gives him a quick wave, glances once at Tyler, then hurries away.

I usher the Tuesdays into the Barn. The front door opens on to an open-plan living area, with sofas and a big TV straight ahead and a kitchen area to the right.

'Very nice,' Mr Tuesday says approvingly. 'From the outside, I wasn't expecting it to be so modern. Eh, Tyler?'

'I guess,' Tyler says with a self-conscious shrug. He pulls out his phone and peers at the screen. A look of disappointment settles over his face. I wonder if he has someone – a girlfriend or boyfriend – back in London.

'Look, your mother's left us a box of groceries,' Mr

Tuesday says, wandering over to the kitchen area. 'That's kind of her.'

'Yeah, and there's some cleaning stuff in the cupboards, and that –' I point to a door under the stairs – 'that's a downstairs loo. Let's go up now.'

'Sure.' If Mr Tuesday is feeling rushed he doesn't show it. He and Tyler follow me up to the first-floor landing.

'Two bedrooms and a bathroom,' I say, pointing to each door in turn.

I check the time. 12.42. I still have eighteen minutes to get to my room and make my call. I tap my fingers against the landing wall while Mr Tuesday and Tyler explore the rooms. I don't know what they're looking at. The bedrooms are plain and empty – apart from the beds, wardrobes and curtains. It couldn't be more different from our house, with its crazy prints and ornaments everywhere.

'Look, Ty,' Mr Tuesday says, peering out of the back bedroom window. 'It's an apple orchard. What varieties do you grow here?'

I stare at him blankly. 'Er, sorry, I don't know.'

'I bet you'll know this . . .' Tyler says. It's the first time he's spoken directly to me.

'What?' I ask, feeling self-conscious.

'Where can I get Wi-Fi?'

‘There isn’t any in the Barn,’ I explain. ‘It’s not great in the house either. Patchy.’

Tyler’s face falls.

‘I know, it sucks. Maybe if you ask Mum she’ll fix it up for you.’ I fidget from foot to foot. 12.47. Thirteen minutes.

‘Well, I think there’s a lot to be said for a little less internet.’ Mr Tuesday chuckles. ‘Eh, Tyler?’

Tyler makes a face. He doesn’t seem wound up though. I’m getting the impression that he and his dad actually get on really well.

‘Just the attic left to see,’ I say, hurrying across the landing. ‘There’s another bedroom up there.’

‘You go on, Tyler, I’m happy with this one.’ Mr Tuesday turns back to the window.

I race up the second set of stairs to the top floor. Tyler lollops after me.

I’m itching to tell him to hurry up.

The Barn’s attic is a big room, though the roof slopes dramatically on either side, meaning the portion you can stand up in isn’t huge. There’s a double bed in the middle of the room and a window seat that runs the length of the huge window. I gaze at the expanse of floor between the window and the bed which, just yesterday, was covered in the fabric for the dress I was making.

'Wow,' Tyler says.

I check the time on my phone again. 12.50. Time to leave.

'There's a shower room too,' I gabble, pointing to a door on the left.

I take a step back, towards the landing.

'Three bathrooms in a house for two people,' Tyler drawls. 'We're not going to smell while we're here, are we?'

He smiles. It transforms his face, all the intensity falling away and his eyes lighting up with warmth. For a second, I'm transfixed. His eyes are beautiful: a hint of gold shining through the brown.

'I have to go,' I say, backing away and hoping he can't see that I'm blushing.

Tyler stares at me. Feeling overwhelmed, I turn and fly out of the room, down the stairs and out of the Barn. Across the shade of the courtyard and on to the lawn, where the sun beats down on my face.

As I enter the house, I can hear Mum greeting her client. 'Welcome, *such* a wonderful day for a reading. Jupiter is in retrograde, the perfect time to reflect on visions, ideals and beliefs. This way.'

I race up to my room and shut the door firmly behind me. It's 12.54. I still have six minutes.

My fingers fumble as I find Rik's number. I hesitate for a moment, then press video call. I need to see his face. It'll be easier to tell if he's lying that way.

I keep my own video off.

The top of the screen fills with a fuzzy picture: the edge of a table, a door opening. It's someone moving. A blur, then a man's face appears. He's younger than Mum and Dad, but still lots older than me. Beads of sweat glint on his forehead.

'Cat? Is that you?' he asks. 'Are you there?'

'Yes,' I say. 'It's me.'

A look of relief fills his face. 'Oh, thank goodness. Cat, I'm Rik Adamski.' The hint of a smile lifts the corners of his mouth. 'I know this is a shock, but it's true. Your dad is alive.'

Hearing the words said out loud whips the ground out from underneath me. I sink on to my bed.

'Cat?' Rik peers more closely at the screen. 'Did you realize your video is off?'

I take a deep breath, trying to focus.

Rik blinks, anxiously, intent on seeing my face. 'Cat? Are you okay?'

'But Dad drowned in a boating accident,' I blurt out. 'The police said so. I . . . I went to his funeral. His boat was so battered from the storm he got caught out in, it couldn't be repaired.' Emotion swells inside me. 'How can he possibly be alive?'

There's a pause. 'Your dad made the boat look like that. He didn't drown,' Rik says. 'Your dad faked his own death.'

4

Faked his own death?

'Cat, are you still there?'

I let the video show my face so Rik can see the disbelief written all over it.

'No.' I shake my head. 'There's no way.'

Rik's expression is intense and deeply serious. 'I know this is a lot to take in, Cat, but think about it. Your dad's body was never found, was it?'

'No, but that's . . . that can happen when you die at sea. Dad wouldn't . . .' I trail off, anger rising through my shock. How dare this man suggest that Dad would have deliberately chosen to leave us? Dad *loved* us. Furious tears prick at my eyes.

'I'm so sorry.' Rik's face creases with sympathy. 'I realize this is overwhelming, but I promise you, Cat, your dad faked his own death.' He pauses. 'He didn't have any choice.'

'No.' An angry sob swells inside me. 'It doesn't make any sense. Dad *wouldn't*.'

'Let me try to explain,' Rik says, his voice urgent. 'It all happened by accident. One day, eighteen months ago, your dad and I were alone in the shop and a woman approached us for a private valuation. She claimed she'd inherited a collection and offered us hundreds of pounds just to examine a few bits of jewellery.' He sighs. 'We should have realized that there was something dodgy going on but . . . well, she was in a hurry and you know your dad . . . always happy to help people.'

I nod, remembering how on our strolls through the village, everyone Dad and I passed would stop to smile and chat with him.

'To cut a long story short,' Rik goes on, 'your dad and I agreed to do the valuation. We started checking over the jewellery and among all the necklaces and rings there was this cheap-looking box with a rusty clasp. It was obvious it hadn't been opened for years, so your dad prised it open carefully and . . .' his voice fills with hushed awe, '. . . and inside we found a huge and priceless blue diamond.'

I frown, unimpressed. What on earth does this have to do with Dad faking his death?

Rik leans closer to the lens, his face filling my screen. 'Someone had wound the diamond with a bit of chain and when your dad held it up, it sparkled in the light like it was on fire. It was by far the most valuable thing either of us had ever seen. Worth millions. The diamond was flawless.'

I can see he's expecting me to be properly wowed by this news, but all I want is to find out about Dad.

'Okay,' I say, 'but why does any of this—?'

'We thought the woman would be delighted to discover she had a priceless diamond on her hands, but as soon as we told her, she got very aggressive. That was when we found out exactly who she was.'

'Who?' I ask.

'Fran Farmer, the head of the Fran Farmer Gang. A bunch of local gangsters, very much under the radar, but up to their eyes in violent crime.' Rik pauses.

A shiver snakes down my spine.

'It turned out that this Blue Fire diamond, as we called it, was part of a haul of stolen goods the gang had smuggled into the country,' Rik goes on. 'Fran Farmer clearly hadn't realized the diamond was even there, let alone that it was so valuable. And she was furious that we'd seen it. She got a couple of her heavies to threaten us . . . Your dad and I were told to keep our mouths shut or *else* . . .'

'So . . . so what happened?' I gulp. Poor Dad; he must have been terrified.

'We did what Farmer asked,' Rik says. 'Your dad and I knew full well we were supposed to report the discovery of any significant gemstones to the authorities, but we were too scared to do it and then . . .' he hesitates.

'Then what?'

'*Disaster.*' Rik lets out a low groan. 'At some point over the next couple of days the diamond was stolen from the gang and Fran Farmer blamed us. Me and your dad.'

'*No!*' I gasp. 'But Dad wouldn't steal anything.'

'Of course he wouldn't,' Rik says. 'And neither would I. My guess is some rival gang member was responsible. Anyway, Fran Farmer was convinced we'd stolen it, and she had a lot of very violent people backing her up.'

I shake my head. Rik sounds like he's describing the plot of an action movie. 'Why didn't you go to the police?' I ask.

'We wanted to,' Rik says. 'But Fran Farmer threatened to kill us and our families if we did.' He pauses. 'She torched my car to show she was serious. It was parked right by my house and she set it on fire.'

I stare at the screen. It's like I'm outside my own body, watching myself listen to him.

'Your dad and I were left with just one option. Going into permanent hiding was the only way to keep the people we loved safe.'

'But—'

'Your dad agonized about his decision, Cat,' Rik says gently. 'It was easier for me; I've got no family apart from an old auntie who was never going to ask any difficult questions. I just went abroad. But for your dad it was different. If he vanished overnight, there would've been a big outcry. Anyway, if the FFG thought he was still alive, they might have used you to get to him. Faking his death – and making the FFG think the Blue Fire diamond drowned with him – was the only way he could protect you. Of course, your dad disappearing also stopped the gangsters searching for me, but you and your mum and sister were the priority.'

'But why didn't Dad tell us?' Tears well in my eyes.

'It was for your own good,' Rik says. 'It was important the FFG believed he was dead and the diamond they thought he'd stolen was at the bottom of the sea. It destroyed your dad to do all this, but he was adamant it was the only way to keep you safe.'

'Where did he go?' I ask, voice rasping. 'Where is he now?'

'I don't know,' Rik says. 'We haven't had any contact since the day I left the country when I swore to him I'd never tell a living soul he was still alive.' He hesitates and when he speaks again his voice is low and troubled. 'I'm only breaking that promise now because I have to.'

'What do you mean?' My head spins, panic rising. 'What's happened?'

Rik sucks in his breath. I lean towards my screen, intent on what he's about to say.

'Fran Farmer has found out your dad faked his death seventeen months ago,' Rik says, his voice low and serious.

My stomach clenches with fear. 'How?' I breathe. 'How did she find out?'

'I don't know,' Rik admits. 'But I got hold of her telephone number before I left the country and every now and then I check in on her messages.'

'You do?' I stare at him.

'I'm good with IT . . . that was a big part of my job at Ballena Jewellery.' Rik shrugs. 'Anyway, it's clear from the messages I've intercepted: Fran Farmer is certain your dad is still alive *and* that he ran off with her diamond.' He looks at me intently. 'She wants the Blue Fire back. And she wants revenge on your dad. *Extreme* revenge.'

'You mean she wants to . . . to kill him?' My heart pounds.

'Yes.' Rik's mouth sets in a thin line.

I stare at him, too shocked, too upset to speak.

'I'm on the other side of the world,' he says. 'Which is most likely the only reason Fran Farmer hasn't caught up with me. She's probably trying to track me down right now, in fact, to find out if I know where your dad and the diamond are. If I come back to help your dad, I'll have a target on my back . . . I'll just make things worse for him.' He sighs. 'There's nothing *I* can do, but *you* . . . your dad talked about you a lot, Cat.'

My heart feels tight in my chest.

'He couldn't bear the thought that one day they might get to you – that you might find out he'd gone away and not understand why he'd had to leave.' He gives me a shaky smile. 'That's why I have your number. Your dad gave it to me, along with things like your birth date and your school . . . everything he could think of so that, if the worst happened, I'd be able to find you and tell you the truth . . . that he *didn't* run off with the diamond and that he's always loved you and your mum and your sister more than his own life.'

I stare at him, a lump in my throat.

'Your dad gave up everything for you, Cat,' Rik says softly. 'And now you're the only person who can help him.'

It takes a second for me to realize what he's just said. 'Me? *How*? What can *I* do?'

Rik leans into the camera, his eyes bright, his gaze intense. 'You need to find your dad. Warn him that the FFG are on his trail. That his life is in danger.'

'But—' I shake my head, overwhelmed by what Rik's suggesting. 'What about the police?'

'No!' Rik's voice rises. 'The FFG have spies everywhere. If anyone informs on them to the police, they'll know.' His gaze darkens. 'Right now they're probably leaving you and your family alone because they don't want to draw attention to themselves. But if they were to find out the police are investigating them anyway, I reckon they'd come after you, use you to draw out your dad. It's how they work.'

'But don't you have friends? People who could help find Dad . . . who know about—'

'No one who's prepared to risk their neck for a man they don't know. And I'm thousands of miles away.' He grimaces. 'I'm sorry . . . if there was anyone else I could ask, I would. I hate to put you in danger, but . . .' He makes a face. 'It's up to you, Cat.'

'What about my mum?' I ask. 'Why not speak to her?'

Rik shakes his head. 'Your mum won't believe anything I say,' he says. 'Your dad told her some lies about me so that if the FFG came around, asking her questions . . . well, it would throw them off the scent.'

'What lies?' I ask.

'He said we'd fallen out, that I was a con man. But your dad was my best friend, Cat. You *have* to believe me. I'm telling the truth. I've got no reason to lie, I just want to help.' He suddenly looks exhausted. 'Look, I've told you everything I know. As soon as I hang up I'm destroying this phone. So you won't be able to call me. But I'll check in with you when I get my next burner. And I'll give you whatever help I can. But I daren't come back to the UK, so it's up to you. You need to find your dad as fast as you can. Find him and warn him, before it's too late.'

'But . . .' I stammer. 'But if he's really alive, he could be anywhere.'

Rik shakes his head. 'I'm certain he's in the UK. Not nearby, but somewhere in Britain. I told him the last time we spoke that he should go abroad, but he said he couldn't . . . *wouldn't* leave the country where his family lived.'

The lump in my throat swells painfully.

'All I can tell you is that he'll be somewhere isolated where he can keep a low profile.' He pauses. 'Okay, I've stayed on this number too long already. I have to go.'

'No, please.' Panic surges inside me. 'I . . . I can't do this.'

'Yes, you can. Your dad told me how smart and determined you are. How the two of you were always on the same wavelength.' Rik gives me a smile of encouragement. 'Which means if anyone can work out where he's chosen to hide, it's you, Cat. You can do this.'

Before I can respond, the screen goes black. I stare down at the blank space where Rik's face had been. The sun is still shining, the warm air filtering in through my open window and the branches of the tree just outside rustling in the breeze.

But everything in my world has changed.

I don't know how much time passes, but I'm still sitting on my bed, trying to take in what's just happened, when Mum's voice trills up from the hall downstairs. 'A wonderful session! You're so open, so connected to the planetary influen—' The dreamy sound of her voice fades. A moment later and the front door shuts. Mum's footsteps pad across the hall again.

'Bess!' she barks, her tone suddenly terse and impatient. 'Mrs Trimble has your lunch ready. Don't make me call you again!'

I unfurl myself. Panic rises inside me as I stand up. It's all very well Rik saying all that stuff about me being smart and determined, but I have no clue how to find Dad. No clue even where to begin. I reach for my phone. Maybe going to the police is too dangerous and telling

Mum a waste of time, but I can't do this by myself. There must be another way.

I find Rik's number and press call. My hand trembles as I hold the phone to my ear.

A long, flat beep sounds. It's dead. My heart sinks – Rik's ditched his burner, just like he said he would. And I have no idea how soon, or if, he'll make contact again.

I'm on my own.

5

I feel sick with fear as I walk over to my bedroom window. Everything Rik said sounded totally convincing, yet now I'm off the phone it's almost impossible to believe any of it is true. I pace across the room, my panic building. Surely Dad can't be alive?

And yet . . . suppose he is?

I sink on to my bed, my head in my hands. My mind darts and dives, trying to find some kind of certainty. And then, like a splash of cold water, it strikes me: I can't know for sure. Not at this point. Not without more evidence.

And this gives me a simple choice: I either decide Rik is lying and ignore his message altogether, or I accept that he might be telling the truth and set out to find and warn Dad.

I sit up, drawing in a deep breath.

Even if there's only a small chance Dad is really still alive, I have to investigate.

I can't take the risk of *not* helping him.

But if Dad is still alive, where on earth could he be hiding? I run over my memories of the last few days before he disappeared, desperately trying to remember any clue he might have dropped. But I can barely recall talking to him at all, let alone anything specific he said.

I do remember that last morning. It was a Saturday, a time when Dad would usually get up early and chivvy me and Bess out of the house and into the car, so that we could drive to the shore and sail off for a few hours in his boat, the *Marvista*. That day was beautiful, the clear blue sky and bright sunshine giving no hint of the storm Dad must have later got caught in. When he appeared in the doorway of my bedroom I was expecting him to give me the usual ten-minute warning to get ready to leave. But he didn't. Instead he stood there, mumbling something about repairs and needing to test the *Marvista* at sea on his own. I didn't take much notice, though I do remember asking:

'So can we go out later, Dad? You, me and Bess?'

Dad said: 'If there's time, Kitterbug.' Then he paused and gave me a strange, sad look. 'You know I love you, Cat, you and your sister . . . more than my life.' And then he turned and walked away.

It was the last time I saw him.

I stand in front of my bedroom window, lost in the memory. That strange look he gave me . . . I've never seen it in this way before, but it seems obvious now that he was saying goodbye. And the words he used, about loving us more than his life. Rik used those exact same words too, as if he'd heard Dad say them.

I try to focus on what I know. If what Rik says is true, Dad probably didn't speak to anyone else about his plan to fake his drowning. But maybe, at some point, he wrote down something about where he was going to go, or what he was going to do.

Yes. Perhaps there'll be some clue among his old possessions.

I hurry downstairs. I'm certain there's a big box of Dad's things in Mum's office. She put a lot of his stuff up in the attic but, months after he disappeared, she would still come across random items buried in a pile of papers or languishing down the back of the sofa. I'm certain that Ballena Jewellery, where he worked, sent things too. I remember Mum cursing once: *It's like they're trying to torment me with these constant reminders.*

As I scurry across the hall and into Mum's office, I hear her in the kitchen, giving Mrs Trimble instructions on the shopping she wants done. Mrs Trimble comes five days a week, doing a couple of hours of cleaning before making lunch, then babysitting Bess until Mum finishes work for the day. Mum often sees clients in the evenings too – but I'm supposed to look after Bess then.

The office is hot and stuffy and, as usual, a total

mess. Unlike the rest of the house, where every surface is crammed with astrological prints and ornaments, the office is cluttered with books and folders and stationery. Mum keeps client files in two big drawer files that stand on either side of a bookcase, slumping under the weight of the books on its shelves. The big, colourful boxes she uses to store things are stacked on the opposite wall.

Naturally, nothing is labelled. I sigh. Typical Mum. As I pull out each box in turn to check its contents, the door creaks. My head jerks up. Thankfully, it's just Bess. She glances momentarily at the array of boxes pulled away from the wall, then shoots me a quick, quizzical look: *What are you doing?* When I don't answer, she shrugs, then curls up on the floor by the bookcase. She gets out her pens and hunches over her drawing.

I pull out another box and take off the lid. It's full of old flyers and leaflets for the astrology shows and conventions that Mum regularly speaks at. I rummage through the paperwork in case any of Dad's old things are in here too.

Maybe it's having to focus on something – or maybe it's the sound of Bess's pens, scratching their way rhythmically across her drawing book, but I start to feel slightly calmer. I just need to focus. Deal with what's in front of me, one step at a time.

Like I do when I'm dress-making. It's the same sequence every time:

Choose pattern. Select fabric. Pin. Cut. Sew. Repeat.

As I lift the lid off the next box, I sense Bess looking at me again and glance over.

She offers me a shy smile. I long to tell her that Dad is still alive and out there. But I stop myself. It wouldn't be fair to get her hopes up. Bess wouldn't understand. *I* don't understand.

'What did you think of the Tuesdays?' I ask instead.

She nods enthusiastically, her smile broadening to a beam.

I grin back, pleased she liked them. 'Yeah, I thought they seemed okay too.'

I turn back to the box. My heart leaps. It's a jumble of Dad's things: leaflets for the courses on woodwork and photography that he talked about starting but never did; holiday brochures of places he wanted to visit. He was always talking about the future – from careers that would fulfil his creative potential to holiday destinations by the sea. I don't remember any of the specific things he said, but I can still see his face when he talked – smiley and shiny-eyed with excitement.

None of that helps me work out where he might be now. I rummage, feeling increasingly desperate, through half-written film reviews – from that time when he fancied becoming a movie critic – to unfinished sketches of me and Bess on his boat.

Without warning, I come to a printed-out selfie of Dad with me and Bess. It's from just before he died; I haven't seen it before, though I remember him taking it. I gaze down at us: Dad with one arm round me and Bess, the other reaching away to take the picture. All three of us are laughing. Bess has our old dog, Pirate, in her arms. She's hugging him close and his silky brown ears flop over her arms as he leans against her.

The memory of Bess's high-pitched, joyful giggle rings in my ears, then passes to silence. I feel suddenly empty, tears pricking at my eyes. It's been ages since I heard my sister laugh.

A gentle hand on my arm. Bess has crept over and is looking up at me, her eyes full of enquiring concern. I show her the picture.

'D'you remember this?' I ask.

Bess takes the photo in her colour-stained fingers. She shakes her head, then shuffles back a little, still looking at it.

I wipe my face and turn my attention back to the box. Right at the bottom, there's a stapled-together print-out of pages with BALLENA JEWELLERY WEBSITE UPDATE – DRAFT TEXT written on the front. And it's dated the same month Dad disappeared. Maybe there'll be a clue in this . . . Something that might indicate where he would go.

I snatch it out of the box.

'Hey,' Tyler's voice from the doorway makes me jump.

I look up. He's lolling against the door frame, filling the space with his broad shoulders. His eyes are still fierce, but there's the hint of a smile on his lips. For a second I stare, transfixed, then shake myself, my irritation rising.

'What are you doing here?' It comes out much snappier than I mean it to.

The smile falls from Tyler's face. He straightens up. 'I was just looking for Wi-Fi,' he says. 'I heard you talking to . . . to Bess.'

'Oh,' I say.

Tyler takes another step inside the room. 'So could I have the password, please?'

I grip the stapled pages more tightly. Tyler's too close and I need to look through these papers. If Dad is alive, I have to find him.

It's overwhelming.

'No,' I snap. 'Sorry, but it's not a good time. I'm busy.'

Across the room, Bess kicks her foot against the wall, telling me I'm being rude.

I ignore her.

Tyler blinks, taken aback. His mouth opens a little, his eyes hardening as they meet mine. 'Right,' he says. 'Bye.' He turns and stalks off.

I watch him go, my heart thudding. Bess kicks at the wall again.

'What?' I glare at her.

She spreads out her arms and widens her eyes. *What is the matter with you?* For a second she looks like a miniature version of Mum.

'None of your business,' I mutter, turning back to the papers.

I put Tyler out of my head as I flick through the pages. There're a load of handwritten red pen marks on the one marked HOME PAGE, but it's mostly a series of captions for different jewellery ranges. I stop on the fifth page, staring at a picture of the little back office I vaguely remember being behind the main shop. Rik and Dad are standing in front of the work bench while the actual jewellers sit, surrounded by their tiny boxes and pots and miniature hammers and chisels. Dad has his hand on Rik's shoulder and the two of them are grinning at each other. So they are friends, just like Rik said. My heart thuds as I flick over the page. This one is headed DRAFT TEXT FOR 'OUR STAFF' SECTION. There's a grainy photo of Dad looking uncharacteristically serious halfway down the page, with the caption:

Our Senior Sales Assistant, Alan Mooney, brings 20 years of experience in the retail industry.

And there, just below Dad, is a picture of Rik. His caption reads:

At 31, Rik Adamski combines two roles, as Junior Sales Assistant and our youngest ever Head of Digital.

There's nothing written in the margins. Nothing here that helps.

Depressed, I chuck the papers back into the box. As I do, a Post-it flutters off the back page. The date on the note is printed at the top: *18 February*. That's the day before Dad disappeared. The handwritten message beneath reads:

Alan – Sandy Williams called @ 3 p.m.

Did Dad get the message? Did he call back? The name means nothing to me. Anyway, Sandy Williams is probably just an ordinary customer – nothing to do with Dad's disappearance.

I shove the boxes roughly back into place and trudge away, feeling hopeless.

Where on earth do I look now?

6

I wake up late the next morning. It took me ages to get to sleep and, even then, I kept waking up and tossing and turning. I open my curtains wide to find a cloudy sky outside. The damp, hot air presses down on my head, Rik's warning humming in my ears:

Find your dad and warn him, before it's too late.

I drag on leggings and a homemade tunic made from soft blue cotton. The photo of Dad, Bess and me on the beach that I took from the office keeps catching my eye. We were so happy that day, it hurts to remember it.

I force myself to go downstairs. I can hear Mum tapping away in her office. She usually spends the early morning replying to emails, working on her social media and her *Truth in the Stars* newsletter. Mrs Trimble is humming to herself in the living room.

I wonder idly where Bess is. On weekdays during term time a tutor comes to the house every morning – Bess hasn't been to proper school since she stopped speaking – and she sees a therapist on Mondays, Wednesdays and Fridays.

However, it's the summer holidays now and the therapist is only coming once a week. Left to her own devices, Bess normally follows Mrs Trimble – or me – around the house, curled up wherever we are with her tongue poking out from between lips as she concentrates on her latest drawing.

I trudge out on to the patio. Bess is at the opposite end of the garden, close to the big oak tree. She's standing with her hands on her hips, her little legs sticking out of her dungarees. They're an old pair of mine and too big for her. She's rolled up the legs and the left hangs lower than the right. She's also tried to plait her hair herself so the braids are uneven too. Next to the huge tree trunk, she looks small and vulnerable as she shuffles from side to side. What is she looking at?

Curious, I wander towards her. Which is when Tyler emerges from behind the oak tree. His long arms are stretched into the air, one leg pointing in front of him. There's a look of intense concentration on his face as he balances himself, then throws himself forward into a cartwheel.

His hands plant firmly. One. Two. His straight legs turn in a perfect circle over his body. He lands lightly on the grass, pauses for just a fraction of a second, then cartwheels again across the lawn.

This time he stands up, grinning at Bess. His smile lights up his whole face. Bess claps her hands, jumping up and down with excitement.

Neither of them have noticed me.

'Your turn, Bess!' Tyler calls. 'Come here!'

My jaw drops as Bess runs over. Tyler talks to her – words I can't hear – as he gestures towards her arms and legs.

Bess is nodding, reaching her arms into the air.

'No!' I shout. Is he insane? Bess is too small to attempt a cartwheel. 'Stop!'

Bess freezes. Tyler looks up. He sees me and that gorgeous smile disappears.

'Come on, Bess,' he calls, his eyes still on me. 'There's nothing to be afraid of.'

Bess hesitates. I can see the fear in her whole body. She's just doing this to please him. To try to impress him.

Fury rises inside me as I break into a run. 'Stop!' I yell again. 'It's not safe.' I reach Bess with my next stride and grab her arm. 'You might break your neck.' I spin her round.

She gazes up at me, her face scarlet with humiliation, her dark eyes defiant. Then she wrenches herself out of my grip and races across the grass, into the house. I turn back to Tyler. He's staring angrily at me, arms folded across his chest.

'You should be ashamed of yourself!' I shout.

'*What?*' Tyler's mouth gapes. 'What the hell is your problem?'

'Me?' Anger roils inside me. 'You're the one encouraging a vulnerable little girl who isn't even seven years old to—'

'To attempt a cartwheel? With me right there to help her?' Tyler's eyes widen. 'You're being ridiculous.'

'And you're being irresponsible,' I snap back. 'You don't know anything about my sister. Or me.'

Tyler's jaw grinds, the muscles moving under the skin. 'I know you're stuck-up,' he says, his eyes narrowing. 'I know you're the rudest person I've ever met.'

We stare at each other. And, suddenly, I know that if I stay here a second longer, I'm going to burst into tears. I turn and run, pelting around the side of the house, across the drive at the front and along the dirt track. I don't stop until I'm in the woods. Then I fall to a heap on the dry earth, hot tears streaming down my face.

I cry so much my heart feels like it will burst. Dad is out there somewhere and I have no idea how to find him. There are horrible strangers in our home and now Bess hates me too.

Things couldn't be worse.

'Cat?'

I look up. Tyler is standing over me, arms folded and a look of concern on his face. He followed me? How embarrassing. I turn away, wiping the snot and tears from my face.

Tyler squats down beside me. 'Are you okay?' He touches my arm, just for a second.

My skin tingles.

I shake my head. 'Everything's wrong.' The words flow out on a sob. I swallow furiously, determined not to cry in front of him.

Tyler settles himself on to the patch of earth beside me. We're close to the stream now, the water bubbles gently and the leaves over our head rustle. I sniff loudly, then wipe my face again. I look up. Tyler is watching me, his eyes full of concern. Slivers of sunlight play across his face, gleaming like emeralds in his eyes and catching the arc of his cheekbone and the square set of his jaw.

I realize I'm staring and look away.

'I didn't mean to upset you,' he says gently. 'I get that you're super-protective of your sister. I just thought that she spends all her time drawing, you know . . . shut up in her own head with the not-talking and . . . I thought she might like to try something new, have a bit of fun. I'm sorry if it scared you.'

I tense, filling with surprise. I hadn't expected an

apology. Or for him to have understood Bess so quickly. I look up at him. There's genuine warmth in his eyes. And suddenly I realize that I was in the wrong too.

'No, *I'm* sorry,' I say, offering him a shaky smile. 'I overreacted. It's fine to show Bess how to cartwheel, it's just . . . she's been through so much.'

'You mean your dad?' Tyler asks.

I nod. 'It was after that she stopped speaking,' I explain, sitting back against a tree. Truth is, I was too caught up in my own, numb grief to notice exactly when Bess retreated into her drawings, answering all questions only with a nod or shake of the head, then backing away.

'Our dog died too, just before Dad,' I explain. 'She was run over. Pirate belonged to all of us, but Bess played with her *all the time.* She was this amazing, crazy terrier with a brown patch over one eye, who never stopped racing around and jumping on everything. We all loved her,' I pause, 'but Bess loved her the most.'

'That's a lot,' Tyler says, awkwardly. 'For both of you.'

I stare at him. 'Yeah,' I say.

'I guess us being here doesn't help.' Tyler makes a face. 'Dad was saying last night that it must be hard for you to have strangers living so on top of you.' The corner of his mouth curls. 'I told him it was hard for me too, though not that politely.'

'You didn't want to come here for the summer?' This hadn't occurred to me before. But now it seems obvious. Tyler is attractive and sophisticated. Everything that Brockledore – and my family – is not.

'No way.' Tyler rolls his eyes. 'Back home there were friends and football and a proper internet connection. Here . . .' he waves his hand. 'Here it's just trees and grass and . . . and bunny rabbits!'

I laugh. Tyler gazes across to the stream.

'Pretty, though.' He looks at me. 'So it's not all bad.' He shuffles back, so he's leaning against a tree. He closes his eyes and holds his face up to the light filtering through the branches.

'So are you really okay?' he asks.

A long moment passes. I stay silent. Most people I know would start speaking to fill the space, but Tyler just carries on leaning against his tree, eyes gently closed. Waiting.

I clear my throat. 'When's your birthday?'

Tyler opens his eyes, glancing at me in surprise. 'Er, the twenty-ninth of April. Why?'

So he's a Taurus. I feel stupid for asking. Mum's always so fascinated by people's birth charts it's easy to forget that most normal people don't really think about their horoscopes.

'Just wondering,' I say, trying to cover my confusion

while desperately looking for a new subject. 'Er, where's your mum?'

'She got cancer and died when I was little.' He stares at the stream in front of us.

'Oh.'

Too late I realize that just because I mentioned losing my dad, it doesn't mean Tyler will want to talk about something so private and painful.

'It's always just been me and Dad,' he says, softly. 'That's why I get what it's like for Bess, all shut up in her own head.'

'No brothers and sisters?' I ask.

Tyler shakes his head. 'What about your dad? How long ago did he die?'

Yesterday morning that would have been a straightforward question to answer. But now . . . I open my mouth to tell Tyler the phrases I've learned to use, the simple script that explains Dad drowned on a boat in a winter storm almost eighteen months ago, and that makes it clear I don't want to be asked anything else. But when I speak, it's not those words that come out.

7

A gentle breeze whooshes through the trees, the only sound around us. Maybe it's the calm of the woods or maybe the concern in Tyler's eyes, but once I've started speaking, I can't stop:

'Dad went out in his boat on his own and there was a storm and he didn't come home,' I say, my voice breathless and my explanation rushing out fast, like it's got a will of its own. 'Mum got more and more worried and then he was officially missing. We kept hoping and hoping and then after two days his boat washed up all battered along the coast and his things were inside, his wallet and his phone, waterlogged and ruined and that's when we knew . . .' I stop, drawing in a deep lungful of air. Tyler nods, his eyes intent on mine.

'They declared him missing, presumed dead, but –' I take a deep breath – 'but yesterday one of Dad's friends from work, Rik Adamski, got in touch. He told me Dad faked his death and is still alive and in hiding from gangsters who want to kill him in revenge for something he didn't do.' I stare at Tyler, my heart pounding.

He stares back, his mouth gaping. 'Whoa,' he says. 'What does your mum say?'

I shrug. 'Rik said she wouldn't believe anything he said, and that I can't tell the police because the gangsters would know.' I can hear the bitterness creeping into my voice. 'So I'm on my own.'

'Are you're sure what this Rik said is all true?' Tyler asks. 'It seems kind of unlikely, don't you think?'

'It does,' I say, nodding. 'But Rik knew all this stuff about me and Dad, and I've seen a picture of them together. They were friends. It's just . . . Rik says he called me on a burner phone, and I don't know when he'll get in touch again, and the gangsters could get to Dad any time.'

Tyler frowns. 'Was your dad, like, a gang member, then? Running with bad people?'

'No.' I make a face. 'Dad wasn't like that. Rik told me they were set up. They'd identified this rare, priceless diamond which it turned out some gangsters had smuggled into the country. The diamond was stolen at some point and the boss of the gang – Fran Farmer – was convinced Rik and Dad did it.' I shake my head. 'I know it sounds crazy, like something out of a movie, but I'm *sure* it was real. I know Dad wouldn't have left us unless he had to, and why would Rik lie about it anyway?'

Tyler frowns. 'So how much was this diamond worth?'

I shake my head. 'Millions, I think. There wasn't time for Rik to explain everything. And now he's gone and . . . and I'm on my own.'

'No, you're not.' He grins and my stomach does a tiny somersault. Is he offering to help me?

I look away, my emotions churning.

Tyler takes out his phone. 'First thing is to make sure this Rik is everything he said he is. Did you find out anything else about him? A wife . . . or a girlfriend?' He looks at me expectantly.

'Um,' I say, 'Rik said he didn't have family, just an old aunt.'

Tyler bends over his screen. I wipe my face. I didn't put on any make-up this morning, so at least that won't be smudging under my eyes, but I must look awful. I run my fingers through my hair too.

A few minutes pass, then Tyler holds out his phone. 'Was this him? It's a guy called Rik Adamski from this area, who seems to have stopped posting seventeen months ago, around the time your dad died.'

I take his phone and peer at the screen. Rik's face stares back at me.

'Yes,' I say, my heart racing. 'That's him.' I scroll down through the pictures. They are mostly selfies of Rik, either inside or outside what look like a variety of pubs.

I come to a pic of Rik with his arm round the shoulders of an elderly lady. She's wearing glasses and, like Rik, a warm smile. But it's not the photo that's caught my attention. It's the caption:

#HappyBirthday, Aunt Sandy – 70 years young! #oops #neveraskalady

I stare at the name: Sandy. Dad's handwritten Post-it flits into my head. I gasp, 'I wonder if that's Sandy Williams,' I say, handing Tyler back his mobile. 'Dad was supposed to call someone with that name the day before he disappeared.'

'Okay, I'll see if I can find a post with her surname.' Tyler taps away.

'And I'll look for Sandy Williams's contact details.' I take out my own mobile and open a search. It's soon obvious there are hundreds of people called Sandy Williams and I set my phone down with a sigh.

Tyler is still scrolling down Rik's Instagram feed. I watch him, liking the way his forehead creases slightly as he concentrates.

'Any luck?' I say.

'Not on the surname,' Tyler says, 'but look . . .' He hands me his phone again.

I gaze down at the screen. It's another photo from

Aunt Sandy's birthday, with Sandy herself in the middle of a group of elderly ladies. The caption reads:

#Sandybirthdaystreetparty

'There.' Tyler points to the far end of the picture. A road sign is just visible to the left of the group. It shows the letters: *Thresha*—

I stare at him. 'Do you think that's where she lives?'

'It must be.' Tyler nods. 'It's her party.'

I turn back to my phone and refine my search. A bird screeches overhead, breaking the silence.

'I've found her!' I say. I show Tyler another series of pictures, this time showing Sandy and her friends outside a front door marked with the number 18.

'*Sandy Williams, 18 Thresham Street, Covington*,' I say out loud.

'Nice work,' Tyler says. He sounds impressed.

'Why, thank you.' I make my voice deliberately formal, hoping he won't notice the blush that warms my cheeks.

We hold each other's gaze for a moment, then I look down at my screen again.

'So . . . I'm thinking maybe Rik's Aunt Sandy might have some clue about where Dad is,' I say. 'There's no phone number to call her on, but Covington is just a few miles away.'

'D'you want us to go over and visit her?' Tyler asks.

For a second I think I've misheard him. Did he say '*us*'?

'I can go on my own,' I say quickly, then bite my lip. Did that sound rude? Tyler's expression doesn't change. 'I . . . I just mean I can handle a visit to an old lady by myself.'

'Course you can.' Tyler smiles at me. 'I just wondered if you fancied some company?'

I shrug, feeling torn. On the one hand I don't want Tyler to think I need his help – and I barely know him. On the other, I have to admit to liking the idea of spending time with him.

I like the idea a lot.

'I really don't mind either way,' Tyler says quickly, stretching out his legs. 'It's just that there's not much else to do around here.'

Oh. So Tyler only wants to come because he's bored. I sigh, inwardly. I should have realized. Why would he be interested in someone like me? He's handsome and full of London smarts and probably has a million mates back home, while I'm short and friendless, with horrible clumpy hair and homemade clothes that I might like but that probably look super-unfashionable to him.

At least he's offering to help. Maybe, in time, we can be friends.

I smile at him. 'Sure,' I say. 'We can go together.'

Friends is enough.

It's more than enough, in fact.

I stand up, brushing bits of grass and earth off my tunic. Now that we have a plan, my heart is beating faster.

I'm on Dad's trail at last.

'The bus to Covington leaves from Brockledore Village,' I explain, checking the time. 'If we hurry we should make it.'

'Great,' Tyler says, jumping to his feet. 'Let's go.'

8

Tyler and I rush to the village, only to find that the bus is running late. We wait at the stop opposite the war memorial. The sun has burned away the earlier clouds and it's a beautiful day, with clear skies and a light breeze. Tyler leans against a tree, peering at his phone.

I, on the other hand, can't stand still.

This time yesterday I was lazing about with Bess, thinking about the vintage dress I was making and getting irritated by Mum. Dad was a sad memory, always there at the back of my mind, but not real, not whole. An absence, not a presence.

Now here I am, pacing up and down while I wait for a bus I rarely catch with a boy I barely know to start tracking down a father I can hardly believe is still alive.

Find your dad and warn him, before it's too late.

'Cat?' I realize Tyler has been speaking.

I look up. He's gazing at me, a look of bewilderment on his face. 'I just checked the timetables on my phone,' he says. 'It says there are only two buses a day.' He frowns.

'A *day*. Ones that go through Brockledore Village. Is that right?'

I grin. 'Yeah, welcome to the countryside.'

The bus approaches. We get on board, which takes a while as the driver chats to everyone in front of us in the queue.

We find seats at the back. Tyler slides in next to me and whispers: 'This is so weird.'

'Why?' I regret the question as soon as I've asked it. I don't want to look stupid in front of him. But Tyler doesn't act like it's a silly question. Instead he frowns. 'I . . . I guess I'm just used to millions of buses and people not talking to each other.'

'In London?'

He nods.

'Where exactly do you live?' I ask.

'Archway,' he says. 'It's in north London. It's . . . well, compared to this it's all traffic and people crammed into flats.' He gazes out of the window. We've already left the village and are zooming along an empty country road, fields on both sides.

'After your mum . . . the cancer . . . Was it hard, just you and your dad?' I ask.

'I guess. I don't really remember.' Tyler sounds awkward. Which I understand. Until our conversation earlier, it's how I've always felt talking about Dad. 'I was thinking . . .' he goes on, clearly trying to change the subject. 'Have you heard of that local gang Rik mentioned before? What was it called?'

'The FFG.' I shake my head. 'Rik said they operate "under the radar". That means in secret, doesn't it?'

Tyler fishes his phone out of his pocket. 'I'll see what I can find.'

'Good idea,' I say. 'Me too.'

We sit, side by side, both intent on our mobiles. I search both the FFG initials and the boss's name: 'Fran Farmer'. No hits that suggest anything linked to a violent, local gang – though when I search for news on local gangs themselves, it's obvious there are plenty of them operating across Devon, smuggling stolen goods past customs and selling them in the towns and cities. I sit back, and snatch a sideways glance at Tyler, frowning in concentration. He catches me looking and grimaces.

'Nothing,' he says.

'I know,' I say. 'But I've found lots of mentions of gangs in the area.'

'Yeah, nobody seems to know who exactly runs them –' Tyler's eyes fill with worry – 'but they sound really dangerous. It's the same in London . . . I've seen about gangs like this on the local news.'

'Have you and your dad got family in London?' I ask.

Tyler shakes his head.

'My family's lived in our house for, like, a hundred years,' I say. 'My grandparents are dead now, but my mum grew up there and her dad did too.'

'Seriously?' Tyler looks like he can't believe such a thing is possible. 'Dad and I have lived in four flats in the past five years.'

'Wow.' I can't imagine what moving around all the time must be like.

'Tyler sits back and gazes at his phone again. I wonder again if he's left someone behind. Someone important to him.

The bus is trundling into Buckton Stanleigh, a small town where lots of girls from my horrible school live. It judders to a standstill at the first stop, on the outskirts of town. I watch, nervously, hoping no one I know gets on board.

There's a bustle of people with shopping bags and pushchairs and then, to my horror, I see Delilah Jenkins in a canary-yellow swing coat, sashaying her way along the aisle. I shrink down in my seat, shielding my face from view. If she sees me she's bound to make a sarcastic comment about that time she glued my cardigan to the desk – she always does. But, to my relief, Delilah strides past us without so much as a glance in my direction. I relax a little. And then, from between my fingers, I catch a glimpse of someone else following Delilah along the aisle, a sheet of long black hair hanging down her back.

No. My heart seems to stop beating.

It's Cindy Cho, who was once my best friend in the whole world.

Until the point where it was clear she wasn't my friend at all.

Is she really mates with Delilah now?

My mind catapults back, slinging snapshots of memory at me: Cindy and me bonding over puppy pics on YouTube on the first day of Year Seven; playing in the snow with Pirate – who Cindy adored almost as much as Bess and I did.

For most of that winter, Cindy and I were inseparable. She'd come back with me after school two or three days a week and we'd walk Pirate, then go back home for platefuls of Mrs Trimble's chocolate-chip cookies.

Then, a year later, Dad died. At first, Cindy was sweet, calling and sending me texts and offering to come round to the house. I noticed her messages, but I didn't reply to any of them. You can't when you're in the middle of a big shock. It's like being in the heart of a tornado. Just trying to stand up takes all your effort. There's no room to notice other people.

I'd had nearly two months off school and was really looking forward to seeing Cindy when I went back after Easter, but it was clear straight away that she'd moved on. Or perhaps that we'd never been as close as I'd imagined in the first place. Whatever it was, she acted like everyone else: wary of what I might say or do. As if I was a dangerous wild animal she didn't know how to handle.

The bus groans and judders and we set off again. Next to me, Tyler is still absorbed in his phone. Over his shoulder I can see he's selecting music, though at this angle I can't work out which tracks. He takes a pair of ear buds from his pocket and inserts one in each ear. I wonder what kind of stuff he listens to? I used to listen to all sorts but, after Dad died, all I wanted to hear for ages were the nineties tunes he used to play around the house. And then, gradually, I stopped listening to those too.

Tyler doesn't look round at me and I stay hunched low in my seat. The bus is almost full now; a murmur of voices humming alongside the rumble of the engine and the gentle hiss from Tyler's headphones. My ears find Delilah's voice as it rises above the chatter.

'Yeah, so, that party was *crazy*,' she says.

'It totally was,' Cindy agrees, enthusiastically.

'I couldn't believe it,' Delilah goes on. '*Everyone* was there. It was *so* great you could make it.'

I shuffle even further down in my seat, horribly aware that Delilah's 'everyone' doesn't include me. I'm glad that with his earbuds in, Tyler isn't likely to hear anything Delilah says – and potentially discover just how friendless I am.

'You *have* to come to the next one too,' Delilah goes on.

'Yeah, er, I'd love to.'

It sounds as if Cindy has had no problem finding a new best friend. The thought is like a stone lodged in my stomach.

A few minutes later the bus slows down as we near the stop by the shopping centre. I raise my hand to my face again, hoping to shield myself from view in case Delilah and Cindy get off.

I'm too late.

'Hey, *Glue Girl*!' The yellow swing coat is right beside me. I glance up, through my fingers. Delilah is standing right next to me, a huge, stupid grin on her face. 'What are *you* doing here?' Delilah asks. Then, without waiting for a reply, she turns back to where she was sitting and calls out: 'Look, Cindy, it's Glue Girl!'

My cheeks burn as Cindy appears beside Delilah.

'Hi, Cat,' Cindy's voice sounds strangled. I'm clearly the last person she wants to see.

‘Hi.’ My mouth shapes itself into a trembly smile.

‘Come on!’ Delilah orders, turning and sauntering away along the aisle.

Cindy and I stare at each other for another fraction of a second, then she gives me an uncertain frown, before hurrying off after Delilah.

The bus stops. I stay hunched in my seat as they get off and we rumble into action once again.

‘You okay?’ Tyler asks. He’s taken out his earbuds and is gazing at me, his eyebrows raised.

‘I’m fine,’ I say quickly.

Tyler hesitates. ‘Did you know those girls?’ The rasp of the music from his earbuds drifts faintly towards us.

‘Not really,’ I lie. ‘Maybe vaguely, from school.’

Tyler’s frown deepens. ‘Why was that first one calling you Gl—?’

‘What are you listening to?’ I interrupt, desperate to change the subject.

Tyler stares at me, thoughtfully, then offers me an earbud and I put it in. A soft, trance-like dance track plays. It’s haunting, beautiful, mesmerizing. Nothing like the music I was expecting. I smile to acknowledge I like it and then the bus passes the sign for Covington and the reason for our journey leaps back into my head along with a fresh wave of anxiety as I remember Rik’s words:

Find your dad and warn him, before it's too late.

'We're here,' I say, grimly.

Tyler nods, suddenly as serious as I am. 'Okay,' he says. 'Let's go and find Aunt Sandy.'

9

We get off the bus into the damp heat of Covington High Road. The stench of traffic fumes and from refuse sacks waiting for collection on the nearby kerb fills the air.

'So where's Thresham Street?' Tyler asks. His T-shirt is sticking to his back from the bus ride. He pulls it free and I catch a glimpse of the toned brown skin of his back. I can feel myself blushing and busy myself with the map on my phone.

'This way,' I say briskly, pointing to the left.

We make our way, taking another left, then a right, then following a long road for five minutes. Thresham Street is a turning on the right, a row of terraced cottages. Number 18 is a small apartment block in the middle. The block is set back from the street with a communal patch of grass in front. A group of mums and little kids are out there, picnicking on rugs. They stare suspiciously at me and Tyler as we walk up to the front door. The name 'Sandy Williams' is printed over the bell for number 4. I press the keypad.

No reply.

'She's not in,' I say, crestfallen.

Tyler glances over his shoulder at the women on the rugs, then presses 3, then 5. Silence.

'What are you doing?' I hiss.

Tyler presses 1 and 2 in quick succession. 'I'm just—'

As he speaks, the door buzzes. Tyler pushes it open, grinning. 'Come on.'

We go inside. The hallway is wide and cool. The concrete floor is scattered with junk mail and two pushchairs are lined up against the back wall, next to a thick glass door leading out into a grubby concrete yard. There are four doors off the hallway. Tyler heads straight over to the one numbered 4 and gives a sharp knock.

No answer.

He grimaces. 'I was hoping maybe it was just her intercom but . . .' he sighs. 'I guess she really isn't in.'

I open the back door, shove one of the pushchairs to hold it in place and walk outside. The concrete yard is surrounded by a high wall. It's empty apart from rubbish bags and litter overflowing from bins. There's a smell of rotting food. A single droopy pot plant beside the far wall does nothing to brighten the place up.

I hurry along the yard, to the window that belongs to flat number 4. A neat living space is visible through the glass: tiny, with a single armchair in front of a small TV. Photos are ranged across the mantelpiece. I shield my eyes from the sun and press my nose against the glass.

In pride of place, in the centre of the mantelpiece, is a picture of Rik.

This is definitely Sandy's flat and, having come all this way, I'm not going home without looking inside.

Tyler strolls up behind me. 'I guess we're stuck with waiting or coming back another time?'

I shake my head, pointing to the latch swinging freely to the side of the window. 'Maybe there's a third option.' I give the window a push. It glides open, revealing enough space for us to climb through. I turn to Tyler, my eyebrows raised. Maybe it's the adrenaline, but I feel suddenly free and unafraid.

All that matters is saving Dad.

Tyler's jaw drops as he looks from me to the open window. 'You want to break in?'

'No,' I say. 'I don't *want* to. But it's not like we'd be stealing anything, and this is *definitely* Rik's aunt, who *definitely* called my dad the day before he disappeared. And, right now, she's the only lead I have for tracking him down.'

Tyler frowns. 'If we get caught—'

'We won't.' The thrill of the risk surges inside me.

'We're not really doing anything wrong. Just investigating. We'll just have a look round, be out again in no time.'

Tyler chuckles. 'You are full of surprises,' he mutters.

I'm not sure what to make of that, so I ignore it.

'Come on, then,' I urge, gripping the window ledge. 'Help me inside.'

Tyler makes a stirrup with his hand. I step into it, clutch the sill and let him hoist me up. I hook my knee over the ledge and clamber awkwardly sideways. For a second, all I can think about is how I really don't want Tyler seeing me splayed clumsily over the window sill, then I remind myself I need to focus on getting into Aunt Sandy's flat.

I extend my leg carefully, looking for a toehold on the sideboard beneath the window. I find a space between a glass vase and a china ornament of a little girl holding a balloon. I rest my foot for a second, then twist my body and leap down. *There.* I land with a clunky thud on the patterned carpet and straighten up, catching my breath.

I move the breakables out of the way while Tyler follows me inside, but it's soon clear I didn't need to worry. His movements are swift and sleek, far smoother and quieter than my own.

'What are we looking for?' Tyler whispers.

'Letters, postcards - something that might tell us where my dad is.'

Tyler wrinkles his nose. 'Won't all that stuff be on her computer . . . or phone?'

'Look around you.' I indicate the cluster of china figurines on the table beside the TV and the doily set to the side of the armchair. 'She's an old lady. Old school.'

Tyler nods and hurries across the room to the pile of magazines on the coffee table. I busy myself with the contents of the sideboard.

After thirty seconds or so I blow out my breath, frustrated. 'This is just cups and coasters.'

'All I've got here are knitting magazines,' Tyler says with a sigh. 'Let's try another room.'

We scuttle along the narrow corridor. It's a tiny flat, with a little bathroom and kitchen on one side, and a bedroom on the other. Tyler dives into the kitchen, exploring the row of cupboards. I turn into the bedroom. There's hardly anywhere to store anything, but I rummage guiltily through the chest of drawers full of neatly folded clothes.

I turn to the bedside table, intending to open its one drawer and take a quick peek inside. But a postcard on the top shelf above the bed catches my eye. It's of a gentle sea, with a boat that looks a lot like the *Marvista* bobbing on its waves. It's just the kind of card Dad would send.

I snatch it down and turn it over.

Happy Birthday!

Regards, Alan

It's definitely from Dad; he's even drawn the tiny sailing boat he always put next to his signature. I turn, intending to show Tyler but, as I move, the unmistakable sound of a key turning in a lock meets my ears.

Tyler is staring at me from the kitchen across the narrow passageway. His eyes are wide with fear. '*Hide!*' he mouths, ducking beside the fridge, out of sight.

I just have time to hurl myself under the bed, when the flat door creaks open and footsteps pad inside.

Aunt Sandy is home.

10

I hold my breath, watching as she walks past. I'm expecting to see old-lady shoes, but Aunt Sandy is wearing orange trainers that peek out from under her black trousers. She grunts as she plonks her shopping bag on the kitchen counter. She must be inches away from Tyler. I imagine him squeezed flat against the side of the fridge. Another step and she'll see him.

But, instead, Aunt Sandy shuffles back into the corridor and heads into the bathroom. As soon as I see the door to that room close behind her, I scramble out from underneath the bed. Tyler emerges from beside the fridge at the same time. We meet in the narrow corridor. I open the front door softly, heart thudding, as the toilet flushes.

Tyler grabs my arm to stop me leaving the flat. Shakes his head.

'*What?*' I mouth. Is he mad? We need to get out of here fast, before Aunt Sandy comes out of the bathroom.

Tyler holds the front door open and calls out 'Hello! Anyone home?'

I stare at him, horrified.

A second later, Aunt Sandy bustles out from the bathroom. She's exactly the same as in her picture – though now she's not smiling.

'Hello?' she says warily.

Tyler gives her his warmest smile. 'Hi, sorry to barge in,' he says, 'the door was open.'

My jaw drops at his daring. He gives me a gentle nudge. 'This is Cat Mooney. She . . . er . . . she knows your nephew, Rik.'

Aunt Sandy frowns. 'I thought I'd shut it behind me,' she says, indicating the door.

There's an awkward pause. I can feel Tyler's gaze on my face. I need to speak, but my tongue is thick in my mouth, my muscles frozen. 'Hi,' I manage, at last.

Aunt Sandy tilts her head to one side. Her eyebrows knit in a suspicious frown. 'So how do you know my Rik?' she asks.

I force myself to smile as I answer. 'He was friends with my dad . . . er, Alan Mooney. I – I'm trying to meet people who knew him . . . my dad, that is . . . to find out more about him.' I stammer to a stop.

A huge beam spreads across Aunt Sandy's face. 'You're Cat? Alan's eldest?'

I nod, astonished that she knows my name.

All the tension in Aunt Sandy's face ebbs away. 'Well, why didn't you say? Come in, come in . . . I'll make you both a cuppa and I've got some chocolate biscuits too.' She ushers us towards the living room. 'I'll just pop the kettle on.'

Tyler and I obediently trot along behind her. I notice the window we climbed through is still open and pull it shut, then turn to Tyler. 'That was a sneaky move with the front door,' I hiss.

He grins at me, the sparkle in his eyes making my stomach flip over. 'Worked, though, didn't it?'

Aunt Sandy bustles in with a plate of chocolate biscuits and sets it down on the sideboard. 'Sit down,' she says.

Tyler and I perch side by side on the tiny couch, waiting in silence while Sandy settles herself into the armchair. The kettle sings in the distance.

'I was so sorry to hear about Alan's passing,' Aunt Sandy says. 'He was a lovely man. So charming, always smiling. A great role model for my Rik.'

I nod, my mouth dry. 'Er . . . when did you last see Rik?' I ask.

Aunt Sandy's mouth dips at the corners. 'He moved away about a year and a half ago. Abroad. For work.'

'The same time my dad died,' I say.

Aunt Sandy nods. 'I was pleased for Rik, getting such

a big IT job, though of course I miss him dreadfully. He's my only family, you see. My younger brother had a girlfriend and she . . .' Sandy sighs. 'She wasn't really cut out for motherhood, so when Rik came along I helped look after him. Then my brother passed and, well, it was just Rik and me.'

I nod. This ties in with what Rik said. 'How often do you hear from him?' I ask, wondering how much Sandy knows about Rik's situation.

'Not very often.' Aunt Sandy sighs. 'He's so busy with his job. They move him all over. He's been . . . oh, I don't know . . . *everywhere*, it seems like. Never in one place for long and always with a different phone number. I can't keep track.'

Tyler and I exchange a meaningful look. It's clear that Sandy has no idea about Rik's real reasons for leaving the country.

'Do have a biscuit.' Sandy points to the plate. Tyler obediently takes a cookie. A crunching sound fills the room.

'Have you spoken to Rik recently?' I ask.

'Not for a few months.' Sandy looks away, lost in her disappointment.

A riptide of anger surges through me. Poor Sandy. And poor Rik and Dad, forced to turn their lives upside down and devastate the people who love them.

‘That’s sad,’ Tyler says with feeling.

Sandy pats the side of her armchair. ‘Ah, well,’ she says. ‘Do have a biscuit, Cat, dear.’

‘Thanks, but I’m okay.’ My mouth feels too dry, like if I tried to eat I’d choke. I swallow hard. I need to ask Sandy about the Post-it note I found with Dad’s work things.

‘Did . . . er, did you speak to my dad, just before he died? I found a message from his work. It said that you’d called him.’

Sandy frowns. ‘Not that I remember . . . no, wait . . . I think I *did* call. Just to pass on a message from Rik.’

I lean forward. Could this be the clue I’ve been waiting for? ‘What was the message?’

‘Oh, I don’t remember after all this time, dear,’ Sandy says, waving her wrinkly hand. ‘Something about Rik being “ready” or . . . or “on track”, yes, that was it. Rik had gone abroad by then, of course, and said he couldn’t call Alan himself for some reason. I really don’t recall the details.’

I sit back, disappointed. More confirmation of what I already know. But no help finding Dad.

‘May I have another biscuit, please?’ Tyler asks.

‘Of course, dear.’ Aunt Sandy gives him a smile, then turns to me, her bright button eyes suddenly sparking.

'You know, it's funny you should have come around today asking about Rik. I had a man here yesterday asking very similar questions: Where was he? When did I last hear from him?'

'Really?' My heart thuds. Could Aunt Sandy's mystery visitor be one of the gangsters after Dad? 'What was his name?'

'He didn't say,' Aunt Sandy explains.

'What did he look like?' Tyler asks.

Aunt Sandy shrugs. 'Average really. Quite smartly dressed. He had a funny tattoo on his wrist. I asked him about it, but he changed the subject.'

'What was the tattoo of?' Tyler asks.

'Like a "T" with another bar halfway down. Like one of those star-sign symbols.'

I sit up. If there's a set of symbols I'm familiar with, it's astrological ones. 'Could you draw it?'

Aunt Sandy fusses about fetching a pen, then turns a box of paper tissues upside down and sketches the symbol on the back:

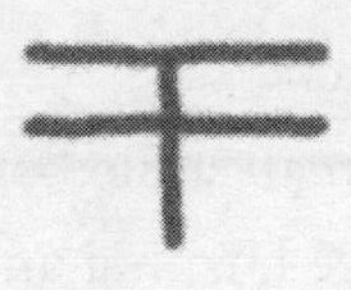

‘Are you sure?’ I ask.

Sandy nods and my heart sinks. I don’t know what the symbol means, but it definitely isn’t anything to do with star signs and horoscopes.

‘I don’t recognize it,’ I say, looking down at my lap. Another false trail.

‘Shall I make some more tea?’ Sandy offers.

I glance at Tyler.

‘Thanks, but we should probably go. Our bus will be here soon,’ he says. ‘Right, Cat?’

I nod, then hesitate. Should I tell Sandy about Dad? Or that Rik – far from enjoying a well-paid, jet-setting IT job – is really on the run from gangsters?

I bite my lip, deciding against it. It would only upset and worry her.

I stand up. ‘Thanks for having us,’ I say. ‘It was very nice to meet you.’

‘Bless you, dear.’ Sandy takes my hand and gives it a squeeze.

Tyler picks up the biscuit plate and our mugs and carries them out to the kitchen. As he disappears from view, Aunt Sandy catches my eye. ‘Handsome boy, that one,’ she says with a small smile.

I turn away, my face burning and hurry after Tyler.

As she shows us out, Aunt Sandy takes my hand again.

'It was so nice to meet you, Cat. Your dad told me how proud he was of you. What a tragedy we've lost him.'

There's a lump in my throat as I follow Tyler out of the apartment block and on to the pavement. It's still warm outside, but clouded over completely and a few spits of rain fall around us. The young mums on the grass have vanished. The only person visible is a man leaning against a motorbike parked on the other side of the road. His face is covered with a black helmet painted with red skulls. We stroll along the street in the opposite direction. I'm lost in dark thoughts. All the effort of coming here and I'm still no closer to Dad.

'That told us *nothing,'* I say, heaving a great sigh.

Tyler's head whips round. 'Yes, it did,' he says. 'It told us lots.'

'Like what?' I stare at him, astonished.

'For one thing, everything Sandy just said stacks up with what Rik told you,' Tyler points out as we turn the corner and head towards the high street. 'We know for sure now that Rik and your dad were friends. That makes everything else Rik said more likely to be true too: that they were wrongly accused of stealing a diamond and went into hiding.'

'Okay,' I concede.

'More importantly,' Tyler goes on, 'we know that

an FFG gangster came to see Sandy yesterday asking questions about Rik.'

'Not necessarily,' I point out. 'I mean, that visitor she had could have been anybody.'

'What about the tattoo she described on the man's wrist?' Tyler draws the symbol in the air as we hurry along. 'Look at the shape it makes.'

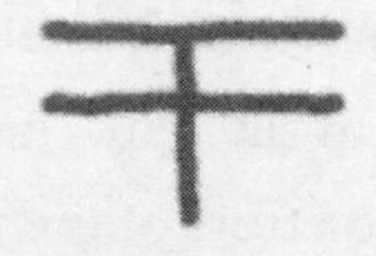

I stare at him, blankly.

'It's two "F"s back to back,' Tyler says.

My jaw drops. 'For Fran Farmer,' I say with a gasp. 'The Fran Farmer Gang.'

Tyler smiles, clearly enjoying my astonishment. 'And don't think the guy *wasn't* a gangster, just because he was nice and polite. He probably didn't get heavy with Sandy because he worked out straight away that she didn't know anything. There was no point causing a big scene or hurting her and drawing attention to himself. But I bet if he'd thought Sandy was hiding something, he'd have forced it out of her.'

His words send a shiver down my spine. We turn

another corner, then cross the road. It's clouding over again, the skies darkening, threatening rain.

'That means Fran Farmer and her people are definitely on Dad's trail,' I say. 'In fact, they're already one day ahead of us.'

Tyler stops walking. I meet his gaze. His eyes are full of concern, his expression deadly serious. 'Then we need to hurry up and work out where your dad is,' he says slowly, 'so you can find him and warn him. Right?'

I nod and we set off again. A gentle rain starts to fall, pattering softly on to our hair and shoulders. I pull the hood of my jacket up. Tyler shoves his hands in his pockets and brushes the wet off his hair. As we cross the next road, I catch sight of the motorbike man with the red skulls helmet from outside Sandy's flat. He's at the end of the next street. I stop as we step on to the pavement. The rumble of his bike sounds low along the road in the distance. Slowly, he's coming closer.

'Do you think that guy is following us?' I hiss.

Tyler follows my gaze. He frowns. 'Maybe.'

We watch together as the bike inches along the road towards us. Then stops.

'Tyler?' My heart thumps, loud, against my ribs.

'If he *is* following us,' Tyler says slowly, 'he's seen that we've seen him.'

The bike lets out a roar and starts moving towards us again.

My heart pounds. Tyler reaches for my hand, his strong fingers press against mine. 'Run!' he cries, tugging me forward. '*Run!*'

11

We pelt along the pavement. Tyler's hand is hot in mine. His legs are longer and he's running faster, almost pulling me off my feet as we turn a corner into a short street full of houses. I'm certain we're just two roads away from the high street now. A large building with a car park in front rises up on the left. Tyler tugs me into the parking area, flying across the gravel to a row of cars in the shade of some trees. Instinctively, we both make for the largest car and dive behind it.

I duck down, trembling.

'You okay?' Tyler whispers.

I nod, then peer anxiously round the rear wheel of the car. There's no sign of the bike rider in his red skulls helmet. 'We lost him,' I say.

Tyler blows out his breath. 'Or more likely we imagined he was following us.' He sounds relieved.

'Right,' I say, though inside I'm not quite so convinced.

We head for the high street. Still feeling spooked, I glance over my shoulder a couple of times but, thankfully, there's no sign of the biker. Tyler must have been right.

'The bus back to Brockledore doesn't go for nearly an hour,' I say, frowning.

Maybe we did imagine we were being followed, but I still don't fancy hanging around here any longer than we have to.

'Why don't we get on the first bus that comes?' Tyler suggests, clearly picking up on my unspoken thoughts. 'We can always switch to another in a few stops.'

'Good idea.' I glance at him. There are beads of sweat on his forehead. Guilt stabs at me. 'I'm sorry,' I stammer. 'I . . . I didn't mean to drag you into all this.'

Tyler meets my gaze, breaking into a huge smile.

'Are you kidding?' He moves closer, his arm almost brushing against mine. My skin erupts in goosebumps. 'I thought living in the country would be boring, but this is way more exciting than London.'

The journey home takes twice as long as the journey out, thanks to our detour. We spend most of the four stuffy bus trips we end up taking talking in low murmurs about Aunt Sandy and her mysterious visitor with the double 'F' tattoo.

'If the FFG suspect Dad's alive,' I say, 'do you think they might come to my house? See if Dad's been in touch with us?'

'I guess,' Tyler says, giving me a worried look. 'Though

I reckon if Fran Farmer thought you knew where he was, she'd have already sent someone to get the information out of you.'

I nod, Rik's words running through my head.

She wants revenge. Extreme revenge.

Up until this point, my search for Dad has felt a little unreal, but now it's suddenly clear that everything Rik warned me about is actually happening. 'Do . . . do you think that if the FFG find my dad and realize he doesn't have the diamond, they'll really kill him, like Rik said?'

I'm hoping Tyler will make a face and say that such thoughts belong in an overdramatic TV show. But instead he just presses his lips together, as if to say: *yeah, I do.*

I sit back, my heart pounding, as the bus swerves around a sharp corner.

Things just got serious.

12

It's almost 6 p.m. by the time we get home. Tyler slips around the side of the house to the Barn. Realizing the boxes of my fabric are still on the front porch from yesterday, I gather them up and go inside. I'm intending to go up to my room and just sit and think for a bit. I'm determined to speed up my efforts to find Dad, but other than scaring the wits out of me, my visit to Rik's Aunt Sandy hasn't brought me any closer to working out where he might be.

As I reach the landing, Mum's voice echoes up the stairs. 'Cat? Is that you?'

I dump my boxes with a sigh, then make my way back down to the hall.

Mum is standing close to the bottom step, hands on her hips. She's obviously been seeing clients – her eye make-up is heavier than usual, all thick black flicks of eyeliner and sparkling orange eyeshadow, and she's wearing one of her more outlandish outfits: a frothy, yellow dress with purple ruffles and a headdress cascading with purple and yellow fronds. The kind of look you might get if you crossed a banana with a peacock.

I catch sight of Bess outside in the garden. She is attempting a cartwheel, a very determined look on her face. Her legs go halfway up then flop down again. Tyler saunters into view and says something that I'm too far away to hear. Bess gives him a huge grin, nodding eagerly and has another go. I smile to myself.

'What on earth, Cat?' Mum strides towards me. Her eyes are the palest blue. Right now they look like chips of ice water. 'I've been trying your phone every ten minutes for the past hour and a half. The locator shows you've been to Covington and back.'

I frown, whipping out my mobile. I put it on silent when Tyler and I 'broke in' to Sandy's flat and, in the excitement of our conversation afterwards, I haven't looked at it since.

'Sorry, Mum,' I say, 'I . . . I just went to visit someone . . .' I hesitate. Should I tell Mum everything? Rik insisted she wouldn't believe anything he said, but it's not just Rik any more. Aunt Sandy's backed up Rik's story. And the man who visited her proves the FFG are on Rik and Dad's trail.

'You went to see a *friend*?' Mum asks, misunderstanding. Her voice softens slightly. 'Why didn't you tell me? I was *worried*. I understand you want a bit of independence, but it's selfish to just go off wherever and whenever you please without letting anyone know. Anything could have happened to you . . .' She sighs, her voice trembling. 'I can't go through not knowing - like before . . .'

She's remembering those terrible two days before Dad's battered boat washed up on the shore. The time that seemed an eternity before we knew – or thought we knew – that he was definitely dead. I look down at the sweeping grey scuff marks across the pale wood floor of the hall. I remember Dad pointing them out when I was younger. *These were made by your mum's family over generations, Cat. When you walk across these marks, you're walking across your own history.*

A sob rises inside me, a wave of fresh pain that rolls up and spills out of me: 'I miss Dad.'

Mum blinks, clearly taken aback. Tears prick at my eyes. Now I've started, I can't stop myself. The words tumble out of me:

'Dad's alive, Mum. His friend told me. He faked his death to protect us. He's *alive*.'

Mum's jaw hardens. 'That isn't funny, Cat.'

'It's not a joke. Dad was framed by gangsters so he had to go into hiding, but now those gangsters have found out he didn't die and they're after him.'

'What?' Mum frowns. 'Slow down. Some gangsters told you Dad faked his death?'

'No. Dad's friend told me.'

'Dad's friend?' Mum echoes. 'What on earth are you talking about? *What* friend?'

I take a deep breath. 'Dad's friend Rik Adamski, from his old work, got in touch with me yesterday. He told me that he and Dad were framed for stealing from a gang of smugglers. *That's* why Dad had to go into hiding.'

Mum stares at me. 'Rik Adamski told you this?'

I nod.

'Why didn't you tell me he'd contacted you?' she asks, her eyes wide with shock.

'I am telling you,' I point out. 'And I already know you don't like him. Rik told me that Dad had to make up some story about him. But it's not true.'

'Isn't it?' Mum raises her eyebrows. 'Well, that's convenient for Rik.'

'You're missing the point, Mum. I met Rik's aunt – she's the person I went to see today.'

'You went to see some stranger's aunt?' Mum's face is stern.

'She – Rik's aunt . . . she confirmed things that he'd said.'

'*What* things?'

We sit down at the kitchen table. It's a relief to tell Mum everything that's happened. I leave nothing out, except the fact that Tyler and I basically broke in to Sandy's flat before she arrived home. There's no point getting myself into even more trouble.

Mum listens without interrupting. As I finish, she sighs heavily.

'Okay, let me tell you about Rik Adamski.' She leans forward. 'He and your dad *weren't* friends, whatever Rik said. According to Dad, he was shady . . . a con man . . . mixed up with some very unsavoury people.' She pauses. 'He was actually fired on Dad's say-so.'

'No, that's not true,' I say. 'If Dad said any of that he was lying to protect you. Rik told me Dad had done that – deliberately made out they weren't friends when they were – in case anyone asked you questions after he disappeared.'

Mum blinks, her pale forehead creasing in a deep frown. 'Oh, Cat,' she says. 'I understand how much you miss Dad, but can't you hear how ridiculous all this sounds?' She sighs. 'Seriously, doesn't what I've just told you make more sense than Rik's lies? Plus I did Rik's birth chart after Dad told me about him. He has Gemini in the ascendant *and* his moon is in Scorpio in the eighth house. Put those together and you're bound to find a liar and a cheat.'

Now who sounds ridiculous?

I look up at her, feeling sullen. 'But why would Rik make up that Dad was still alive?' I ask. 'And why after all this time?'

Mum shrugs. 'Perhaps he's been away or . . . or in prison. Or perhaps he just got sacked from yet another job and blames Dad for where he's ended up and thought he'd take it out on you?'

'You're saying he'd make up a story like that for revenge?'

'It's possible,' Mum says. 'Remember that moon sign of his. People with Scorpio in the eighth are almost always mean and manipulative. I've seen it a million times.'

'But what about his aunt?'

'She didn't think Dad was alive, did she?'

'No . . .' I concede reluctantly. 'But there was this man on a bike. He . . . he might have been watching us.' I stammer to a halt, aware that I'm clutching at straws in my attempt to convince her.

'*Might?*' Mum frowns. 'What does that mean? Did he approach you? Did he follow you?'

I shake my head, falling silent.

'I'm so sorry, Cat,' Mum says slowly, 'but you need to face reality. Dad . . . Dad's gone and I *know* that you're hurting but—'

'This isn't about me *hurting*.' Her words rub against me like the fine sandpaper I use to keep my sewing needles and scissors sharp. 'This is about saving Dad's life. We need to find him before the FFG track him down.'

Mum reaches across and pats my hand. 'I want you to put this whole story out of your head.'

'I can't,' I say. 'I *won't*.'

'You have to,' Mum persists. 'Do you have Rik Adamski's number? We should report him for harassment.'

I shake my head. 'He said he used a burner phone.'

'Of course he did.' Mum rolls her eyes. 'Now I need to get on with my work. I have clients to organize and a speech to write.' She gets up. 'I meant what I said. You need to let Rik and his stupid lies go.' She pauses. 'I want you to promise me that you'll tell me *immediately* if he calls you again. Okay?'

I give her a sulky nod, though I've got no intention of keeping my word. Mum's wrong. I *know* she is.

'Okay, then.' Mum gives me a final, worried look, then heads off to her office. I hurry up to my room, where I lie on my bed, thoughts whirling through my head. If Rik really was lying about him and Dad being close friends, how come he knew so much about me? Mum would probably say he'd looked on my social media. But that doesn't explain how he knew about

'Kitterbug'. Or the FFG going round to Aunt Sandy and asking questions.

No. Whatever Mum says, I'm certain Dad is out there somewhere, and I'm going to find him. And fast.

Whatever it takes.

13

I wake up the next day to find Bess standing over me, a new drawing clutched in her hand. She gives a little skip when she sees my eyes are open and proudly displays her picture. I'm expecting another dog and, indeed, there is a Pirate-like puppy, complete with brown patch over one eye, to the side of her main drawing. But the focus of the picture is a man – clearly meant to be Mr Tuesday, down to his khaki cargo shorts and big smile. I wriggle on to my elbows and peer more closely. A woman stands next to Mr Tuesday. Her head is wound round with a purple scarf. Wild red curls spring out of it at all angles. She's wearing a dress full of colourful swirls with long pink fringing flying out from the arms.

'Is that Mum?' I ask.

Bess nods, beaming with delight. Her hair isn't plaited yet and falls, soft and golden, over her shoulders. I stare at her sweet, heart-shaped face. It's not how Bess means it, I'm sure, but it's like she's drawn a picture of her mum and dad.

Except, of course, that Mr Tuesday isn't her dad.

Anger rises inside me, not at Bess but at the situation . . . the way Mum is in denial, the way that she won't even admit the possibility Dad might still be alive.

I force myself to smile at Bess and tell her what a brilliant picture she's done, then I dress quickly, determined to find Tyler as soon as possible. I put on a green A-line dress that I made from an old silk kimono of Mum's and pin back my fringe with a vintage jade-green hairclip.

Standing back, I examine myself in the mirror. I messed up the stitching on the side seam of this dress, but, thanks to the way the silk falls in folds, you can't really tell. It's a pretty shape and colour, but it can't disguise my awkwardness. I was aiming for 'cool and quirky' but I'm probably just signalling 'trying too hard'.

I heave a sigh, altering the hairclip so that more of my fringe falls over my face. Then I turn away from the mirror, trying not to think about how much less attractive than Tyler I am. He'd never be interested in me in a million years . . .

Mrs Trimble is chatting to Bess in the kitchen when I wander downstairs. 'Now let's put in the eggs,' she says. 'Did you whisk up all three?'

I reach the back door and shuffle my feet into my sliders.

'Ah, Cat, good, you're up.' Mum stands in her office door. She's wearing cut-off jeans and a bright pink top – her 'non-client' clothes for those days when she isn't seeing people at the house.

'I need to do something,' I say, putting my hand on the back-door handle.

'Not so fast.' Mum grins. She's not wearing any make-up and her eyes look smaller than usual without the long black flicks and frosted eyeshadow. 'Come with me; I want to talk to you.'

I trudge reluctantly across the hall and follow her into her office. It's the usual cluttered mess of scattered papers and bulging files.

'I'm doing the keynote speech at the Mercury Rising Astrological Convention next week and I haven't even begun writing the thing,' Mum confides. 'I want to make a start today, but there's masses of admin to catch up on.' She waves her arm to indicate the room. I frown. What is she driving at? 'I think it will be good for you,' Mum continues, 'not to mention a huge help to me, for you to spend the next few days helping out with my office work.' She smiles brightly.

Is she serious? My frown deepens.

'Come on, Cat. It will take your mind off all this nonsense about Dad and this awful Rik character.'

I chew on my lip, feeling mutinous. I have no intention of 'taking my mind' off trying to find Dad. In fact, what I want to do now – more than anything – is go around to the Barn, get Tyler and talk it all through with him. He was so smart yesterday figuring out the FFG tattoo. I'm sure he'll have a suggestion for what I should do next.

'I can't, Mum,' I say. 'I . . . I don't feel well,' I lie. 'I think I have a temperature.'

Mum's eyes narrow. She takes a step towards me and feels my forehead with the back of her hand. 'Nonsense.' She gives me a beady stare. My heart sinks. It's not a look her clients ever see, but I know that expression all too well. It means she's made up her mind, and nothing will deflect her. 'Come on, now, Cat,' she says, briskly, 'let me show you what I need you to do.'

I pull the keyboard of Mum's computer towards me. I've only been at work for an hour and I'm already bored and hot, my top sticking to my back. I open the website email and groan. There are seventy-two new emails, most of which will be enquiries from people wanting to either make an appointment with Mum, or find out more about her work. My job is to sift through these, printing out the requests for private readings and drafting replies to the others. I delete the obvious crackpots who just want to meet Mum because she used to be a D-list celebrity, such as:

As a fellow traveller on the Spiritual Superhighway, I would love to meet, connect and share my thoughts on the influence of the Venus retrograde on modern society.

I also delete the hateful messages. To be fair, the worst of these appear on Mum's social media, which she deals with herself, but there are always a few emails too.

Some of these are semi-religious:

Know that you are doing the work of the devil.

Others are simply scornful, with bad spelling:

Your a loony and totel witch.

That sort of thing.

It takes nearly two more hours to plough through them all. Mum checks in on me several times, then says I can have an hour off for lunch. I grab a sandwich from the pile Mrs Trimble has made and stroll outside. I wonder, idly, where Bess is. Normally, by this time in the day, she'd have sought me out and curled up nearby to draw or play silently with her menagerie of dolls and soft toy animals.

Mostly, however, I'm thinking about finding Dad – and wondering where Tyler is. I gulp down my sandwich and wander across the lawn towards the Barn. I see him before he sees me. He's squatting in the courtyard, digging away at the weeds that peek up between the gravel around the mosaic. He's hunched over, the muscles in his arms flexing as he works. Mr Tuesday is leaning against the sundial in the centre, examining the piece of paper in his hands.

'There's a lot to do,' he says. 'The only area that doesn't need work is this.' He indicates the inner circle of star-shaped tiles that surround the sundial. 'So here's the plan: once we've cleared out the weeds and the broken tiles, we can start work on the repairs – and the replacements for the missing star signs.' He points to the three big gaps in the horoscope that surrounds the sundial, then holds up the piece of paper. 'The outline designs for those are on this.'

'What do they look like?' Tyler asks, glancing up.

'See for yourself.' Mr Tuesday offers him the paper.

Neither of them have noticed I'm here. I take a step closer and realize, with a jolt of surprise, that Bess is here too, sitting at the far edge of the courtyard on her rug. As usual, she's surrounded by a cluster of her favourite toys plus, of course, her drawing book and pens. She's concentrating fiercely on her picture.

Like the others, she hasn't noticed me.

Tyler walks over to his dad and takes the piece of paper. They're both wearing long cargo shorts and trainers, but whereas Mr Tuesday's shoes are worn and weather-beaten, Tyler's are clean and new. I gaze down at the dress I chose so carefully earlier. Out here in the sunlight, I realize it's badly creased and that the crooked seam is more obvious than I'd thought. I tug the skirt straight, feeling self-conscious.

Across the courtyard, Tyler is peering intently at the paper with the designs for the three missing star signs.

'According to these outlines –' Mr Tuesday scratches his head – 'we need to put in a couple of fishes swimming in opposite directions on the right side, then a lion's head and what looks like some sort of lobster on the left.'

'What do they mean?' Tyler asks.

Mr Tuesday shrugs, then glances across at Bess. 'Hey, Bess, any idea what these star signs are?'

Bess scampers over. Mr Tuesday lowers the paper so she can take a look. She wrinkles her nose and shakes her head. Mr Tuesday laughs and Bess grins back. It strikes me that I've seen her smile more in the two days that the Tuesdays have been here than in the whole of the previous seventeen months.

'Hey, Cat!' Tyler looks up and sees me at last.

'Hi!' I wander over, trying to look like I'm just on a casual stroll. 'Hi, Mr Tuesday. Hey, Bess.'

Bess looks up at me, her dark eyes registering surprise at the super-casual tone I'm using. My stomach gives a twist. She can always tell when I'm feeling self-conscious.

'Hello there,' Mr Tuesday says cheerily. 'We were just looking at the designs for the mosaic renovation. Afraid I'm not very up on star signs.'

'Oh,' I say. 'Um . . . well, the fishes are Pisces. Then the lion is Leo, and the other one isn't a lobster, it's a crab. For Cancer.' I break off, suddenly feeling awkward that I've said the word Tyler's mum died from. I look down, my cheeks burning.

Mr Tuesday nods sagely. 'Well, there's a thing.'

I can feel Tyler's eyes on my face.

Mr Tuesday gives him a nudge. 'Wanna take a break, son? You've been at it for hours.'

Tyler nods. I look up.

'I'll get us a drink,' he says.

He disappears inside, while Bess shows Mr Tuesday her drawing. He's incredibly gentle with her, taking far more time to examine each picture than Mum ever does.

'This is a great one,' he murmurs. 'Had a pup like that when I was a boy.'

There's a stillness about him, a patient calmness which Mum doesn't have at all. And it's different from Dad, too, who was always getting us to run about and play and *do* stuff.

Tyler reappears with three cartons of juice. He gives one to Bess and hands me another.

'Your mum was very kind to provide us with all that food,' Mr Tuesday says. 'We won't need to shop for days.'

It's the second time he's mentioned the groceries. Should I tell him that it was almost certainly Mrs Trimble who went shopping for them? I decide against; talking about it would just be embarrassing. I shield my eyes from the sun. 'Shall we take these into the shade?' I ask Tyler.

He nods and we wander around the side of the Barn to the cool of the orchard. We sit down opposite each other, each of us with our back against a gnarly tree trunk.

'What's up?' Tyler asks.

I smile to myself. Clearly Bess isn't the only one who can sense when I'm upset.

'I told Mum everything . . . about Dad, what Rik said, talking to Rik's aunt, the guy on the bike . . .'

'And?'

I sigh. 'She's certain Rik's made up everything to get some weird kind of revenge on Dad. She was furious that he'd got in touch with me,' I explain. 'Rik warned me she'd been fed a load of lies about him. She refuses to trust anything he says.'

It suddenly occurs to me that, in the cold light of day, Tyler might have come to the same conclusion.

'Right.' Tyler takes a sip of his juice. He puts it carefully on the grass beside him.

'I don't buy that Rik was lying,' he says at last.

'I don't either,' I say, feeling relieved.

'For lots of reasons, but mostly because it doesn't make sense that Rik would do something so convoluted after so much time,' Tyler says. 'Anyway, if Rik was lying about everything, why did the FFG visit his aunt?' He takes another gulp of his drink.

'Exactly.'

We sit in silence for a minute, the only sound the breeze rustling in the trees above.

'So what d'you want to do now?' Tyler asks.

'I guess I need to look for clues to where Dad might have gone.' I make a face. 'I just don't know where to begin.'

Tyler nods. 'What about his old belongings? Did he have a laptop?'

I shake my head. 'He used the PC in Mum's office sometimes. He had a phone, of course, but, like I told you, that was found in his boat when it washed up on shore. It was wet from the sea and the salt . . . damaged beyond repair.'

'What about the rest of his stuff?' Tyler persists.

'There's the box in Mum's office that I've already been through,' I explain. 'And some more in the attic.'

'Shall we look there, then?' Tyler stands up. He has a way of moving that's muscular, but graceful.

I hesitate. Part of me wants to look alone. Letting Tyler see my family's private things feels uncomfortable. But Tyler is looking at me expectantly, with those intense brown-gold eyes of his.

Anyway, searching through everything will be quicker if there are two of us.

'Sure.' I scramble to my feet. 'Let's go.'

I lead Tyler across the lawn and into our house. He follows me to the end of the first-floor landing, where I open the little door that leads up to our attic. Tyler has to duck as he walks up the narrow stairs. I switch on the light on the beam at the top.

The attic is old and dusty and full of stuff from not just my childhood and Mum's, but loads of her family before her. It's crammed from floor to ceiling with boxes and bags spilling open with everything from old, often broken toys to moth-eaten curtains. Bess's old pushchair lies on top of an ancient set of skittles, while cobwebs festoon the three large trunks tipped on their ends in the corner.

'Where're your dad's things?' Tyler asks, looking around. 'Are they at the front?'

I sigh, the enormity of the task ahead hitting me. 'They could be anywhere,' I say helplessly. 'Mum chucks stuff up here every six months or so. She just shoves things wherever there's a space. No labels. It's all random.'

Tyler whistles, running his hand through his hair.

'I know,' I say. 'It's going to take ages, but it's all there is to go on.'

Tyler reaches across and squeezes my shoulder. His touch sends a tingle through my whole body.

'Don't worry, Cat,' he says. And I realize it's the first time he's actually spoken my name out loud. 'We'll do it together.'

14

It feels weird letting Tyler help me, I'm so used to doing everything by myself. Still, there's no way I'd be able to get through the mountain of stuff in the attic on my own. We don't have much time: I'm stuck in Mum's office most of the day, working on her appointments and emails. Meanwhile Tyler is helping his dad with the mosaic renovation. As soon as we're both free, we head up to the attic and open endless bags and boxes.

By the end of the second afternoon, we've found nothing connected with Dad, let alone anything that will give us a clue as to his current whereabouts. Just a load of old toys and clothes plus some ancient and mostly broken household equipment, as well as furniture and ornaments from Mum's childhood and before.

I catch sight of my reflection in an old zodiac-themed mirror with cracks running through Scorpio and Capricorn. I'm so shocked by the dust creating crazy peaks in my hair that I move too fast trying to brush it out, knock over an ancient vacuum cleaner and, in jumping away so that it doesn't fall on my toes, bang my forehead on a beam.

'Ouch!' I let out a yelp.

Tyler races over. 'You okay?'

'Yeah,' I say, seriously embarrassed. 'I'm fine.'

'Let me see.' Tyler peers closely. So closely I can count his eyelashes. My heart thuds and I pray he can't hear it. He runs his finger, very gently, over my forehead. I close my eyes, my skin tingling where he's touched it. 'Ah, there's a little bump,' he says.

In my imagination he's about to lean just that fraction closer and brush his lips against mine. Every muscle in my body tenses, my nerve endings sparking like fireworks. But then I open my eyes and find that he is already turning away, going back to the box he's been examining.

I swallow down my disappointment. I have to get used to the idea that Tyler just sees me as a friend and hide the strange, raw feeling I sometimes have around him, like my skin is inside out.

That evening Rik messages me. Like all his texts, it comes from a different number than the one before, but essentially asks the same questions:

How are you getting on? Any leads?

I message back straight away, explaining we're looking through Dad's things but haven't yet found anything that indicates where he might be hiding. I also tell Rik about visiting his Aunt Sandy – though I decide not to mention the mysterious motorbike rider in the red skulls helmet.

The FFG are definitely on your and Dad's trail – they went to see Sandy the day before we did.

Rik texts immediately:

That's not good. Please be careful

It's not exactly a reassuring message, but it helps to know that he's out there, feeling concern and offering support. Especially when I'm getting neither from Mum.

She has no idea that we're up here. She's distracted and busy, either seeing clients or working on her talk for the upcoming astrology convention. She asks a couple of times if Rik has been in touch again. I tell her he hasn't. What's the point of being honest? Mum would only make a fuss and order me not to speak to him again.

The third day of our attic search and we're still only about halfway through all the bags and boxes. There's a constant knot in my stomach. The gangsters who think Dad stole their diamond could be getting closer and closer to finding him. For all I know they could have found him already and killed him. *No.* I can't let myself think that. But it's hard to stay positive.

'Doesn't your mum ever throw anything away?' Tyler asks, despairingly.

'She says she's never had to,' I explain, 'because she's lived here her whole life.'

'I can't imagine how weird that would be,' Tyler mutters.

'I gaze at his face. His left side is in the shadow thrown by the overhead light, but his eyes still gleam intently.

'After your mum, did your dad ever meet anyone else?' I ask.

Tyler shakes his head. 'No,' he says. 'We've never even had a pet. It's always just been the two of us. I don't even have any grandparents any more.'

I turn back to my rummaging in a crate of ancient wooden tennis rackets, wondering what such a tiny family would feel like. As I peer into the corners of the crate, Tyler gives a low whistle.

'Look,' he says. 'These must be your dad's.' I glance up and he shoves the box he's examining towards me. My heart leaps. Here's a boat Dad made once from a model kit I bought him with my pocket money. Underneath it is a folder. I open it eagerly. Inside are all Dad's sailing certificates going back to when he was a child.

Tyler is rummaging deeper in the box. He pulls out two trophies, then peers at the labels more closely. His face falls. 'Oh, but they're really old.'

I take a look at the dates. 'Yeah, they're from when Dad was a teenager.' I rustle around in the papers at the bottom of the box, but they're all school-related things of Mum's, plus a few baby pictures of me. My heart sinks. There's nothing here that helps.

Tyler pulls out another box and lifts the lid. As he sets it down on the grimy attic floor he glances up at me. 'Did your dad grow up by the sea?' he asks.

'Yeah, North Devon. He used to say that if you can sail there you can sail anywhere in the world.'

'I've never been on a boat,' Tyler confesses, his cheeks pinking a little.

'Really?' I ask. 'Dad used to take me and Bess out every weekend. He had a little sailing boat. The *Marvista*.'

'The *what*?'

'*Marvista*,' I repeat. 'It's Italian, no . . . Spanish. Whatever. It means . . . sea view.' I stop, eyes widening as the significance of this shoots into my veins. 'Oh my God.'

'What?' Tyler asks, looking up. 'Cat?'

'I've just remembered something.' My mind claws at

the memory, trying to see it more clearly. 'I remember Dad arguing with Mum about how he'd like us to move closer to the seashore and Mum saying she'd never leave this house, that she's Brockledore born and bred.' I meet Tyler's gaze, suddenly certain. 'If Dad had to give up everything . . . his life, his work, his family . . . I think that living by the sea would be the one thing that would make it bearable.'

'Okay, but . . .'

'It makes sense. He loved the sea. He loved the *Marvista*. In his drawings, next to his signature, he always drew a boat,' I say, a grin creeping across my face. 'Mum always says that Dad was forever trying new things and not sticking at anything, but boats, sailing - he *always* loved those.'

Tyler stares at me. 'I don't—'

I leap up. 'I know I can't prove it, but I'd bet *anything* that wherever Dad is living, it's near the sea.'

'Okay, but . . .' Tyler frowns. 'I hate to point this out, but Britain is an island – there are *masses* of places near the sea.'

He's right. For a second, I feel the hope and excitement start to ebb away. Then an image of the brochures I found in Mum's office springs into my head. I race over to the attic door. 'I've got an idea. You carry on looking here.' I hurry away, down to Mum's office and drag out the box. I'd thought I'd seen two or three print-outs from websites of home rentals by the sea. In fact, now I'm properly looking, there are ten separate bundles. Each one of these contains at least a hundred potential places that Dad could have rented. It's better than the whole of Britain, but it's still an overwhelming number to investigate.

At least it's a start.

Clutching the print-outs I race back up to the attic. I quickly explain my idea.

'So . . .' I finish. 'If there was just some way to link the places Dad had looked at with the time period just before he disappeared . . .' I trail off, the enormity of the challenge overwhelming me again.

'But there is.' Tyler's eyes shine bright with excitement. Even with the dirty smudges on his cheek and T-shirt, his face is ridiculously handsome.

'What?' I ask.

For an answer, Tyler delves into the box behind him and brings out a heap of paper.

'These are mostly credit card statements and paper receipts,' he explains. 'If we can just find the ones from the couple of weeks before he died . . .'

I gasp. 'We'll be able to work out what he was spending money on when he knew he needed to fake his death.'

We stare at each other. Tyler grins, moving a tiny bit closer to me. This time, I'm careful not to misread him. I take a step away. Tyler hesitates for a second, then puts half the papers in front of me.

'Here,' he says. 'You sort through those. I'll do the rest.'

We scan the papers fast, checking each sheet and putting it back in the box if it's too old. After ten minutes we're left with one credit card statement and five receipts.

I snatch up the statement and read the list of names Dad had bought from. It's just food shops and the local pub. Nothing that suggests he was preparing to leave home for ever. Nothing that indicates any kind of forward planning whatsoever, let alone anything connected to the seashore.

My heart sinks. Maybe I've got this all wrong. I force myself to read to the very bottom of the page. The last item is dated the day Dad died. It's a payment for fifty pounds to Farraday Inc.

'What's Farraday Inc?'

Tyler shakes his head.

I hand him a bunch of cottage rental print-outs. 'See if you can find the name Farraday anywhere.'

We both start looking, scanning each page carefully.

'These are all things like cottages-on-the-coast.com,' Tyler complains. 'Nothing like Farraday.'

I keep looking, my excitement building. The name

doesn't come up on the first three batches of paper I examine. And then I turn to the fourth – SEAVIEW MOBILE HOMES – LONG-TERM LETS. I open it at the back, intending to flick forwards. *There*, at the bottom of the info page in tiny print is the name Farraday Inc.

'I've found it!' I thrust the page at Tyler. 'What's a long-term let?'

'When you rent somewhere for a long time, I think, rather than just on holiday.' Tyler pauses. 'Do you think your dad would have rented a mobile home to live in?'

'If it was by the sea, yes, but *where* exactly?' I scan the pages eagerly. Seaview Mobile Homes offers long-term lets at three trailer parks: one just a few miles away, near Torquay; another, larger, place just outside Cardiff in Wales and a third, much smaller place on the coast near the village of Saltcliff in Norfolk, on the east coast of England. 'Dad wouldn't stay in Devon,' I reason. 'Rik was adamant he'd leave the area. And the Welsh park is too big, too close to a big city. Rik was sure Dad would have gone somewhere really isolated.'

'That leaves Norfolk,' Tyler says.

Nodding, I snatch up my phone and, with trembling fingers, dial the number for the Saltcliff park.

'Hello? How may I help?' The woman on the end of the phone sounds bored and irritable.

'I'm looking for Alan Mooney,' I say, trying to sound more confident than I feel. 'He booked . . . that is, I think he might be living in your mobile-home park.'

'I see.' There's a short pause, then the woman says she'll check her database. A minute later she's back. 'No Alan Mooney lives here,' she says briskly.

'Oh . . .' I frown. 'Okay, but could you check back over, say, the past year and a half?'

The woman makes an exasperated clicking sound with her tongue. 'Hold the line.' Another minute and she's back again. 'No, no one of that name has lived here in the past two years. I've just done a scan of the files.' She sighs, impatiently. 'Was there anything else?'

I tell her there isn't and ring off. Despair mounting, I turn to Tyler. 'What do we do now?' I ask. 'Dad isn't in the Norfolk mobile-home park after all.'

Tyler frowns. 'You don't know that,' he points out. 'You just know that no one called Alan Mooney lives there. Stands to reason your dad would have used a different name to avoid arousing suspicion. He'd left all his ID behind anyway.'

'You're right.' Hope surges inside me.

'Not that it helps much,' Tyler goes on glumly, 'unless we know what name he *is* using.'

'We don't need his name,' I say, a small smile creeping

across my face. 'Not if we go there and look for him in person.'

'Go to Norfolk?' Tyler's jaw drops. 'But that's right on the other side of England.'

'I know,' I say. 'But I can't see another option.' I hesitate. 'You don't have to come . . . I can go on my—'

'Of course I'm coming,' Tyler interrupts. He grins at me, determined. I smile back. 'But how are we going to get there?'

The smile falls from my face. 'I have no idea.'

15

Half an hour passes and we still can't see a way to get to Norfolk. Tyler and I sit on the dusty attic floor and look at the challenge from every angle.

'It's too far to go there and back in one day,' Tyler says, tapping at his phone. 'We'd have to get to London first, then it's another two and a half hours from London to Norwich . . . plus an hour on the bus to Overstrand and then a three-mile walk to the mobile-home park at Saltcliff.'

'We'd have to stay overnight somewhere,' I say with a sigh.

'I don't have the money for that,' Tyler says. 'Not on top of all the buses and trains we'd need to catch.'

'I should pay, it's my dad we're looking for.'

Tyler frowns. Before he can speak, I hurry on. 'Never mind the money, Mum would never agree to me going all that way. She'll be furious if we sneak off.'

'Yeah, my dad wouldn't be too pleased either.' Tyler makes a face.

I bite my lip, unsure how to express what I want to say next. 'I . . . um . . . even if we can't get there, I really appreciate you saying you'll come with.'

'Don't sweat it.' Tyler smiles shyly. 'And we will get there. It's gonna be an adventure.'

'Cat? Where *are* you?' Mum's imperious cry blasts up the stairs. 'Come *here*!'

We head downstairs. It's late – Bess is already sitting at the kitchen table, tucking into the tea that Mrs Trimble has left for her. Tyler slips away, out of the back door, just as Mum emerges from her office.

'There you are,' she snaps. 'Didn't you hear me calling?'

'Yes,' I say, instantly riled. 'That's why I came down.'

Mum gives an exasperated tut, then shoos me into the kitchen. She flaps around, looking for something, while I join Bess at the table and help myself to some fish pie.

'Mmm, creamy,' I say, smacking my lips as I swallow a mouthful of mashed potato.

Bess gives a silent giggle, her eyes crinkling.

'Cat.' Mum sounds a low warning from across the room. 'Oh, I hate it when Neptune is in transit. I can't find *anything.*' She pauses. 'Do you know where Mrs Trimble might have put the scissors?'

'Drawers to the left of the cooker,' I say. 'Second one down.'

Mum stares at me for a second, then turns away and rummages in the drawer.

I grin at Bess. Truth is, I know where the scissors are because I borrowed them last week to cut a piece of fabric I needed for my dress. It's weird to think that, just a few days ago, dress-making was the most important thing in my summer.

Mum retrieves the scissors with a surprised sniff, then heads back to her office. Bess and I finish eating, and I load the plates in the dishwasher. Mum comes back in just as I'm rinsing our glasses. She replaces the scissors in the drawer and trudges over to the fridge, where she heaves another weary sigh as she pulls out a bottle of wine and unscrews the cap. 'I'm exhausted,' she moans, reaching for a glass and letting the wine glug into it. 'This keynote address will be the death of me. I can't believe I have to have it ready *and* myself packed up in just two days.' She shudders. 'If only my Mercury was in something helpful like Gemini or Libra.' She sighs. 'It's the thought of the journey too. All that way into the stink of London.'

I straighten up from the sink, an idea sparking inside my head.

'What about letting me come with you to London?' I ask.

Mum stares at me, clearly taken aback. 'To the convention?' she asks.

'You're driving anyway, so there'd be plenty of room in the car. And I could help with all your admin. Give out information on your stall while you're doing readings and talking to people.' There's no way I'm really intending to help her out at the convention, of course. But it can't be far from there to Liverpool Street Station, where – I've already discovered – trains leave for Norfolk.

Mum leans against the counter. 'I guess you *would* be a help,' she says. 'I mean, I know they'll give me a volunteer but . . .'

'But I'd be much better,' I point out. 'I know how all your stuff works.'

'That's true.' Mum nods. 'The accommodation wouldn't be a problem either. They've lined me up a flat near Alexandra Palace – that's where the convention is – and there's a pull-out sofa bed, so . . . I mean, I'll have to socialize a bit in the evenings, but you're old enough to be left alone for a few hours, and it would save me paying Mrs Trimble to stay over, so maybe . . .'

'Oh, please, Mum,' I say. 'It would be so much fun. And it's not like we're going on any other kind of holiday.'

'You'd have to be responsible for Bess, of course.'

My jaw drops. 'Bess?'

Mum gives a nod. 'Of course, I can hardly leave her behind.'

I frown. Bess wasn't part of my plan at all. It's one thing plotting to give Mum the slip and make my way to Norfolk for the day – but leaving Bess behind means abandoning her to face Mum's hysteria after I've gone.

Well, it can't be helped.

I leave Mum sipping her wine at the kitchen table and hurry over to the Barn. I cross the courtyard, carefully avoiding the section that Mr Tuesday has fenced off. The mosaic is starting to take shape. The missing astrological symbols are still absent, of course, but overall it looks tidier and brighter, with all the weeds gone and about a quarter of the damaged tiles replaced.

I hesitate outside the Barn. Through the window I can see Tyler, shovelling in the final forkful from a bowl of pasta. His free arm is resting on the kitchen table. The muscles under his T-shirt are clearly defined, even in the gentle glow of the indoor light.

I push down the longing that fills me. There's no point me wishing Tyler would miraculously discover he likes me.

I hurry to the back door which is propped open with a shoe – presumably to let some air in. I give it a soft tap, then ease it open and peer into the room.

'Hello there, Cat,' Mr Tuesday says, his face wreathed in a smile. 'Haven't seen you all day.'

'Mum's got me working hard on her appointments and stuff,' I say, still standing in the doorway. I can feel Tyler's eyes on my face, but I'm deliberately not looking at him. I'm certain that, whenever I do, he can see just how much I like him and I don't want to expose myself any more than I already have. 'Er . . .' I hesitate. 'I just wanted a quick word with Tyler.'

'Sure . . . go on, son,' says Mr Tuesday. 'I'll clear the dishes.'

I let myself look at Tyler at last, as he stands up and lopes over to the door. He holds it open, as if inviting me properly inside, but I beckon him out to the courtyard.

'What's up?' he says, softly, letting the door swing shut behind him. His golden-brown eyes gleam in the dying light. 'Are you okay? You look weird.'

Great.

I pull myself together. 'I just found a way for us to get to Norfolk,' I whisper. 'Well, to London, anyway. Mum's agreed to take me with her to the convention she's speaking at. She's driving up, first thing the day after tomorrow.' I explain how I've offered to help Mum with her admin and her stall at the convention centre. 'Once we're in London, we just need to get the train to Norfolk, then the bus, then walk to the mobile-home park and . . . and find my dad. I've looked at the times. We can be back in London by evening.'

As I speak, a frown creases Tyler's forehead. 'That's brilliant, Cat,' he says slowly. 'But I don't see how I fit in – your mum won't want me with you.'

'I've thought of that,' I say eagerly. 'The convention's at Alexandra Palace, in North London. It can't be that far from where you live. I thought you could say you wanted to go back. Stay at a friend's? Or . . . or see your girlfriend?'

Tyler nods. Does that mean he *does* have a girlfriend in London? Or just that he agrees with my plan?

'That could work,' he murmurs. 'I'll have to set it up properly. Dad'll want to check it's okay with whoever I stay with, but . . .' He grins and my heart gives a little skip. 'Yeah, that'll work.'

We stand in the courtyard, smiling at each other. Tyler seems like he wants to say something so I wait, my whole body tingling with pleasure that he seems so delighted.

'Wow,' he says finally. 'It'll be amazing to get back to London for a bit. I mean, I know we'll be off to Norfolk on one of the days, but I'll have another to see my mates. It'll be brilliant.'

The smile falls from my face. Of course. It makes total

sense that seeing his real friends is what he's really looking forward to.

I shouldn't have expected anything else.

16

The drive to London is like one of those fairground rides where you start out all excited and hopeful and end up desperate to get off because you're feeling so sick.

It's Mum's fault, of course. She's told Mr Tuesday that she's 'absolutely delighted' to be giving Tyler a lift to London, but nearly four hours into the journey it's embarrassingly obvious that she'd rather he wasn't here.

We've barely reached the outskirts of the city, but Mum's already mentioned the fact she needs to drop Tyler off five times.

'I'm very happy to be doing it, of course, but on top of getting to Alexandra Palace . . . well, I don't know the area and the driving in London is terribly aggressive with all those one-way systems.'

'You can just leave me at Alexandra Palace,' Tyler says, shifting awkwardly in the passenger seat. I'd hoped we could ride together in the back, but Mum insisted Bess and I sat there and that Tyler was up front with her.

'Nonsense,' Mum trills, her jaw clenched. 'I promised

your dad I'd take you right to your friend's door. It's no imposition at all.'

The closer we drive, the worse things get. I was Bess's age on my last visit and don't remember the city at all. As we negotiate the endless streets full of cars and vans and buses, Mum misses turn after turn, sitting hunched over the steering wheel. Bess, who has spent the journey drawing and listening to stories on her headphones, is now, thankfully, asleep. Mum, meanwhile, gets in more and more of a flap.

'Oh, this is so confusing! Oh my goodness and now I have to do this detour for you, Tyler. Which of course I'm totally happy to do, but . . . Aaagh!' she shrieks, making Tyler and me both jump. 'That car behind nearly hit us!'

In front of me, Tyler stiffens, clearly terrified by her driving.

'Jeez, Mum!' I mutter.

'Stop attacking me, Cat.' Mum takes both hands off the wheel, waving them angrily in the air. 'This is just the downside of having Sagittarius in the eighth house and Capricorn rising. It's not my fault I find this . . . this *onslaught* so overwhelming.' She sighs. 'I'm sorry, Tyler, but I'm going to have to drop you at the Palace after all.'

'That's fine,' Tyler says, sounding relieved he will soon be let out of the car.

'He said it would be fine over an hour ago,' I can't help but comment.

'Will you *please* stop being so aggressive, Cat,' Mum snaps. She glances across at Tyler. 'As soon as I did that one's birth chart I knew she'd be difficult. It's her having her Sun *and* Mars in Aries. Same as her dad. And not just a temper, but a *sarcastic* one.' She glares at me in the rear-view mirror.

My face burns with embarrassment. I'm used to Mum saying stuff like this, but Tyler is looking at her – not for the first time – like she's utterly mad.

It's gone 3.30 p.m. by the time we arrive at our apartment. After the busy streets on the way in, I'm astonished by how quiet and leafy it is here. I'd imagined the whole of London would be stylish and exciting, but the road where we're staying, close to the convention, feels a lot like towns in Devon, though maybe with more houses packed in together. And definitely more cars. I can't help but feel a little disappointed it's not more glamorous.

As Mum rummages among her bags in the boot, muttering to herself about 'London parking', I go over to Tyler.

'Is it like this where you're from?' I ask.

'What do you mean?' He stares at me, the sun lighting his caramel skin, making his eyes look more golden than usual.

'Just rows of houses.' I pause. 'I thought there'd be more shops and . . . and atmosphere, more *buzz*.'

'Did you?' Tyler gives me a wry smile. 'London is a lot of different places.'

I frown, unsure what he means. 'So is where you're from more like the centre?' I gabble. 'Like it is around Oxford Street and the big department stores? Where they have shops like Liberty with loads of amazing fabrics?'

It's the most I've said all journey.

'No,' he says shortly. 'Where I'm from is nothing like that.' He gazes at me curiously. I wish I knew what he was thinking. Then he lowers his voice. 'See you tomorrow, 9 a.m.' A second later, he shouts a 'thanks for the lift, Mrs Mooney' at Mum and strides away.

I watch him go. He doesn't look back. Clearly, it doesn't even occur to him that he might want to.

Mum shouts at me to help with the bags and she, Bess and I take our stuff into the apartment. She's still grumpy, complaining that the flat is too small and lacks 'a spiritual vibe'. Of course, half an hour later, when the convention co-ordinator turns up with a young volunteer totally in awe of Mum's celebrity status, Mum is all smiles and enthusiasm.

I wish the people who think she's so serene and easy-going could see how bad-tempered and demanding she gets when there isn't an audience around to impress.

A car is coming to pick us up at 8 a.m. tomorrow, so that Mum can set up her stand before the convention opens at 10.

'Oh, it sounds just wonderful,' she coos. 'Thanks *so* much for all your hard work.' She reaches out and pulls Bess, hiding behind her, a little closer. 'I'm so lucky to have so many people looking after me. Including these two beautiful angels.' She indicates me and Bess.

Bess gives the co-ordinator a shy smile. I scowl, earning a sharp prod in the back from Mum.

'See you tomorrow,' Mum says cheerfully, as the others leave. 'Can't wait!'

As soon as the door of the flat shuts behind them, she turns to me and snaps:

'Make your sister a snack. I'm going to have a bath.' And sashays off to the bathroom.

She's in a slightly better mood once she's washed and changed. We order in a takeaway which we eat in front of the TV. I glance every now and then at my phone, wondering if Tyler will message me. Of course he doesn't. He's probably out with his friends. Maybe even the girlfriend I'm sure he must have, who he hasn't told me about. Nobody as good-looking and kind as him could be single, especially coming from somewhere as full of people as London.

I do get a text from Rik, on yet another new number.

Rik here. Any update?

I hesitate before writing back. I don't want to sound too excited, in case the Saltcliff lead is wrong. In the end I decide to be positive, but not too specific:

Think Dad might be in Norfolk, going tomorrow

Rik's message pings back straight away:

Will contact you again tomorrow. Good luck!

As the evening wears on, my nerves build. My excitement at getting closer to Dad weaves in and out of the fear that we'll be too late. That maybe if two teenagers can figure out that he's hiding in a mobile home in Norfolk, then maybe a skilful and ruthless bunch of gangsters will have got to him first.

I wake to the sound of the kettle boiling. Mum is already up and dressed – in her most extreme outfit: a blue and purple volcano of frothy chiffon with a matching headdress that spouts long strips of coloured silk all the way down her back.

My heart starts to thud as the car taking us to the

convention sets off. I'm expecting the journey to take a while, but five minutes later we're in the car park, high on a hill. Mum has explained that this isn't a real palace, but it's still enormous, with huge arches on either side of the entrance, and a massive glass window above it. You can see all over London from just outside the building, but there's no time to take in the view. Mum hurries Bess and me inside, issuing instructions about where on her stand to set out the astrological ornaments and how to divide all her leaflets into the appropriate piles.

Bess and I work obediently for about half an hour, while Mum greets person after person. She seems to know almost everyone exhibiting at the convention. It's a massive room. I can only see the surrounding stalls, but they burst with colour: two of them have sun-splash and star sign posters and piles of books, while a third strains under the weight of its rows of crystals.

I check the time. Quarter to nine. Mum has been whisked off for a cup of tea by the volunteer who showed up yesterday. She left Bess and me with strict instructions to store all the extra pamphlets in neat, organized piles under the table. I shove the lot into the corner. It's time to go and meet Tyler outside.

I glance at my sister, feeling guilty. I'm not so much worried about her safety. She's sat inside the stall with her back to the table, hunched over her latest drawing of a puppy. She's not even visible from the exhibition floor.

No, it's more that when Mum gets back from her cup of tea and discovers I've gone, she'll be furious. And, by going, I'm leaving Bess to deal with that all by herself.

My phone pings. It's Tyler. He's already outside. I squat down next to Bess and tap her shoulder. She looks up.

'I have to go . . .' I say. I'd been going to pretend I was just going in search of a bathroom, but looking into Bess's clear eyes I know I can't lie to her. I hesitate, then say: 'Don't worry about me.'

Bess frowns. Her eyes glint in the overhead light as she stamps her foot. *No.* She's clearly telling me. She stamps again. *No.*

'Stay here till Mum gets back.' I straighten up, guilt still tugging at my chest. I tell myself that it's worth upsetting Bess in this moment, if I can find Dad alive, and so make her happy forever.

I turn and hurry away, following the signs to the main exit. Tyler's text says he's at the bus stop just outside. I race out to the terrace. It was overcast when we woke up, but the sun has burned all the clouds away and London is spread out before me, its mass of buildings going on for miles, into a clear blue sky.

As I run down the steps to the pavement, I see the bus

stop across the road to the right. There's a knot of people waiting, but I spot Tyler straight away. He raises his arm and waves as he sees me. My heart gives a little leap of hope.

This is it. The start of my quest to find Dad.

Tyler waves harder, beckoning me to move faster. A big red bus trundles towards us. Tyler holds his arm out to stop it.

I race across the road as the bus reaches the stop. The central doors open and a slew of people in colourful outfits stream out. Panting for breath, I weave my way through them to the front of the bus. I lose sight of Tyler in the crowd for a moment. There he is, holding out the Travelcard he'd promised he'd get for me. His eyes flare as he sees me . . . Is that surprise? Excitement? I can't read his expression. Someone behind me is shoving me in the back. I barely have a chance to grab the Travelcard before I'm hustled on board. I tap the card on the pad by the driver and move inside the bus. People stream on. I spot Tyler over their heads – he's made it on. The door of the bus shuts, the engine roaring into life. I'm forced further down the bus as the people between us swarm past me to the seats at the back. As the bus moves away I turn around, expecting to see Tyler right there: alone and smiling at me.

He's there all right, but he's neither smiling nor alone.

My jaw drops as the bus picks up speed, hurtling down the hill away from the Palace. Because there, standing beside Tyler, with her chin jutting forward and a defiant glint in her eyes, is Bess.

17

Tyler ushers Bess towards me, his eyes wide with shock.

'You brought your little sister?' he hisses. 'What happened to "she's not even seven", "she's vulnerable"?'

'I *didn't* bring her,' I gasp, as the bus zooms past a stop.

I crouch down so I'm face to face with Bess. 'Why did you follow me?' I demand.

Bess lifts one shoulder then drops it in a sulky shrug.

'What were you thinking?' My voice rises. 'This was really selfish of you. Really—' I stop, my breath catching in my throat.

I sound just like Mum.

I look out of the window. The bus is sailing past the next stop now, gathering speed as it hurtles down the hill. Bess kicks at the floor, scowling.

'Can we take her back?' Tyler asks.

I shake my head. 'There's no time if we're going to make our train. Anyway, Mum will have noticed we've gone by now.'

I glance around. We're standing in the middle of the

bus by the double exit doors. There's a smattering of other passengers, but none of them are taking any notice of us.

'Come on.' I take Bess's hand and guide her towards the long seat at the very back of the bus. Tyler sits on my other side.

'What are we going to do?' he asks.

'She'll have to come to Norfolk with us,' I say with a sigh. Bess looks up at me, a sad, sulky expression on her face. I put my arm round her. 'It's okay, Bess. Sorry I got cross. I wouldn't have wanted to be left behind at that stupid exhibition either.'

Bess folds her arms and stares out of the window. I decide there and then that I won't tell her we're on a mission to find Dad. There's no point raising her hopes until I know for sure he's at the mobile-home park. 'You have to promise me you'll do whatever Tyler and I tell you.' Bess says nothing, just kicks her foot listlessly against the seat in front. Which is, luckily, empty.

'There's no need to be like that,' I say, feeling annoyed again.

Bess sticks her tongue out at me. I go to stick mine out back, then remember Tyler is sitting on my other side. So, instead, I blow out a frustrated breath and lean back in my seat.

I love my sister, but having Bess with us is going to

slow us down and make us stand out from other teenagers enjoying a bit of time away from home. Plus, it could be dangerous for her, especially if we encounter any FFG gangsters.

And, of course, it means I won't get to be alone with Tyler. I scowl to myself. Not that being alone with him will make any difference to how he feels about me.

The bus turns on to the main road.

'We should be at Finsbury Park in about ten minutes,' Tyler says. 'Then we have to go on the tube to get to Liverpool Street . . .' He hesitates. 'You should probably let your mum know you're okay.'

I nod, taking out my mobile and sending Mum a brief text saying that I'm really sorry and I know she'll be furious, but I won't be able to help out on her exhibition stand as Bess and I have gone out for the day. I don't mention Tyler – no point getting him into trouble too. Then I remove the SIM and slide the phone into my shirt pocket.

'Why are you doing that?' Tyler asks.

'The price of me having a mobile has always been Mum insisting she could track it at any given time, night or day.' I glance anxiously at Tyler. 'I know, it's really uncool.'

He shrugs. 'She'll be worried.'

'I can't imagine your dad tracking your movements,' I say with a smile.

'Nah, my dad would call something like that an invasion of privacy,' Tyler says. 'He's all about taking responsibility. Stuff like that.' He grins, then lets his hand rest lightly on mine, before sitting back in his seat. The brief press of his palm makes my skin fizz.

I try to focus on what lies ahead. We might be just hours away from finding Dad. I try to picture the moment I see him. What will I say? How it will feel?

I can't imagine it; all I know is that I'm suddenly brimming with nervous excitement.

And hope.

We emerge from the hot and smelly underground into Liverpool Street Station. I tell Bess to stay close, but she's already gripping my hand tightly. Neither of us have ever seen so many people packed into a single place.

'I'll get the tickets,' I say, heading over to the ticket machine. I know how these work from the shopping trips Mum and I do to Exeter.

Tyler rummages in his pocket and draws out a couple of crumpled notes. 'Let me pay for mine,' he says.

'No, it's fine,' I say. 'You're only here to help me, I should pay.'

'I can manage,' he says, firmly.

'Okay.' I shrug, turning back to the machine.

Our train leaves in twenty minutes, so there's plenty of time. We buy drinks and sandwiches with our leftover cash then stand, watching the noticeboard for our platform number.

I get the sudden sense I'm being watched. I tug Bess, already huddled at my side, even closer. There are far too many people here to keep track of. It would be easy for someone to have followed us without us knowing. A shudder runs down my spine. I spin round, my eyes flickering over the people nearby. No. I'm just spooked. Imagining things.

At least I hope I am.

The train to Norfolk is surprisingly empty, though our carriage is hot and stuffy. After about an hour, Bess falls asleep, her mouth open and a strand of hair sticking damply to her pale cheek.

'When did you say Bess stopped speaking?' Tyler asks, looking over at her.

'Just after we found out Dad was missing . . .' My mind drifts back to that terrible moment, when the police arrived on our doorstep, all serious faces and solemn voices. Even though I couldn't hear their exact words, I knew what they were telling her. 'Bess was worse back then,' I go on. 'Nowadays I sometimes think she actually *wants* to speak, but . . . but it's like she's stuck in a room and doesn't know how to open the door to get out.'

'I was younger than Bess when my mum died.' Tyler's voice – soft and low – brings me back to the swaying train carriage. I glance at him and he gives me a small, sad smile. 'It's hard when you're little. You just don't understand what's going on.'

'But you didn't stop speaking, did you?' I ask.

Tyler shakes his head. 'Everyone grieves in their own way,' he says with a sigh. 'That's what Dad always says anyway.'

I sit back, gazing out of the window at the trees and fields rushing past. For the first time since we ran away from Alexandra Palace, I feel calmer. Less anxious. Maybe it wasn't such a terrible thing to bring Bess with us, after all. I'm going to find – and warn – Dad at the mobile-home park. I'm sure of it. And, though I don't know what's going to happen when we do, maybe it will help Bess start talking again.

And if that can happen, anything can.

18

The sun is shining brightly by the time we get to Norfolk. It's almost 12.30 p.m. and we only have a few minutes to find our bus. After a panicky race across the tarmac we make it just in time. The bus itself reminds me of the ones in Devon, though everything else is very different. The roads are wider for a start, and the sky somehow bigger. Around Brockledore it's all twisty, hedge-lined lanes over dips and hills, with farmed fields beyond. Here, the land is mostly open and flat. I've never seen anywhere that stretches out so far.

Gradually, the bus empties out. By the time we reach the end of the line, we're the only people left on board. It's 1.30 p.m. – and we still have a long walk ahead of us. I'd allowed an hour for the three-mile hike to Saltcliff, but having Bess with us means it could easily take twice as long. Fresh butterflies flutter in my belly. We're going to be pushing it to get back to London tonight.

'Come on, Bess,' I urge, taking her by the hand. 'We need to get going.'

I hurry along, checking Tyler's phone's map app to make sure we're walking in the right direction. Tyler hasn't said much during the journey, but as I hand him back his mobile, he leans in close and whispers in my ear.

'You nervous?'

His breath is hot against my skin. It makes my whole body shiver. Trying not to show how unsettled I feel by his walking so close to me, I make a face.

'About possibly meeting my dead dad after a year and a half?' I say, lowering my voice so that Bess doesn't hear. 'Nah, not nervous at all.'

Tyler grins, then falls back. Bess turns, flapping a piece of paper at him. She's clearly hankering to show him the dog drawing she did on the bus. I tell her it will have to wait until we stop and tug her after me. She resists, pulling back, and my mobile, nestling in my shirt pocket, bumps against my chest. Part of me wants to put the SIM in and call Mum. I know she'll be worried about us. But she'll also be mad. And likely to demand we come straight back.

So I leave my phone in my pocket.

'Come *on*, Bess.'

She gives me a sulky look, but speeds up.

The road we're on is dusty and flat, the sun fierce overhead. For the first forty-five minutes we move briskly, Bess keeping up fairly well. Then the land rises steeply, forcing us to slow down. Even though Tyler half carries Bess up the hill, it still takes another half an hour to reach the summit. Suddenly, we're at the top of a cliff, the sea spread out in front of us – blue and sparkling, like it's covered with tiny stars.

'*Marvista*,' I say under my breath. *Sea view.*

There's no question. Dad would love it here.

The cliff runs for miles in either direction. A few stony beaches are visible in the distance. They are all completely deserted.

'You'd think there'd be more tourists,' Tyler says. 'I guess it's cold, though.'

He's right. The wind whips at our faces, making the air far chillier than it was earlier in London.

'All the more perfect for Dad,' I murmur. 'Come on, let's keep walking. We must be nearly at the mobile-home park by now.'

We follow the clifftop path for about fifteen minutes. It's a sheer drop to the sea below and I make sure Bess stays well away from it. The wind pummels our faces and we have to yell to hear each other. We pass a huge white rock, then a series of smaller ones. Tyler, with his long strides, ends up a little ahead of us. I hang back, helping Bess clamber over the uneven ground.

'Over here!' Tyler calls.

Bess and I look up. He's pointing to a trailer positioned between two long fences. The word 'Office' is printed on the door. A tatty banner trailing across the top reads:

SALTCLIFF SEAVIEW MOBILE-HOME PARK – LONG LETS

This is it.

Bess prods me, eyebrows raised. From the look of impatient curiosity on her face, it's clear she wants to know why we're here. I hesitate. Is it time to come clean? To let her know we're looking for Dad? That I'm almost certain he's on the other side of the fence, inside this mobile-home park?

My heart beats faster. Not until I know for sure that he's here. 'I can't,' I say. 'Not yet. Soon.'

Bess stamps her foot, her expressive face screwed up with irritation.

'What's up?' Tyler asks.

'I'm going to see what they know in this office.' I hurry away, leaving Bess to Tyler. I stop at the trailer door and take out my phone.

I hesitate for a second, then put the SIM back in. Doing so means I'll connect to the internet and Mum will be able to see where I am, but I don't have a choice. I have to be able to show whoever's inside a pic of Dad. The phone fires up. A bunch of missed calls and furious messages from Mum flash on to the screen. There's also one from Rik.

How you getting on?

I delete them all – there'll be time to contact Mum and Rik later, when I actually have some news – then I knock on the door.

No reply.

I wait a second, then try the handle. It opens smoothly. I step up and go inside.

The trailer is cramped and gloomy. There's a living area at one end and a table in the middle. Someone has attempted to make the table look like an official reception area, with a notepad, laptop computer and pot of pens.

'May I help you?' A middle-aged woman with grey hair and a yellow cardigan that hangs loosely off her shoulders appears from the bathroom at the end of the trailer. She frowns at me. 'Mum and Dad outside?'

'No,' I say. 'Actually I'm *looking* for my dad. I called a few days ago. I think he might be living here.'

'Oh, right.' The woman sounds uninterested. From the bored tone of her voice, I'm pretty certain she's the same person I spoke to before on the phone. She wanders over. There's a lopsided name badge pinned to her chest. It reads *Yvonne*. 'What's your dad's name?'

'Alan Mooney,' I say. 'But . . . but I think he's calling himself something different now.' I wince, aware how weird that sounds.

'Really?' Yvonne raises her eyebrows. 'Is that so?'

'Let me show you his picture.' I hand her my phone, a screen grab of that picture of Dad, Bess and me on the beach on the screen.

Yvonne sits heavily at the seat behind the table. She wrinkles her nose as she peers at Dad's picture. 'No, I don't recognize him.' She taps her fingers against the table, then looks up at me. 'If he was here, he left before I arrived back in May.'

Is she telling the truth? It's impossible to know.

'You've had a wasted journey, I'm afraid,' she says, a hint of sympathy creeping into her voice.

'Can I just go into the mobile-home park and look around?' I point to the door opposite the one I came through, marked 'caravans this way'.

'Sorry, love, but that's against health and safety.'

'But—'

'No unaccompanied minors allowed,' Yvonne says briskly. 'I'm afraid you'll have to leave.' She peers out of the window. 'Is your mum with you?'

'Er, yes,' I lie, feeling crushed. I can't believe that I've come all this way, only to fail at the final hurdle.

I retrace my steps away from the office trailer, to where Tyler and Bess are waiting back at the big white rock.

Bess glares at me, clearly still furious that she has no idea what we're doing here.

'What happened?' Tyler asks.

I draw him to one side, so Bess can't hear us. 'There's a woman inside who says she doesn't know Dad from his picture, but I can't tell if she's lying. She could be covering for him . . . or maybe Dad changed his appearance.' I hesitate. 'Or maybe she's right and he isn't here. Either way, I need to take a look in the trailer park, find out for sure. I just don't know how to get past her and through to the actual mobile homes.'

'Mmm, maybe we don't have to get *you* past her,' Tyler says slowly. 'Maybe we just get *her* out of your way.'

I raise my eyebrows. 'What do you mean?'

Tyler grins. 'We just have to work as a team.'

19

So much for working 'as a team'. My getting into the mobile-home park depends on Bess playing along with Tyler's plan and, so far, she's refusing. Her combo of sulky shrugs and accusing glares make it clear she's going to have nothing to do with his (admittedly crazy-sounding) idea until I tell her why we're here.

I crouch down so we're level with each other and gaze into her dark eyes. Sometimes Bess's eyes are soft, like chocolate. Right now they are hard, like conkers.

'I promise I will tell you soon,' I say. 'I just want to make sure before I say anything.'

She purses her lips.

'Please, Bess,' I say. 'It will *so* be worth it in the end, it'll be the *best* thing you could imagine.' I smile at her, ignoring the worry that twists in my guts.

Her eyes brighten. She points to her drawing book, at her latest puppy picture.

'Better than a dog,' I say, grinning. 'The most brilliant surprise *ever*.'

Bess shrugs, but I can see the excitement building in her eyes. I stand back and let Tyler explains what he needs her to do. He goes over it a couple of times, in that calm, patient way of his that is so like Mr Tuesday's.

'I think we're ready,' he says, looking up at me with a smile.

I stare anxiously at Bess. 'Are you sure you know what to do?' I ask.

Bess rolls her eyes at me, then gives Tyler a cheeky grin.

Tyler chuckles. 'I think she's got it.'

Bess nods furiously.

'Okay,' I say, still feeling a little reluctant. To be honest, I'd rather not have to involve Bess or Tyler – even though he's helped to get us this far – but I can't see another option. 'Okay, I'll see you both back here.' I point to the big white rock beside us. 'Don't forget.'

Bess stamps her foot again. Tyler chuckles. 'Yeah,' he says. 'Bess and I know. Now . . . get in position, okay?'

I give Bess a swift salute, then hurry away. My breath is rapid and shallow as I make my way along the cliff path. Around the bend and the office trailer comes into view again. There's no sign of Yvonne at the window. Moving as fast and as quietly as I can, I scuttle across the dry, compacted earth and crouch down at the side of the trailer. From here, I'll be able to see Yvonne coming out, but she won't see me.

It's a sheltered spot, between the high fence and the trailer, the air hot and still. It's quiet too, just the occasional clank from inside the mobile-home park and a couple of squawking seagulls overhead. I wait. Several long seconds pass. And then, exactly as planned, Tyler and Bess appear. Tyler glances around to check I'm in the right place, then leads Bess to the opposite side of the trailer. As if on cue, Bess drops to the ground, clutching her ankle. Tyler says something to her that I can't hear and Bess starts rocking to and fro. I catch sight of her face, her mouth twisted in what looks like agony. Apart from the fact that she's making no sound, her pretend injury looks completely convincing.

Tyler straightens up. 'Help!' he shrieks. He races over to the trailer door and pounds hard. 'Help! My sister's hurt. Help!'

I hold my breath. Two seconds pass. Three. Four. Five. Tyler bangs on the door again.

It opens slowly. Yvonne appears, frowning as she peers over at Bess. 'Help, she tripped!' Tyler is gabbling. He sounds totally panicked. 'I think she might have broken her ankle.'

Leaving the trailer door open, Yvonne hurries over to

where Bess is now writhing on the ground. Bess needs to pull back a little. She's on the verge of overdoing it. As if she's heard my thoughts, Bess checks her movements. Yvonne reaches her and bends down. She gently presses Bess's ankle. She's speaking. I can't hear the words, but her low murmur is gentle and soothing.

She's taken the bait. It's time for me to move.

I slide out from my hiding place and creep round the front of the trailer. Yvonne has her back to me. Tyler is talking now. I catch the words 'doesn't speak', then I slip inside. I've done it! I hurry over to the door on the other side of the office that says 'caravans this way' and tug at the handle.

The relief that washed over me just seconds before now vanishes.

The door is locked.

Heart pounding, I look wildly around. There's no sign of the keys on the desk. Has Yvonne taken them outside with her? I glance through the window. Yvonne is nodding, Tyler still talking. The plan is for him to urge Bess to try putting a little weight on her ankle. Soon it will become clear Bess isn't badly hurt. She and Tyler will then leave and Yvonne will return to the trailer.

I need to move fast.

I gaze at the kitchen shelves and the settee covered in

clothes and the pile of magazines on the floor. Yvonne wouldn't have had much time to put the keys anywhere after locking the door. If they are here, they can't be far away.

I try to focus. Where do people put keys? They hang them on pegs, but there aren't any here.

And they put them in drawers. Of course. I hurry around the other side of the desk. Pull open the top drawer.

There. Lying on top of a well-thumbed accounts book is a keyring with three keys. They clink as I snatch them up. My heart is in my mouth as I hurry round the desk and fit the first key in the door. Then the second. Neither fits.

Yvonne's voice echoes towards me. 'I have some arnica cream in the trailer,' she's saying.

She's on her way back here. Her footsteps sound on the steps just outside. My fingers fumble as I try the third key in the lock. *Yes.* It turns smoothly.

Pulse racing, I slip through the door, pulling it shut behind me.

20

I gaze around the mobile-home park. The trailers are spread out in fan-shaped rows. It's quiet, nobody in sight. I glance anxiously back at the office door. Yvonne must be back inside now. Hopefully Tyler and Bess are already on their way to our meeting place.

I hurry away. As soon as I'm past the first caravan I start to see people: a man in a tracksuit hanging out some washing to the left; a woman with a toddler sitting on a rug and a bunch of rusty-looking cars are parked over to the right. In front of them a cluster of loungers are arranged with a view of the sea beyond the cliff edge. They're occupied by three grey-haired women, all with their backs to me. Maybe one of these ladies will know Dad.

As I scurry past the outer circle of caravans, I realize that there's a wire security fence at the cliff edge. The air is freezing, in spite of the sun, and the salt wind whistles around my ears. The mobile homes themselves are old and grubby-looking, but the sea beyond is sparkling and beautiful.

I reach the knot of elderly ladies. They're still sitting with their backs to me, chatting away. I move within view and one of them looks up. She has bright, twinkling eyes and greets me with a cheery smile.

'Hello, there, you all right, pet?'

I nod, hurrying over. 'I'm just wondering if you know my dad?' I ask, taking out my phone. 'I think he lives here.'

I hold the photo of Dad in front of the first woman's face. She fusses for a second, fetching glasses from her handbag.

'No, I don't know him.' She hands the phone to her neighbour who stares at the screen for a while, then shakes her head slowly.

'Sorry,' she says.

She passes the phone along to the final lady, the one with the twinkling eyes. She gazes for a moment at the picture of Dad, then looks up. 'I don't recognize him,' she says. 'Has he just moved here?'

'I . . . I . . . No,' I say. 'I think he moved here about a year and a half ago.'

'Ah, that explains it.' Twinkling Eyes offers me a sympathetic look. 'We've all only been here three months or so, just before Yvonne took over in the office. He must have left before we came.'

Her words feel like a slap to the face. I'd been so focused on the idea that Dad came here after faking his death, I'd completely forgotten that he might, later, have moved on again.

My disappointment must show on my face.

'Oh, pet,' Twinkling Eyes says in a concerned tone. 'I'm sorry. What's your dad's name?'

'Alan, but . . .'

I stop in the face of her blank expression, unable to admit that I have no idea that my father is almost certainly using a different name now. Instead I smile awkwardly, then back away. I hurry to the woman with the toddler and then to the man who has finished hanging out his washing.

Neither of them recognizes either Dad's picture or his name. I stand, my face whipped by the wind, staring at Dad's image on my screen. Up until this moment I was convinced he was going to be here. What was that certainty based on after all? A single conversation with Rik. A guess based on a boat's name and a few holiday brochures.

And all the longing and hope in my heart.

Tears prick at my eyes, as a wave of doubt washes through my body. And then the laundry man points me to a caravan opposite, surrounded by potted plants of all shapes and colours. 'Try Mac,' he suggests. 'He's an old-timer. If anyone'll remember your dad, it's him.'

I trudge miserably over, glancing at the office trailer as I pass. There's no sign of Yvonne right now, but she could appear at any moment. What am I going to do if I can't find Dad? I think of Mum with a pang of guilt. She's bound to be worrying, especially about Bess, and by now will be *beyond* furious with me. She's probably telling everyone at the convention about my Grand Fire Trine, which apparently accounts for me being determined to the point of pig-headed.

I round the plants trailer to find an elderly man with a bristling white beard and a stoop, pottering around a small table. He's busy setting out a row of shallow plastic trays and a batch of tiny green plants and doesn't notice me approach.

'Hello,' I say. 'Mac?'

He looks up. 'Hello, there.' Mac's face is deeply lined, but there's a bright curiosity in his eyes as he looks at me. 'What can I do for you?'

'I'm trying to find my dad.' It's hard to keep the emotion out of my voice as I hand over the picture of Dad yet again.

Mac pushes his glasses up his nose and takes a close look. He stares at the screen for a good few moments, then hands the phone back to me.

'This is your father?' There's a wary note to his voice.

I nod.

'What's his name, then? His full name?' The words aren't a casual enquiry. They sound like a challenge. A test.

It suddenly strikes me that Dad would have made anyone who does know him swear to keep his presence a secret. I hesitate. Rik insisted from the start I shouldn't tell anyone Dad was alive. But standing here in front of Mac, with the salt wind blowing in my hair, I can't see another option. This is my last shot at getting to the truth.

'Dad's real name is Alan Mooney.' My heart thuds, hard, against my ribs. 'But he probably used a different name here. He . . . he's in hiding.'

Mac's weather-beaten face wrinkles further as he considers me. 'And what's *your* name?'

'Cat.' The wind whips a strand of hair in front of my eyes. 'Please tell me if my dad's here.' My desperation rises. '*Please.* I have a little sister, Bess, and she's with me and I know my dad would want us to find him. He's in terrible danger and . . . and I *have* to warn him.' I stop, sucking in my breath.

Have I said too much?

Mac peers closely at me, his eyes like blue buttons. 'Yeah, I thought I recognized you.'

'You did?' I hold his gaze. 'You do?'

'Yes.' He smiles. And for a second it feels like the whole world shrinks to his kindly blue eyes. 'Your dad *was* here. For over a year. And very proud of you he was too. And your little sister. The only thing he kept from his old life was that photo you just showed me: him on the beach with the two of you . . . and your dog.'

The wind picks up, battering against my cheeks, then just as suddenly dies away again. My heart feels like it has stopped beating. Here, at last, is proof that Dad did go into hiding.

Which surely means that my journey hasn't been in vain.

My wonderful dad is still alive.

21

For a few moments I forget where I'm standing. I forget Yvonne in the office trailer. I even forget Tyler and Bess waiting outside along the cliff path.

Mac gazes at me, concern in his eyes. 'Are you all right? You've gone very pale.'

I nod, though in reality it feels like the sea is thundering in my ears and that my legs might give way under me.

'It's probably shock at hearing about your dad,' Mac muses. 'Let me get you a glass of water.' He peers at me. 'Are you hungry? Would you like something to eat?'

'No, thank you.' I take a juddering breath. 'Do you know where Dad is now?'

Mac makes a face. 'I'm afraid I don't,' he says. 'Alan didn't say. Said it was safer for both of us that way. He told me what happened to him, in confidence, of course.' Mac shakes his head. 'Nasty business.'

'So . . .' I'm struggling to focus on the details I need. 'When exactly did he leave here?'

'About six months back, I reckon it was.'

'*Six months* ago?' A sinking feeling lands in my stomach. How on earth am I going to trace Dad now?

I lean against the table where Mac is potting his plants. He watches me with a worried expression. 'Wait here,' he says. He disappears inside his mobile home.

The wind whips around my head as I try to think about what on earth I'm going to do next. My brain is all over the place. One second I'm brimming up with excitement that Dad is really out there. The next I'm overwhelmed with the desperate frustration that I'm as far away from finding him as ever.

Mac reappears after a minute or so, a large paper bag in his hand. 'Some rolls and cheese and a couple of apples,' he says gruffly. 'For you and the little one. I put two cans of pop in too.'

I take the bag. 'Thank you,' I say, forcing myself to focus. 'Are you sure you don't have any idea where Dad went? No clue at all?'

'Well, there is one thing I can tell you,' Mac says. 'Your dad's a great one for helping people, as you'll know, and, while he was here, he did a bit of carpentry work for a young mum with a little boy. Julie Walker. She left the caravan park before he did, so that's a good while back now, but she might remember something as to where he went. I don't have an address for her, but I think she mentioned she was moving to Hallerton East. Tiny place along the coast.'

I nod. It's not much to go on, but it's better than nothing.

'I'd better get back to Bess,' I say. 'Thanks for this.' I hold up the bag.

'Good luck,' Mac says gruffly. 'And give my best to your dad if you find him. Great guy. No matter how low he was feeling, he always had a smile on his face.'

'Oh, thank you!' Overwhelmed, I dart forward and give him a swift, impulsive hug. Mac smiles, raising his hand as I hurry away.

My head is still spinning as I cross the dry earth towards the trailer. I'm not even properly thinking about Yvonne being inside it until I reach the door and curl my fingers over the door handle.

The paper bag Mac gave me dangles from my other hand. I grip it more tightly, suddenly aware that as soon as I open the door Yvonne will see me and realize I've been in the mobile-home park. I brace myself, ready to run, then lever down the handle.

I leap up the steps and into the trailer. Yvonne is sitting behind her desk. She rises up, her mouth a shocked 'O'.

I dart across the trailer to the door opposite.

'What do you think you're doing?' Yvonne rears up, out of her seat.

I fling open the door and hurl myself out and across the hard ground. As I reach the cliff path I shoot a look over my shoulder. Yvonne is still inside the trailer, thank goodness. Clearly I'm not worth chasing. I slow down a little, jogging along the path to the big white rock. As I dart behind it, Bess is coming out of a passable cartwheel. She stands up, looking pleased with herself.

'That was brilliant, Bess!' Tyler says, unaware that I'm behind him.

'It was,' I add, catching my breath.

Tyler spins round, his face lighting up as he sees me. 'What happened?' He rushes towards me. 'Are you okay?'

I can't hold back the feelings surging inside me any longer. I drop the paper bag on the floor, seeing nothing except the concern on his face. And then, in floods of tears, I hurl myself into his arms.

Tyler holds me as I sob, his hand stroking my back. The warm touch of his arms around me makes me feel stronger.

A small hand tugs at my elbow.

Tyler slides away as I glance down at Bess. She's gazing up at me with big, round, worried eyes. I can read her thoughts as easily as if she were able to speak them:

What's going on? Why have we come all this way? How come you're so upset?

I fill up again with sadness.

'Oh, Bess.' I crouch down. 'I'll tell you what we're doing here soon, but I . . . I can't just yet—Ow!'

I clutch my ankle, where Bess has just kicked it.

She folds her arms and glares at me.

Tell me. Now.

'She knows it's something big,' Tyler says softly. 'And she has been waiting all day.'

I nod, slowly. I might be certain now that Dad is alive, but I'm still a long way from finding him and I don't want to raise Bess's hopes until I know she'll be able to see him again. I couldn't bear her to get excited, only to feel devastated if I can't track Dad down for her. 'I'm sorry, Bess, but you're going to have to be patient and wait just a little bit longer.'

Bess stares at me, her lips pressed together in fury. She lifts her foot as if about to kick me again. I scramble backwards, standing up. She stamps her foot on the ground.

I reach for her hand, but she shoves it behind her back. I gaze at her, feeling helpless, then offer her a roll and a thick wedge of cheese out of the paper bag. She takes the food. For a second I think she's going to throw it at me, then she turns and stomps over to a small rock. She sits down with her back to me, munching hungrily.

'What happened?' Tyler asks quietly, so Bess won't overhear. 'Wasn't your dad in the mobile-home park?'

'No,' I say, turning to him. 'Apparently Dad moved out six months ago and I don't have an address. But I spoke to a friend of his who gave me the name of someone else who might know more. He wasn't sure of her exact address, but it's a tiny place, he said: Hallerton East.'

I suddenly remember I haven't taken the SIM out of my phone. 'I'll look for the place, while you look up buses back, yeah? Then we'll switch off our mobiles again.'

'Okay.' Tyler nods.

I take out my phone. There are two new messages from Mum along with yet another missed call. I groan, reading the texts.

'Your mum?' Tyler asks.

'Yeah. She was cross. Then she was worried. Now she's panicking.' I sigh.

'My dad's annoyed too,' Tyler says. 'I've sent him a message saying I'm with you on a day trip and I'm fine. He's not very happy that I ditched London without telling him.'

Tyler and I sit hunched over our phones. After a few minutes we've found out that Hallerton East is about an hour's walk away, and that the last bus from there back to Norwich leaves at 7 p.m. So long as we make that bus, we should get to Norwich with plenty of time to catch a late train to London. I double-check our route, then send Mum another message saying Bess and I are still fine and I'm sorry for upsetting her and she's not to worry.

Remembering Rik's earlier message, I also text him saying:

On Dad's trail, will message again later

Then I switch off my phone and remove the SIM again.

I'm too churned up to eat, but I offer Tyler the bag of food and he takes an apple. While he's biting into it, I wander over to where Bess is still sitting next to the small rock.

'Come on, Bess,' I say. 'We just have to walk a bit further.'

She makes a face at me but stands up.

The three of us walk on. It's slow-going with Bess beside us. If she isn't trudging silently, dragging her feet, she's noticing an interesting flower or an oddly shaped rock and stopping to investigate.

After the way she got so cross earlier, I don't have the heart to chivvy her along. We make our way back to the main road, follow that for a bit, then veer off inland. As we head along a footpath through a copse of trees, Bess skips back from a frothy-headed plant she's been examining and takes Tyler's hand. The three of us keep walking through the woods. The path forks and there are various twists and turns, but I'm certain we're still on track, even though it's taking longer than I thought.

And then I check the time. I'm shocked to see it's nearly six o'clock. I turn to Tyler.

'Do you think we've missed Hallerton East?' I ask, my anxiety rising. 'It looked tiny on the map, we could have easily gone past it.'

'We'd have seen a sign, wouldn't we?' He sounds tired and frustrated. 'Or can't small places in the country be bothered with signposts?'

He smiles, but it's not funny. If we don't get back on track we'll miss the 7 p.m. bus to Norwich and then the train to London, at which point Mum – who is already worried sick and furious with me – will probably explode with fear and rage and my life will be basically over and I *still* won't have found Dad.

'Don't laugh at me for being from the country,' I snap.

'I'm not,' Tyler shoots back. 'That's not what I said at all.'

'Yes, it is,' I insist, knowing that it wasn't, and feeling even more irritated. 'It's not my fault we have no idea where we're going.'

'Well, it isn't mine, either.' Tyler glares at me.

A tense moment passes. I'm suddenly aware of Bess watching us, her grubby hands clasped tightly together. Tyler obviously clocks her too, because he swings himself round and grins at her.

'Hey, Bess,' he calls. 'Fancy a piggy-back?'

She looks up, grinning at him.

'Come on, then.' Tyler hoists her on to his broad back and sets off.

We're moving faster than before, but the route is more confusing. Out of the wood, we take a path alongside a wide stretch of marshland. After almost another half-hour I'm certain we've gone wrong somewhere. We definitely should have reached Hallerton East by now. Away from the marshland and on the verge of another wood, I take out my phone again to check our location. But this time when I put in the SIM, there's no phone signal. And no internet connection either.

'I can't get anything here,' I say despairingly.

Tyler frowns. 'This doesn't feel like the right way.'

'No,' I agree.

Our eyes meet. Neither of us want to say it, especially not in front of Bess, but I can see Tyler is thinking the same thing that I am.

We're lost.

22

Bess is almost asleep on Tyler's back as we try to retrace our steps. There's still no signal and the sun is now low over the distant trees. I check the time again. It's just gone 7 p.m.

'We've missed the bus back to Norwich.' I groan. 'There's no way we can get back to London tonight.'

Tyler nods. 'Bess can't go on much further anyway,' he says. 'She's exhausted.'

'Mum's going to be furious,' I mutter.

'My dad will be too.' Tyler grimaces. 'I guess we better look for somewhere to spend the night.'

I stare at him. 'You mean out in the open?'

Tyler shrugs. 'What other choice do we have?'

He's right. We carry on walking, trudging past wheat fields and through another wood. Thick clouds gather overhead. They darken the sky and make the air cooler than it has been all day. Out of the trees, a rickety iron shelter appears on the left. There's a rusty bit of farm equipment in the corner, clearly broken, and a scattering of small, square bales of hay.

I check the time. It's a quarter to eight and Bess is struggling to keep her eyes open. Tyler is basically holding her up as she walks. I look at the shelter, then at Tyler.

'What do you think . . . ?'

Tyler shrugs. 'I guess it's better than nothing.' We make our way under the shelter. I settle Bess on a hay bale and cover her with my jacket. Tyler lays his over her too. She blinks up at me with round, sleepy eyes. A pang of guilt grips me. Thank goodness she's too exhausted to be scared about being out here, in the open all night. A second later, her breathing softens and deepens. She's asleep.

I flop on to the ground next to her, my back against the hay bale. Tyler sits down beside me.

We look at each other. I can feel the tension from our earlier argument in the air around us.

I take a deep breath. 'I'm sorry I overreacted earlier.'

Tyler gives me a rueful smile. 'You weren't the only one,' he says. 'Sorry I got cross too.'

I smile back, feeling relieved. A bird screeches overhead. I peer at my phone. Still no signal.

'Do you think I should try to send my mum another message?' I ask. 'Explain that we'll be back tomorrow, in case the signal comes and goes?'

'She's going to love that.' Tyler grimaces. 'Still, you

should. Otherwise they'll call the police. I'll send one to my dad too. Hopefully one of them will get through.'

I flop on to the ground and write a text explaining that we're going to have to spend the night away, asking Mum to let Mr Tuesday know – and reassuring her, again, that Bess is fine. I press send, even though there's no signal. The message flashes that it's failed.

The light is starting to fade now. Insects buzz in the faint last rays of sun. It's nowhere near as warm as it was earlier, but there's no wind here. I can't even smell the sea any more.

Tyler sits down beside me. 'I meant to ask earlier,' he says. 'What name did that Mac guy say your dad is using now?'

I stare at him, heart sinking. 'I didn't think to ask him.' I groan. 'God, I'm so stupid.' I put my head in my hands, feeling crushed.

'No, you're not.' Tyler's fingers curl around mine.

I look up.

'Listen, whatever name your dad was using, he probably changed it again when he moved on from the trailer park. I mean, if he didn't tell Mac where he was going, why would he have said what he was going to call himself when he got there?'

I smile. 'Thanks for being here,' I say.

'Are you kidding?' Tyler grins. 'This is great. A night

out under the stars. I mean, I could do with a burger and chips, but . . .'

I sigh. We finished Mac's offering hours ago. I ate less than the others and hunger is now seriously gnawing at my stomach.

'Don't,' I groan. 'I'm starving.'

We sit in silence for a little while. The only sound is the wind across the field and the gentle sound of Bess's breathing. Night falls and the farm equipment in the corner casts a shadow in the moonlight. It looks like a claw. I shiver.

'Cold?' Tyler asks, huddling closer.

He puts his arm around my shoulders and I let myself sink against him, feeling the warmth of his chest through his top. To my surprise, it feels like the most natural thing in the world.

Tyler pulls at the nearest bale of hay, packing the soft yellow strands on either side of us. 'If we stay close to each other, we'll be okay,' he says.

I snort. 'Does that line work for you often?'

I've never spoken to him like this before – all confident and bantering. For a second I freeze, worried he'll be offended. But Tyler just laughs, then draws me closer and I relax against him again.

I'm happy, I realize, even though it's dark and cold and my sister's only little and shouldn't be spending the night outside like this and I'm still feeling frightened that the FFG will find Dad before we do, not to mention guilty that Mum is bound to be worrying about us.

I'm happier, in fact, than I've felt for a long time, perhaps since Dad went missing. I'm doing what I need to do. And Tyler has his arms around me. And even if that doesn't mean to him quite what I wish it did, it still feels good. I gaze up at the sky. It looks like a mass of sequins cast over a big black shawl. I haven't seen a clear sky full of stars like that since Dad took me out in the *Marvista* a few weeks before he disappeared.

'There's Orion's Belt, Kitterbug,' he had said, pointing to the night sky. 'And there's Polaris, the North Star. It's bright, so it's easy to spot and once you've found it you can always work out where you are.'

'The star to bring you home,' I murmur, remembering Dad's words.

'What's that?' Tyler asks.

'The stars have shapes. I was just finding the Little Dipper,' I explain, leaning away from him to indicate the right spot in the sky. 'It's like a spoon with a long handle. Polaris is at the end. *There.* It's super-bright, so you can use it to work out where you're going.'

Tyler follows my pointing finger. 'Wow,' he says, shifting closer to me. 'So which way is that?'

He points in the direction we were walking earlier.

'North-west.' I make a face. 'Which explains where we were going wrong earlier. We should have stayed more directly north. '

'At least we know now.' Tyler leans back against the hay bale, his arm back around me. I hesitate, trying to work out whether or not Tyler will really be interested if I tell him more about the stars.

His breathing grows shallow and even. I glance round. He's already asleep.

I don't remember dropping off myself, but when I wake in the dark, a few hours later, Tyler is still holding me, hay packed around us. I raise my head enough to see Bess on her soft pallet, snuggled up under our jackets.

Tyler murmurs in his sleep, then nuzzles into my neck. His eyes are softly closed, his expression peaceful. And then he shifts, just a fraction. His lips brush past mine before he settles into the new position, still fast asleep.

It's an accident. The tiniest kiss. But my lips are on fire where his touched them.

I'm certain I'll never get back to sleep.

23

I'm woken by the familiar tug of Bess's hand on my arm. I sit up, feeling stiff and frozen. The dawn sky is wide with a grey, pinkish light. There's no sign of Tyler. I get up, looking around.

'Did you see where he went?' I ask.

Bess indicates the field opposite ours. She's shivering with cold, her eyes wide with a mix of anxiety and indignation.

'Hey, this is, like, the craziest most fun adventure *ever*, isn't it?' I say, smiling to reassure her.

She stares at me, clearly unconvinced, then shivers again. Feeling guilty, I draw Tyler's jacket tightly around her and rub up and down her arms. A moment later, Tyler appears from behind a tree and lopes over. I run my fingers through my hair, watching the easy way he walks and wishing we had something to eat or drink.

'I thought there might be a signal over there, but there isn't,' Tyler says, sinking down to the ground beside me. 'On the plus side, the message to my dad that we're all okay but we wouldn't be back last night went through at about midnight.'

'Did he reply?' I ask, meaning: *is he mad?*

'No.' Tyler chews on his lip. 'I guess there was only a signal for a few moments.'

I check my phone, but the text to Mum still hasn't sent. I make a face. 'I hope your dad passed on your message,' I say, 'because my phone didn't send mine.' I sigh. 'At least we know which direction to go in.'

'Let's keep moving.'

We walk on, warming gradually as the sun rises. Tyler clearly has no memory of our accidental kiss in the middle of the night. Neither of us talks much; we're all severely hungry and thirsty. Bess drags her feet. She hasn't smiled since we got up and still seems both anxious and grumpy.

I can't really blame her.

After another half-hour we find a main road and, at last, a sign:

Hallerton East ½ mile

An arrow points the way. 'This is it,' I say.

Tyler gives me an encouraging nod.

We walk on, in single file, through the trees. It's now almost 6 a.m. and the sun is properly up. There are dark clouds in the far distance and a crispness to the air, but overhead the skies are clear and blue, daylight filtering prettily through the trees. The growing warmth of the day barely registers. I forget how hungry and thirsty I am. My nerves are building. Even if we can find Julie Walker, there's no guarantee she'll have any idea where Dad is. It's another long shot.

And, after all this effort, the thought that it might be a dead end fills me with despair.

We emerge from the little wood, to find ourselves on a small, rough dirt path. We walk along the track, past a series of small houses. Another open field appears ahead, with the sea – dark, distant clouds still hovering above the water – visible beyond.

'Is this an actual place?' Tyler sounds astonished. He looks back along the short track. 'I didn't know villages could be this small.'

'I guess we have to knock on some of the doors, see if anyone knows a Julie Walker.'

We turn around and retrace our steps. Bess looks up at me enquiringly. She wants to know why we're here. I carefully avoid meeting her gaze. She stops walking, her arms folded, bad-temperedly, across her chest. A man is just getting into his car outside the second house on the right.

'Excuse me,' I ask. 'We're looking for Julie? Julie Walker?'

'Next house up on the left,' the man says.

Hope surges through me. I meet Tyler's surprised gaze.

'Looks like she's here, then,' he says.

I nod, my nerves shredding as we reach the next house, Bess trudging gloomily a few paces behind us. I knock lightly on the door.

Nobody answers. I wait. Tyler walks along the front of the house, then hurries back.

'I can hear a kid talking around the back. There's a side passage . . .' He looks at me enquiringly.

I nod. 'Maybe I should go alone first, see if Julie's here?' I say, softly. 'I'll come back and get you and Bess if it's okay. Yeah?'

'Sure.' Tyler says.

I glance at Bess. She scowls at me, then looks away.

I hurry past the front of the house. It's a small cottage. Through the window I can see two sofas covered with children's toys. Mac had said Julie was a young mum. Feeling more hopeful, I peer round the rough stone wall of the cottage into the garden beyond. A little boy is playing on a climbing frame in the middle of a large patch of scrubby grass. A young woman with long blonde hair in a ponytail is standing with her back to me, watching him. She's holding a baby, its chubby arms clutching at her neck, its little face peering over her shoulder. The baby sees me and smiles.

Is this Julie? Mac only mentioned her having a little boy.

I take a step towards her.

'Hello!' I call out. 'Julie?'

The woman turns and walks over. She's smiling, though there's a slight wariness in her bright blue eyes. Strands of her fair hair fall on to her shoulders. The baby clutches at them with his chubby fists.

'I'm Julie. Can I help you?' she asks.

'I'm looking for . . . for my dad,' I say. 'A guy called Mac from the caravan park at Saltcliff – he said you knew my dad too, and that you might know where he was.'

Julie blinks at me. 'Are . . . are you *Cat*?' she asks, her eyes rounding in shock.

I nod, my throat tight. So Dad's shown her my picture, just like he did with Mac.

We stare at each other.

'Do . . . do you know where my dad might be?' I ask.

Julie studies me intently. 'He always wondered if one day you might come looking for him,' she says.

'Really?' My heart leaps. 'Dad said that?'

Julie gives me a soft smile. 'He made me promise I'd never tell anyone his real name; he was terrified someone would find out about his past,' she says. There's something down-to-earth about her. A calming quality that reminds me a bit of Mr Tuesday. 'I'm not supposed to talk to anyone about him,' she goes on, 'but I know he'd want me to make an exception for you.'

I nod, hanging on her words. This is what Rik said from the start. That I was the only person who could track Dad down. I swell with pride and excitement.

'So . . . ?' I prompt.

'Your dad lives here,' Julie says, indicating the house behind her.

I stare at her. Is she serious?

The baby in her arms wriggles, letting out a complaining yelp.

'Er, this is Finn,' she says, waving the baby's hand at me. 'He's always on the move, aren't you, Finny?' She glances back at me and there's something guarded, suddenly, in her expression.

I peer at Finn. A horrifying thought strikes me.

Could he be Dad's baby?

No *way.* I shunt the idea away, my cheeks burning.

'Your dad's not at home right now, though,' Julie goes on. 'He's down on the beach, but it's easy enough to find.'

'How . . . how do I get there?' I stammer.

'Down the track to your right, into the old town. There's a few shops, most of them boarded up, but stay on the road till you get to the sea. There's a bus shelter on the right. Your dad'll be in the next bay along from there, tinkering with his boat on the beach.' She pauses. 'I'd call and let him you're coming, but the signal's rubbish here.'

I stand still for a moment, unable to take in the fact that after all my searching, I'm so close to actually seeing Dad again. I want to ask Julie about Finn before I leave, but I can't find the words so instead I say a hoarse thank you, then go back to the front of the house.

Tyler looks up as I appear. He must be able to see the emotion on my face, but he doesn't ask me anything until we're walking along the track and Bess has, once again, fallen behind us, dragging her feet as she plods along.

'What happened?' he whispers.

I tell Tyler quietly about Julie and Finn. 'I think I should talk to Dad first, then talk to Bess before the two of them see each other. So they both have a bit of time to get their heads around it.'

Tyler nods. We follow the road down to the shore. It's a small stony bay, with a bus shelter in front and high rocks rising up on either side. The tide is out, just as Julie said it would be, and the beach stretches towards the water. I gaze to the right. Is Dad really there? Just around the high rocks in the next bay?

'How about I take Bess for a walk?' Tyler whispers.

'You can come and find us once you've spoken to your dad. He can wait while you tell Bess that he's . . . that you've found him. Then we can take her to meet him.'

I nod.

'Come on, Bess,' Tyler says in a loud, cheerful voice. 'Let's see if you can cartwheel as well as me on the beach.'

Bess shoots him a sulky look, but follows him across the stones. She doesn't give me a backward glance. I guess she's still mad at me for not telling her why we're here. Or perhaps she's just completely fed up about being made to wander around for such a long time.

Hopefully, once she sees Dad she'll forget everything else. I take a deep breath, praying that Dad will really be in the next bay. My legs start shaking as I make my way past the high rocks and into the bay on the right.

I stop, stock still. Even though I've been expecting him, it feels like someone chucked a bucket of seawater in my face.

Dad is right there, just a few metres away. He's bent over a little boat, sanding the hull. I watch the familiar movement. His hair – longer than I remember – falls over his face and he brushes it back.

It's really him. The same. And yet not the same. I want to move, to run towards him, but my feet are stuck to the ground.

And then something makes Dad look up and he sees me. His jaw drops.

I force my shaky legs to start moving towards him as Dad takes one step, then another, then breaks into a run, crunching across the stones, closing the space between us. He stops in front of me and peers, in wonder, at my face, as if he's looking at something he thought he had lost for ever.

'Kitterbug?' His voice is hoarse. 'Is that really you?'

24

My heart pounds as we stare at each other.

Dad is looking at me like I'm not real. Like I'm a ghost.

'You're the ghost,' I want to say. But no words come out. As if – the thought flickers like a match sparking and dying – as if I were Bess, my voice caught in my throat.

We're still standing on the stony beach, eyes on each other's faces. Time slows down. There are more lines on his face than in my memory. More grey hair than in any of the photos.

'Cat?' Dad says at last. He takes another step forward. He's right in front of me now, filling my vision. He clutches me by both arms. 'How did . . . ?' His voice is hoarse. 'How are you here?'

I nod, still unable to speak. The wind roars in off the sea. A seagull squawks.

'Oh, Cat.' Dad pulls me into a hug. I close my eyes, letting his arms enfold me, breathing in his familiar scent of sawdust and soap, now combined with something else . . . a deeper, muskier smell I don't remember.

The hug feels familiar and yet strange.

What it doesn't do, is make me feel safe, like his hugs used to. Too much has happened. I pull away.

'Dad?' I say, finding my voice at last. But I don't know where to begin. There are too many questions in my head.

Dad nods, as if he understands. 'How did you find me?' he asks.

'The brochures. Your credit card stuff. And the *Marvista*,' I explain. 'I knew you'd go somewhere near the sea. That got me to the caravan park at Saltcliff, then your friend Mac mentioned Julie and . . . here I am.'

A slow smile spreads across Dad's face. 'Clever Cat,' he says.

His praise used to make me feel like I was glowing inside, but right now I'm numb. My mind flashes back to the little cottage up the hill. And the baby in Julie's arms.

'Are you and Julie?' I ask. 'Is she . . . is her . . . ?'

'No, Kitterbug, of course not.' Dad makes a face as if the relationship I'm hinting at would be totally crazy. 'Julie's a good friend. She's just putting me up for a bit.' He pauses, looking around. 'I can't believe you found me. Are you here on your own?' His eyes fill with alarm. Where's your mum?'

'She doesn't know I'm here,' I explain. 'I'm with my friend Tyler – and . . . and with Bess.'

'Bess is here?' Dad's eyes light up with shocked delight.

'She's along in the next bay.' I point. 'You need to come with me and we'll get her and you can explain everything to us both.'

'No.' Dad shakes his head, his face clouding over. 'No, Cat. I don't think Bess should see me. It's too confusing and upsetting for a little child.'

'She's almost seven, Dad.' There's a thick lump in my throat. 'She's not *that* little.'

'I know,' he says, sounding sadder than I've ever heard anyone.

'Don't you want to see her?' My voice is small and fragile. I'd thought that when I saw Dad everything would fall into place. That after seventeen months of wishing he was alive, to have the ultimate proof that he *was* alive would be the most amazing thing ever. That all I'd feel would be joy.

Instead I feel more churned up than ever.

'Of course I do.' Dad rubs his forehead. 'It's just . . . things are complicated.'

'I know about the Blue Fire diamond,' I blurt out. 'I know you were framed for stealing it.'

Dad blinks rapidly. 'What?'

'That's why I'm here,' I go on. 'The FFG know you're still alive. They want the diamond and – Dad, when

Fran Farmer finds out you don't have it, she'll kill you for real.'

'Wait. Slow down.' Dad holds up his hand to stop me speaking. 'What's the . . . FFG? Who is Fran Farmer?'

I stare at him, bewildered. 'Fran Farmer is the head of the FFG. The gang of smugglers who think you and Rik stole the Blue Fire diamond from them.'

'The gang of . . . ? Me and Rik?' Dad shakes his head. 'What are you talking about?'

I look into his eyes as the wind whirls around our heads and the sea crashes behind us. A terrible feeling of helplessness washes over me. 'Rik told me,' I say. 'He called me about ten days ago and said you were still alive.'

'Rik knows I'm alive?' Dad's tanned face turns several shades paler.

I frown. 'Of course.'

'I don't understand.' Dad shakes his head. 'What else did he say?'

'He said a group of gangsters, the Fran Farmer Gang, think you and Rik stole their diamond, the Blue Fire.'

'But that's crazy,' Dad splutters.

My stomach twists into knots. 'No,' I insist. 'It's true. Fran Farmer has found out you're still alive and she's after you. She still thinks you have the Blue Fire and when she finds out you don't, she's going to take "extreme revenge".' Dad's jaw drops. 'Rik wants to *help*. He told me to find you and warn—'

'Cat.' Dad clutches my arm. 'Listen to me very carefully. Whatever Rik has told you, it's a lie.' His eyes glint in the sunlight. 'There was no gang. No smugglers. The FFG and Fran . . . whoever . . . Rik must have made them up.'

'What?' Blood thunders against my temples. 'I don't understand. If there are no gangsters, then—?'

'The Blue Fire diamond came into the shop for valuation, as part of a batch of unclaimed jewellery and ornaments. Mostly junk . . .' Dad frowns, as if it's costing him a lot to remember. 'Rik and I were on our own in the shop. I soon realized there was a priceless diamond in the mix, did a bit of research, and told Rik what an amazing find it was. I explained that by law we had to report it to the police. Rik got nasty, said no way were we handing it over.'

I reel back. 'But . . .'

'Rik and I argued. He got violent. Threatening me. Threatening *you*. I was petrified. I backed down completely, let him take it.' Dad gives a weary shake of the head. 'Maybe I should have left things there, but I was furious. The Blue Fire belongs to the *world*. Not to a violent thief like Rik.'

'What did you do?' My voice is hoarse. 'Did you tell Mum?'

'No, well, not the full story, I didn't want to drag her into it,' Dad explains. 'I only told her Rik was a con man, which is true, just not the whole truth.'

My hand flies to my mouth, fear pulsing through me. Mum had been right to doubt Rik and I hadn't believed her. All this while, I thought he was helping me.

Instead he was tricking and manipulating me – just like he did with Dad.

'I made an anonymous call to the police,' Dad goes on. 'I tipped them off about Rik being a thief. So they went to his house looking for stolen goods.'

'And they found the diamond?' I ask breathlessly.

'No.' Dad says. 'Not the diamond, but they *did* discover a load of other stuff. Enough to arrest Rik and send him to prison.' He sighs. 'I thought that was an end to it.'

'But . . . ?'

'But then Rik got a message to me from jail,' Dad goes on, grimly. 'He accused me of fitting him up. I denied it, but he was still suspicious. Still furious. He ordered me to fetch the Blue Fire from where he'd hidden it, and use my contacts to sell it on the black market. I tried to refuse, but he got really nasty. Said he had people watching me . . . watching the house . . . to make sure I did what he wanted.'

'Oh, Dad,' I breathe.

Dad brushes his hair off his face. 'I carried on saying

I wouldn't have anything to do with his criminal plan.' He hesitates. 'And . . . and that's when Rik had Pirate killed.'

'*What?*' I stare at him, as the whole world spins and reassembles inside my head. I see Pirate in my mind's eye, bounding enthusiastically across our back garden, then rolling on to his back, offering his tummy for Bess to tickle. 'I . . . I thought Pirate was run over by accident?'

'No, that was Rik. It was a message. A *clear* message. Next time it would be you. Or Bess.' Dad pats my shoulder. 'So you see, I was in this impossible position. Either I committed a crime that could send me to jail, away from everyone I cared about – or else Rik would kill you . . . my family. My wonderful girls.'

I stare at him, sick to my stomach. 'Do you really think Rik would go that far?'

'Yes.' He grips my shoulder more tightly, looking deep into my eyes. 'He's more dangerous than you can imagine, Cat. He basically gave me twenty-four hours to fence the diamond. Or you were all dead.'

I gulp. 'So what did you do?'

'There was only one option – at least that's how it felt at the time,' Dad explains. 'I told Rik I'd do what he suggested, then I ran. I had to make him think I'd drowned while trying to make a getaway with the diamond.'

I nod slowly, taking this in. 'So the diamond is at the bottom of the sea?'

'No. When it came to it, I couldn't destroy something so beautiful and valuable, but as far as Rik was concerned, it was gone.' He pauses. 'And I was gone too.'

The sea beyond us swells and crashes on the shore. A seagull squawks overhead.

'I still don't understand. Why didn't you tell us?' I ask slowly. 'You could have explained you had to leave.'

'I couldn't burden you girls with such a huge secret,' he says softly.

'Right.' A sudden, resentful anger whips up inside me. Maybe Bess would have been too little, but *I* would have understood. 'Did you think you were protecting us again? Is that it?'

There's a long pause. 'Oh, Cat, I'm so sorry.' Dad's lip trembles. 'Maybe I got it wrong, but I promise you I was only trying to do the right thing.'

I shake my head. 'And what about Mum?' I ask. 'Why didn't you tell her?'

A shadow passes over Dad's face. 'Your mum and I . . . we hadn't been in a good place for a long time.'

I don't know what to make of that. I want to tell him he's wrong, that I can remember him and Mum laughing together, even holding hands. But then I think of some of the mean things I've heard Mum say about him recently. Perhaps they really weren't happy together.

'It was *her* fault, wasn't it?' I ask. 'She's so selfish and—'

'No, Cat,' Dad interrupts. 'Your Mum did her best. I didn't make things easy. I was in and out of work . . . I put her through a lot, and we drifted apart.'

The wind gusts against my face: cold and relentless. 'I don't see how "drifting apart" justifies—'

'What I don't understand is how Rik found out I was still alive,' Dad says, changing the subject abruptly. 'I mean, he's great with tech, but I was really careful. I came off all my social media, only spent cash . . .' He shakes his head. 'The only time I went online was to look at what *you* were doing.'

'You did?' My voice blows away on the brisk sea breeze.

'I couldn't resist it.' Dad makes a regretful face at me. 'I followed you on Instagram, "liked" all those dresses you made.'

'I bet that's how Rik found you.' An empty misery settles in my guts. 'Through *me*.'

Dad meets my gaze. 'None of this is your fault, Cat. Rik is ruthless and he had help. Heavies to carry out his threats. You've been on your own.'

'No,' I say, thinking of Tyler. 'I've had help too.'

‘Plus, Rik’s filled your head full of lies, making up stories about gangsters . . .’ Dad shakes his head.

‘Rik wasn’t the only one,’ I say, remembering the visit Tyler and I made to Aunt Sandy and her mysterious visitor with the back-to-back ‘F’ tattoo.

‘I went to see Sandy Williams,’ I blurt out. ‘She said you and Rik were friends. She had a birthday card from you.’

Dad nods. ‘Rik and I *were* friends at first, when he joined Ballena Jewellery as Head of Digital. I told him all about you. And I did meet Sandy a couple of times. But after I called the cops on Rik, I realized she was up to her neck in his crimes too.’

‘She was?’ My eyes widen. ‘She said a man had come to see her, asking questions. We got the impression he was an FFG gangster.’

‘I expect she was just trying to back up Rik’s story, make sure you believed him,’ Dad says wearily.

So Sandy made up the man with the tattoo. She lied to Tyler and me, pretending to care about Dad . . . pretending to care about me. My head spins.

‘So, why did she call you the day before you disappeared?’ I ask, remembering the note I found among Dad’s old work things.

‘To threaten me,’ Dad hesitates. ‘She might look like a

harmless old lady, but I'm pretty sure Sandy was the one Rik got to kill Pirate.'

I gasp.

'What matters now,' Dad says, giving my shoulder a gentle shake, 'is that you fetch Bess and go back to your mother. Forget that you saw me. Lie to Rik, lie to everyone.'

'No.' Tears rush into my eyes. How can Dad ask me to do that? 'I *can't*.'

'You must,' he says desperately. 'Look, Cat, I'd do anything to be able to come back home, but I won't put you and Bess and Mum in danger.'

'But what about you?' I ask. 'Rik's not going to stop until he finds you.'

Dad peers into my eyes. 'He doesn't know you're here, does he?'

'Not *exactly* where we are,' I say. 'But he knows we're in Norfolk.'

'That's bad. Very bad.' A horrified look crosses Dad's face. 'Wait. How did Rik get your number?'

I frown. 'He said you gave it to him.'

'No . . . I'd *never*!' Dad's eyes widen. 'Rik must have got hold of it by hacking your account. Do you have your phone with you now?' he asks.

'Yes.' I take it out of my pocket. 'But there's no service,

there hasn't been since last night. And yesterday I took the SIM out, so Mum couldn't track me, which means Rik won't have been able to eith—'

Dad grabs my shoulders again. 'Did you put the SIM back in at any point?' he asks. 'Think carefully, Cat. It's really important. Rik could easily have tracked you on your phone.'

'I put it back in a couple of times, but the only time there was a signal was when I was at the mobile-home park at Saltcliff. But I only used the phone for a few minutes. I did send Rik a text but it didn't say where we—'

'Damn.' Dad picks up his jacket and starts walking across the beach. 'Come on,' he orders. 'You need to get out of here. Remember, you haven't seen me. It's all been dead ends.'

'Nobody at the mobile-home park knows where you are,' I protest, running along beside him. 'Even Mac – and he was literally the only person I spoke to who had a clue who you were, so— Oh, God, do you think Rik would hurt Mac?'

'I'm certain he would,' Dad says, pulling on his jacket.

We reach the rock face that divides this bit of beach from the next bay, where Tyler and Bess are waiting. Dad pulls me to him in a swift hug. His jacket is rough and damp against my cheek.

'What are you going to do?' I ask, as Dad draws away.

'Deal with Rik once and for all.' He clenches his jaw. His face sets so hard I barely recognize him.

Cold terror sweeps through me. 'What does "deal with" mean?'

'The less you know, the better.' Dad takes a step away from me.

I stare at him. What's happened to the smiling dad of my memories? 'Why don't you just go and get the diamond and give it to Rik?'

Dad gives a hollow laugh. 'It's too late for that now. Believe me, Cat, I know the man. He'll want his revenge on me, whatever I do now.' He pauses. 'It's him or me.'

Tears prick at my eyes. 'So how . . . how can I get hold of you?'

Dad shakes his head. 'Things have gone too far. Rik's crossed a line by involving you. Until I've dealt with him, it's safer for you if you can't reach me. I'm so sorry.' He turns away.

My stomach heaves. A sour, panicky feeling. 'Dad!' I call. He turns, his eyes glittering with fear and impatience. I can't bear it. I'm losing him all over again. 'Where did you put the Blue Fire diamond?' I ask, desperate to keep him talking, even if just for a few more minutes. 'You can't have had long to hide it. Where did you leave it?'

Dad frowns. 'It's better you don't know.'

'Please, Dad,' I say, a sob catching in my throat. 'Tell me and I'll go.'

'No.' His mouth trembles. 'Please, Cat, don't make this any harder than—'

'Just one clue,' I say.

'Then you'll leave?' Dad nods. 'Okay, then. It's at home, under the stars.'

What the hell does that mean?

But before I can ask him, he turns away and breaks into a run. At the top of the beach, he darts right on to the road, lost behind the small row of shops that lead back up the hill.

I want to race after him. But there's no point. I trudge along the stony beach, wind whipping at my eyes. I reach the end of the rock face that leads around to the next bay, and I glance back, desperately hoping that Dad will have changed his mind. That he'll be right there, in front of me, telling me he's coming home with me and Bess.

But the beach is deserted.

The only sound is the wind roaring off the sea.

And Dad is nowhere to be seen.

25

I stumble past the rock face, into the next bay. There's no sign of Tyler and Bess, but the beach here is small. They've probably gone on to the bay after this one, past the line of rocks ahead. It's not easy to walk. My feet sink into the stones, sucked down with each step. The sea, stretched out on my right, is grey and angry. Dark clouds, which were way out to sea earlier, are now gathering overhead. The wind blasts across my face.

I'm barely aware of any of these things.

I found Dad.

And now he's gone again. On the run once more, because of me.

Tears mingle with the saltwater spray that mists on my cheeks. A million emotions battle inside me: fury at Rik for tricking me, an even greater rage at myself for being tricked. And a hollow, empty feeling, where the joy of finding Dad alive should be.

He's okay, I tell myself. I should be happy. Except his life is in danger and I've made that worse and now he can't even spend time with me, or see Bess . . . and it's all thanks to Rik.

Loathing rises inside me, a hatred like I've never felt before. Rik threatened Dad and all of us, had our poor dog killed, ripped my family apart. All for a useless diamond.

I stop walking and turn to face the sea as it tumbles towards the shore. I can taste the salt on my lips, feel it sticking against my skin. It's raining on the horizon, the sky dark as steel. I can smell the storm that's coming.

Thoughts tumble over each other in my head. How could I have believed Rik's story about the FFG? Even though Aunt Sandy seemed to back up everything he said, I should still have . . . I catch my breath as it hits me. Aunt Sandy wasn't the only one who helped me believe Rik was on my side. It was *Tyler* who claimed that the back-to-back 'F' tattoo of her mysterious visitor stood for Fran Farmer.

A new horror seizes me. Tyler and his dad arrived the very day Rik made contact.

Was that really a coincidence?

Is Tyler part of Rik's plan to manipulate me? Find the diamond? Kill Dad?

And I've left him with Bess.

Fear grips my whole body. I break into a run, racing along the stony beach. There's nobody here. The rain is moving closer to the land, the early morning sky overhead low and dark. The tide is coming in fast. I reach the end of this bay and hurtle on to the next. It's even narrower than the one before. The sea is getting closer; the cliffs are high on all sides.

Where are Tyler and Bess?

Just as I'm about to scream in panic, I spot them at the far end of the bay. Can't Tyler see the water already lapping at the rock face just beyond them? Can't he see the tide is coming in? Or is he intending to lure me and Bess under the waves as part of Rik's evil plan: to punish Dad by killing us?

'Bess!' I yell as loud as I can, but the wind whips the sound away. I push myself harder, running as fast as I can towards her.

'Hey!' I yell, now just a few strides behind. 'Bess!'

She hears me at last. So does Tyler. They both turn. Bess's face lights up as she sees me. It's like all her earlier anger has vanished.

'What happened?' Tyler shouts over the wind.

I glance at Bess, a fresh misery twisting inside me as I think about how, now, there's no way I can tell her about Dad. My feelings must show on my face because, as she looks at me, the brightness fades from her eyes. She turns away, picking up a stone and throwing it at the waves licking their way up the beach. The first spits of rain start to fall.

'What happened? Tyler asks again, hurrying over.

'Why did you take Bess out of the first bay?' I demand.

Tyler frowns. 'We just kept walking. What's the—?'

'Are you working with Rik?'

His frown deepens. '*What?*'

'Are you spying for him?'

'No.' He stares at me, shocked. 'Of course I'm not.'

I hesitate. Take a quick look around. The water is rising fast, now splashing against the rock face that leads to the next bay. Talking to Tyler will have to wait.

'The tide's coming in.' I dash forward and grab Bess by the arm. 'We need to go back.'

'No, we don't,' Tyler says, still frowning at me. 'Bess and I passed a couple of girls a few minutes ago. They said there are steps up the cliff out of here in the next bay.'

I hesitate again, unsure whether to trust him.

'Come on,' Tyler urges.

'Okay,' I say reluctantly.

The three of us hurry along the beach. The wind is building. The spots of rain become thick, fat drops. The waves are bigger than ever, crashing against the rock face that we need to pass to get to the next bay. The three of us stand, watching for a second as the water pulls back, sucking at the stones, then rolls forward again. Bess looks anxiously up at me.

'Fancy going on my back?' Tyler asks.

She nods. I hesitate. Should I let Tyler take her? But Tyler has already crouched down. Bess clambers on. Her little legs in their blue leggings stick out on either side of his jacket. She's squinting into the wind and rain, strands of hair blowing out of yesterday's plaits. There's a grubby smear down one cheek and her hands, clutching at Tyler's neck, are filthy. I feel a pang of guilt. I've put Bess in this position. I should never have brought Tyler, or let Bess stay with us.

I should never have come myself.

Tyler sets off, bracing himself as a wave smashes against his legs. His trousers are wet from the knees down. I follow, wading into the ankle-deep water. It's hard to balance when the waves pull back. I keep my eyes fixed on Bess, willing her to hold Tyler tightly. Seconds later and we're through to the next bay. There's a rumble of thunder and a flash of lightning. Rain comes at us like arrows, thrown from every direction, stabbing at our faces. I shield my eyes and look for the steps Tyler mentioned, as Bess scrambles down from his back.

This bay is even narrower than the last, only a thin strip of beach separates the sea on one side of us from the high, sheer rock face on the other.

'I can't see the steps!' I yell, grabbing Tyler's arm. 'Where are they?'

He peers through the downpour. Points to the far corner of the beach. My stomach clenches in horror. Tyler's right. The steps are there, but we're cut off from them by the water. I glance back, at the way we came. The sea is already flowing over the area we've just walked across.

'You've put us in danger!' I yell over the wind.

Tyler throws me an angry look. 'I'm trying to get us out of it!' he shouts back.

I take a deep breath. Whatever Tyler has or hasn't done, I should have spotted the rising water levels before encouraging him to take Bess for a walk along the beach. Dad warned me a million times how fast tides can come in.

'We'll have to wade through the water to the steps,' I say. 'We can swim if we have to.'

'*What?*' Tyler's eyes widen. 'I can't swim.'

Is he serious? Panic rises inside me. Is this another trick?

'Okay,' I say, trying to focus. 'You're taller than us, you can probably walk all the way. It shouldn't be that deep.' I grab Bess's salt-sticky palm. She is freezing. 'You go ahead. We'll follow.'

Tyler nods, puts Bess down and sets off. Bess looks up

at me. Her jaw is clenched, her expression determined, but I can see the fear behind her eyes.

'We just need to get to the steps.' I point across the bay. 'It's going to be fine.'

So long as the water is shallow and the current is weak.

I don't say these thoughts out loud.

Ahead of us, Tyler is already wading through the first bit of water. He turns and gives us a thumbs up. Clutching Bess's hand tightly, I follow Tyler's route, watching where he goes. Another few metres and we're almost at the steps. Ahead of us, Tyler sinks, suddenly, into the water. It's up to his thighs. I gasp, gripping Bess's hand more tightly. Tyler's thighs correspond roughly to Bess's neck. Rain pounds on our heads. My clothes are plastered to my skin. Bess's fingers are slippery with wet and cold. I glance down at her. Her little face is screwed up with concentration.

'Come on!' I yell. 'We can do this!'

I take the next step. The seabed disappears from under me. I lose my footing. Sinking below the water. I'm clutching for Bess's hand but it's gone. Sea in my mouth. Churned up grit masking my vision. I flail, trying to find my feet – to find Bess. The current sucks at me, pulling me away. *Where is she?* Panic whirls like a tornado in my head. I claw at the water, fighting for the surface. For air.

For Bess.

The dark wetness covers me. Arms and legs flailing. I find my feet. Stand. The water is only to my thighs, I'm okay. Panicked, I look around. Tyler is still ploughing ahead, almost at the steps. But there's no sign of Bess. My eyes sting with salt.

'Bess?' I yell. '*Bess!*'

She must be underneath the water.

I draw air deep into my lungs and plunge under again. I scrabble around with my arms, wild with fear. I can't see a thing; it's too dark from the grit churned up by the waves. I *have* to find her. I can't come up for air until I find her. A silent scream sounds from the depths of my heart.

Bess!

26

Black water. Blood pulsating at my temples. Dirt, salt and fear in my mouth. I am desperate to breathe, but I'm not giving up. I scrabble and pull at the water. Bess must be here.

She *has* to be.

Strong hands grab at my hair. Find my shoulder, my arm. Hands under my armpits, lifting me up. I can't fight against them.

I stand up, spluttering.

Tyler stands in front of me, sea water rolling off his face.

'Bess!' I shriek, pulling away.

'I've got her. She's okay.' He points behind him, through the rain.

Bess is there, shivering on the steps that lead up out of the beach. I blink the water out of my eyes.

'She's fine,' Tyler says. 'She's safe.'

I set off, wading fiercely towards her. The rain is still pummelling at my face, my soaked clothes clinging to every bit of me. I don't care. Bess is okay.

I don't know how long it takes to reach the steps, but at last I clamber on to the slippery rock. Bess falls into my arms.

I hold her tightly. There are no words for the relief.

'Come on!' Tyler yells above us. 'The tide's still rising. We need to keep moving.'

I grip Bess's hand again and lead her up the steps. They are steep for her small legs and, at first, the wind buffets us so hard we have to keep stopping to brace against it. I try to position Bess on my inside, but she slips constantly on the steps, her hands red from scrabbling for purchase. We're both crying, tears streaming down our faces. Below us, Tyler climbs watchfully, constantly looking up to check Bess is okay.

It feels like hours pass as we climb, but it's only minutes. And then, as we're almost at the top, the wind drops and the sun comes out, glistening on the sea spread out beneath us. I stop to enjoy the warmth on my face.

'Okay?' Tyler asks.

I turn and look deep into his eyes, at the gold that glints in the brown. And suddenly I know that, whatever else is true, I should never have doubted Tyler. He's a friend. A good friend.

On top of which he, literally, just saved my life. And probably Bess's.

I open my mouth to say 'thank you', but before I can speak an urgent shout cuts through the air.

'Hey there! Are you all right?'

A moment later we reach the top and the steps turn into a path that winds away in a gradual slope.

A dark-skinned, tanned, slender man in a V-neck T-shirt and jeans is peering down at us from the path at the top of the cliff, a blanket in his hand. 'We saw you on the steps, the little one struggling,' he calls out. 'Did you get cut off by the tide?'

I nod, suddenly overwhelmed with exhaustion. The man hurries down to us. He puts the blanket round Bess and picks her up, carrying her up to the top. A woman with flame-coloured curls is waiting at the end of the path. Two small boys fidget beside her, shifting from leg to leg as they watch us. The man turns as he reaches them, beckoning us on.

'Are you okay?' The woman bustles forward, her boys clutching at her legs. 'I'm Emma. This is Roshan.' The man gives us a broad, warm smile.

Tyler and I say our names. Bess, of course, doesn't speak. She's still lying in Roshan's arms, her eyes tight shut.

'And that's my sister, Bess,' I say.

Emma stares at us, frowning as she takes in how soaked we are. She's got a kind, round face, and a smile as warm as her husband's.

'Come on,' she says. 'Our holiday place is just around the corner. You can't stay in these wet things. And you'll be wanting to call your parents. Let them know you're okay.'

Tyler and I exchange a look. As we follow Roshan and Emma across the dry earth, past the shrubs that lead to a little lane, I realize that my backpack is gone along with everything inside it.

'I've lost my phone. My purse. Keys. Everything,' I whisper to Tyler.

'Me too,' he says.

Emma and Roshan's holiday cottage is set back from the lane. Emma ushers us inside, pointing me to the bathroom upstairs. She fetches clothes – her oldest boy's for Bess and a pair of cream shorts and a striped top of hers for me – and starts a bath running.

I have no idea where Tyler is, but Emma assures me Roshan is sorting some dry clothes for him. 'He'll be using the downstairs shower,' she says. 'I'll leave you now. Get some porridge on for you. You look like you could do with some warm food inside you. Do you have your mum's number? Or Tyler's parents'? I can give them a call, if you want, to let them know you're safe.'

I shake my head. 'I don't know her number off by heart, but I know where she is. When you get hold of her, will you ask her to let Tyler's dad know he's okay too?'

Emma nods, then looks at me expectantly.

'My mum's at a convention . . . at Alexandra Palace in London,' I say. 'Her name's Petronella Mooney.'

Emma's eyes light up. 'The astrologer?'

I nod.

'That's . . . Wow, that's amazing. Gosh, I remember seeing her on TV *years* ago.' Emma grins, wrinkling her freckly nose in delight. 'Aren't you lucky having a mother like that? But what are you doing here on your own?' She eyes me with intense curiosity.

I mumble something about a day out and how we got lost and had to spend the night in the open. Horrified – but apparently satisfied by my explanation – Emma scuttles away, leaving me to wrap Bess in one of the big fluffy towels on the rail. Bess is as excitable now as she was terrified on the steps up the cliff, just a little while earlier. She keeps jumping up and down, refusing to co-operate as I try to persuade her into the shorts and cotton top Emma has left for her.

Not for the first time, I get the strong sense that she is dying to open her mouth and speak, but I'm too tired to work out how to help her find a way to do it. At last she's dressed and I'm free to put on dry clothes myself. Emma's top is only a bit too big for me and I can hold up her shorts with the belt she left.

The two of us head downstairs. Tyler is already sitting at the kitchen table, in a brown V-neck jumper that looks really weird on him. The two small boys wriggle on their chairs, gazing up at him. Bess sits next to me, suddenly shy again. She yawns and I'm guiltily aware of how exhausted she must be: her face is pale and there are dark shadows under her eyes.

Emma presents us with steaming bowls of porridge. It's not until I'm eating that I realize how hungry I am.

'Thank you so much,' I say. 'This is really kind of you.'

'Of course,' Emma says.

'Couldn't leave you out there in the elements,' Roshan adds. 'Are you here on holiday?'

'Cat's mother is the astrologer Petronella Mooney.' Emma says, bursting with enthusiasm. 'I've just put in a call to the convention she's speaking at. Hopefully they'll find her and she'll call back soon.'

Great.

Roshan looks confused. One of the little boys starts banging a toy car against the table top.

'Mum's in London,' I explain, giving Tyler a sideways gaze. I hope he understands that I don't want to explain the whole story, however nice Roshan and Emma are.

'We just thought it would be fun to come to the seaside,' Tyler says, instantly getting it. I smile at him.

Roshan chuckles. 'That's backfired a bit, I'd say.'

'Let them eat, Roshan,' Emma urges.

By the time we've finished our porridge, Bess is almost asleep, her head drooping towards the table. The two little boys are now both running an entire racetrack of cars between the various plates and bowls.

'She's dead on her feet, poor thing,' Emma says. 'Roshan, take the boys up to the playground. Let the little one here get some rest.'

A few minutes later, Roshan and the boys leave. The little holiday cottage is suddenly silent. Emma settles Bess on the sofa, covering her with a blanket. As she comes back into the kitchen, Tyler and I offer to help clear up the meal we've just eaten, but Emma shoos us outside.

'Get some sun on your face out front,' she says. 'You've had a shock. I'll be here with Bess. I'll come and get you when your mum rings.'

Outside the sky is clear and the sun shining brightly. The terror of the rising tide and the earlier storm seem like a dream.

Tyler and I sit down at the little wooden table in the front garden. My whole body feels bruised and wrung out.

'That was intense, earlier,' Tyler says quietly. 'In the water, I mean.'

I nod. I'm not intending to speak, but suddenly the words in my head are flowing out of my mouth. 'I thought Bess was dead.'

Tyler looks at me, then reaches across the table. His fingers curl over mine: warm and muscular. My skin fires with goosebumps. 'I thought *you* were.' He shifts a tiny bit closer. 'And before that I thought you'd gone mad. You were ranting about me spying for Rik or something? What on earth did your dad say to you?'

'I'm sorry,' I mumble. 'I was just upset.'

'Okay.' Tyler is still looking at me. 'So what happened with your dad?'

I tell Tyler everything Dad said. Tyler listens, his eyes widening with shock as I outline the full extent of Rik's lies.

'So,' he says slowly, when I finish. 'So . . . your dad had to disappear in a hurry. He couldn't bear the idea of Rik having the Blue Fire diamond *or* of dumping it at sea, so he hid it somewhere in your house?'

'Exactly,' I say. 'And now Rik knows Dad's alive, he's convinced Dad still has the diamond and he wants it back. If he finds Dad, he'll force him to hand over the diamond.'

'Right.' Tyler sits back. 'But rather than hand it over, your dad says he's going to "deal with" Rik.' He hesitates. 'What does *that* mean?'

'I don't know,' I admit. 'I'm scared Dad's going to get hurt. But he won't go to the police. He says Rik's too dangerous. He . . . he says Rik had our dog – Pirate, I told you about him – killed while he was in jail.'

Tyler's eyes widen in horror. 'Seriously?'

I nod. 'That's why Dad doesn't want to give Rik the diamond,' I explain. 'Rik's too angry. Dad says that Rik will want revenge whatever happens now.' I hesitate, an idea occurring. 'Unless . . .'

'What?' Tyler raises his eyebrows.

'Maybe I can do a deal with Rik,' I say.

Tyler stares at me sceptically. 'A deal? With an insane and violent con man thief?'

'If I could find the diamond, maybe *I* could convince Rik to leave Dad alone,' I say.

'But . . . ?'

'Think about it,' I persist. 'Rik still doesn't know where Dad is. And he won't find out now that Dad knows he's on his tail. So maybe if *I* offer Rik the diamond, on condition he stops looking for Dad, he'll agree.' I bite my lip. 'I can't see a better option. It's the only possible way we get Rik to leave Dad alone.'

Free to come home to me and Mum and Bess so we can be a family again.

I don't speak this last thought out loud, but it's

what Dad said he wanted earlier. And the hope of it fills me.

'Okay.' Tyler still doesn't sound convinced. 'Where in your house did your dad leave the diamond?'

I make a face. 'He wouldn't tell me,' I say. 'He doesn't want me involved. Says it's too dangerous.'

'What do *you* want?' Tyler asks.

I turn to face him. 'I want to get Rik out of our lives once and for all,' I say. 'I want to find the diamond and save Dad.'

'Okay,' Tyler sits up. 'What did your dad say about the diamond, *exactly*?'

'He just said it was "at home, under the stars".' I look hopefully at Tyler. 'Do you think that means it's hidden outside, in the garden?'

Tyler laughs. 'Under the stars literally means everywhere, doesn't it? But, yeah, I guess outside, though it would take months to dig up your entire garden.' He makes a face. 'I can't see your mum letting that happen. As it is, she'll probably be so mad with me for coming on this trip, she'll give my dad the sack.'

He looks genuinely worried.

'No,' I say, 'she won't blame your dad. Or you. She'll just be furious with me.'

There's a long pause.

'I don't regret it,' Tyler says softly. 'Any of it.'

'Cat!' Emma's voice from the cottage door makes us both jump. I spin round. She's holding out a mobile phone. 'It's your mum,' she says. 'She wants to speak to you.'

27

My whole body is tensed for Mum to explode down the phone at me. I take the mobile Emma offers. She slips back inside the cottage, a sympathetic smile on her lips.

I glance back at Tyler who grimaces. He's expecting the worst too.

I brace myself and put the phone to my ear.

'Hello, Mum.'

I'm expecting her to yell. To scream. Instead there's just the jerky sound of her breathing.

'Mum?'

'Oh, Cat. You're all right?' I frown, barely able to make out her words. 'You're really okay?'

'Yes, we're all fine,' I say. 'Bess is asleep. Emma and Roshan have been really nice and—' The rest of my sentence is drowned out as Mum bursts into tears.

I walk over to the little wooden table, the phone still at my ear as an emotion I'm not used to feeling around Mum worms its way into my head: guilt.

'I was so frightened, Cat,' Mum wails, her voice

cracking. 'I mean, I was furious at first, especially after your first message, but then by the second I was starting to worry and . . . and when you didn't come back last night—'

'I'm sorry,' I say. 'I did send a message saying we were okay last night . . . but there wasn't a signal. We'd got lost and—'

'Tyler managed to get a message that you were fine through to *his* dad,' Mum says, a note of accusation in her voice. 'Which was – on the one hand – a relief, but on the other meant that the police search wasn't—'

'The police were searching for us?' I ask.

'Of course they were.' Mum breaks down again. 'I went over and over your chart all night. At first I couldn't see anything, but then I realized Mercury was in retrograde and . . . well, you know what a foreshadowing of doom that is . . .'

'I'm sorry,' I say again. 'I . . . I just *had* to come here.'

'Why? What on earth are you doing in Norfolk?' Mum's voice sharpens. 'And what possessed you to take Bess with you?'

'Bess wasn't meant to come,' I explain quickly. 'She followed us. And . . . and . . . we're here for Dad.'

A sharp intake of breath on the other end of the line.

'Mum, I've seen him. We talked. He's alive. He's okay.'

Silence.

'Mum?' Suddenly I desperately need her to believe me. 'Mum, I found him. It's true, what I told you: he was framed, he had to go into hiding to protect us. But you were right about Rik, he was the one who framed him and . . .' I trail off.

Mum lets out a long sigh. 'I understand you're grieving, Cat. I'm very aware. But . . .' She pauses and I can hear the struggle in her voice to keep her temper. 'This fantasy about Dad has to stop.'

'It's not a—'

'I know we didn't have a . . . a body, but I *saw* the wreck of Dad's boat. All the authorities *agreed* he must be dead.' Mum's voice rises. 'Why are you putting me through this?'

'Mum, *listen*—'

'Once we're home I'm going to find an astrological counsellor for you to speak to. Perhaps they will be able to—'

'No.' I'm practically shouting. 'No, Mum, I don't need to speak to someone, I'm not imagining Dad.'

There's an ominous silence on the other end of the line.

'Is Tyler all right?' Mum's voice is sharp, as if she's both hurt and angry. 'His father drove up here first thing this morning, you know.' She sighs. 'This . . . expedition of yours is having far-reaching consequences.'

'But—'

'I've arranged for a local taxi service to come and pick you up,' Mum goes on, clearly determined to ignore everything I'm telling her about Dad. 'Mr Tuesday and I will be waiting for you at Alexandra Palace. As soon as you get here, we'll drive home.' She pauses. 'And, for your own good, you are grounded for the rest of the summer.'

The line goes dead.

I sink on to the bench next to the wooden table, trying to get my head around Mum's refusal to believe me. Does she really think I'm hallucinating about Dad? Or, worse, making up a story deliberately to upset her? Tyler sits beside me, looking worried.

Emma wanders over from the cottage doorway. I hand her the phone.

'Everything all right?' she asks. 'Your mother sounded upset but very grateful you were okay. Gosh, she was so lovely. I used to watch her when I was a teenager and she was on that morning show on TV. She's really got the gift, hasn't she? Does she do your charts for your birthdays? Look into the future for you?'

I gaze up at her smiling, eager face.

'Not really,' I say.

'Ah, well.' Emma smiles. 'I expect she doesn't want to impose herself. She's very sensitive like that, isn't she? Now I better get your little sister up and your wet clothes in a bag. Your mum's sending a car but I expect you already know that.' She disappears inside.

'Cat?' Tyler asks. 'Hey, are you all right?' He shuffles closer along the bench. I lean against him. His body feels like the only stable thing in the whole world. He puts his arm round me and strokes my shoulder. 'What did your mum say?'

I outline our conversation, getting more emotional as I speak. 'I get that she's mad, but why doesn't she believe I saw Dad?'

Tyler shrugs. 'Maybe she thinks you're making him up to justify running away,' he suggests. 'I talked to my dad just now and he didn't believe it either. He's swallowed your mum's version that you're . . . I dunno . . . having some sort of bereavement crisis breakdown. I told him you'd seen your dad, but he got all serious and asked if Bess and I had seen him too. And when I had to admit that we hadn't, he got sad and said you must be very troubled.'

'Great,' I mutter.

We sit on the cottage doorstep, lost in our own thoughts. I can't make sense of it all: Dad is alive, but Mum doesn't believe it. And Rik still wants the diamond – and revenge.

For all that's happened, I'm right back where I started a week ago: Dad's life is in danger and I'm the only one that can help him.

I have to find that diamond.

As Roshan and the little boys arrive home, Bess appears from inside the cottage, her hair neatly brushed and the shadows gone from under her eyes. She sits beside me, sucking her thumb, which I haven't seen her do for years.

Guilt bites at me again.

'We're going home soon, Bess,' I tell her.

She nods, curling up against my side and staring at the little boys, now playing across the grass. After all her jumping around earlier, she seems to have withdrawn again. Or maybe she's just shy around Emma and Roshan's kids.

'I'm going to look for the Blue Fire diamond as soon as we get back,' I mutter to Tyler. I hesitate. The person I used to be would never have asked the question now on my lips, but that's not who I am any more. 'Will you help me?'

'Try and stop me,' he says, a smile spreading slowly across his face.

28

By the time the taxi Mum has sent delivers us all the way back to Alexandra Palace, it's almost 2 p.m. I sleep through quite a bit of the hot journey and wake, feeling disoriented, to find myself back in the car park outside the exhibition centre exactly twenty-nine hours after leaving it.

Mum and Mr Tuesday are waiting for us. Neither of them say anything as they herd us towards their respective cars. Tyler casts me a sympathetic look as his dad orders him into their battered estate. I watch him disappear as Mum, Bess and I reach our car. It's fully packed, ready for the journey home.

'Weren't you supposed to be at the astrology show for another two days?' I ask, as I get into the front seat beside Mum.

She slams her door, tight-lipped, and reverses out of her parking space. 'I was also supposed to be giving the keynote speech, but that wasn't possible either,' she says, her voice tight and clipped, as we turn on to the road,

London spread out in front of us. It's a perfect summer's day, clouds scudding across a bright blue sky.

I frown. 'Why couldn't you do your speech?'

'Why do you think?' Mum glares at me. 'It's not possible to concentrate when your children have run away. I was terrified. Not to mention humiliated.'

'I'm so sorry, Mum,' I say awkwardly. 'I would have said something, it's just . . . you'd never have let me go, so—'

'Of course I wouldn't!' Mum explodes. 'It was dangerous! You ended up sleeping outside in the middle of the country, where you could have been attacked by someone under a negative aspect . . . or by wolves.'

'There aren't any—'

'Letting your sister get caught out in a high tide, when you *know* how tides work.'

I fall silent, guilt stabbing at me again.

'And all the time I'm worried sick about the two of you. And as for the embarrassment of having to tell Tyler's dad you'd run off with his son . . .'

'You make it sound like—'

'And the utter, *utter* humiliation of *everyone* at the convention knowing that I can't keep track of my own children, who I've been boasting are the apple of my eye and the best, most helpful daughters ever born to woman.'

Mum heaves a shuddering sigh and turns the car sharply. 'Not to mention having to deal with that . . . that Emma, who was kind enough to look after you all, but talked non-stop. I bet *her* Mercury is in Gemini.' She tuts. 'Thanks to you, Cat, I've had to offer the wretched woman free readings for six months. So *that's* an expense. And don't get me started on the cost of the taxi that brought you back to London.' She scowls. 'It's all coming out of your allowance, *that* much I promise you.'

I look out of the window. Through her reflection in the wing mirror I can see Bess is gazing out of the window. She's already put on her headphones and has that dreamy look on her face that she always gets when she listens to a story. Earlier today, I'd thought she might be on the verge of speaking at last, but now that seems as far away as ever. The miserable knot inside me tightens.

As we drive on, my thoughts flicker to the conversation I had with Dad. I glance at Mum.

'Were you having problems . . . you and Dad? Before . . . before he went?' I ask quietly.

Mum's head whips round. She stares at me, clearly startled, then turns to face the road ahead again, her jaw clenched.

'*Were* you?' I ask.

Mum takes a deep breath. 'It was a difficult time,' she says, then peers at her satnav.

I wait, expectantly, for her to say more. But, instead, she starts gabbling away about the route out of London.

Clearly, there's no point trying to get her to talk about Dad.

I close my eyes and focus on the only thing that makes sense right now: working out where the Blue Fire diamond is hidden.

Tyler's right that 'under the stars' could mean literally anywhere. But Dad said the diamond was hidden 'at home'. That means outside or . . . *of course* . . . the attic: that's at the very top of the house. What could be more obviously 'under the stars'?

Tyler and I have already looked through a lot of the bags and boxes up there, but there are quite a few more. And plenty of nooks and crannies ideal for hiding a gemstone. I'm itching to tell Tyler, but he's in his dad's car and, as neither of us have a phone any more, there's no way I can communicate with him.

'Mum?' I say softly, as she pauses from her satnav-related rant to take a right-hand turn. 'I lost my mobile in the sea. Do you think—?'

'If you're about to ask me for a new one you can stop right there,' Mum cuts in. 'You won't need a phone for the rest of the summer, remember? You're grounded. When it comes to going-back-to-school time, we'll see. Maybe a cheap one for emergencies.' She sniffs. 'And I'm seriously considering booking you in for a course of astrological counselling sessions.'

I stare at her, horrified, then press my lips together. There's no point arguing with her now, while she's still so angry. Ten minutes later Mum pulls off at a motorway services garage. I get out of the car and look around for Tyler as Mum fills up with petrol. I don't have any real hope he'll be here – we lost sight of the Tuesdays within a few minutes of leaving Alexandra Palace.

'Don't even think about asking me for crisps or sweets,' Mum says, misinterpreting why I've stepped out of the car.

'I'm not,' I say, stung. 'I just need the loo.'

Mum shrugs, then peers into the back seat, where Bess is now busily drawing a new picture. 'Don't be long,' she says. 'I'm not leaving Bess on her own.'

I hurry away, following the signs around the outside of the building to the ladies. I'm in and out quickly. As I walk away from the toilet, a motorbike screeches to a stop in front of me. I spring back, startled. The rider jumps off. His helmet is painted with red skulls.

Panic rising, I try to sidestep the man, but he stretches out his arm, barring my way.

My stomach lurches into my mouth as, with his free hand, the man angrily wrenches off his helmet.

Rik.

29

In person, Rik is shorter, thinner and more mean-looking than he seemed on my phone screen. Sweaty from his bike helmet, his mousy-brown hair is plastered to the sides of his head and his grey eyes glare into mine like pencil points.

'Are you all right, Cat?' he asks.

He's trying to sound concerned, but I can hear the tension in his voice. A shiver runs down my spine.

'You said you were abroad.' I take a step back. 'How come you're here?

'I flew into the UK late last night,' Rik says, smoothing his hair off his face.

He's lying. I glance at the red skulls helmet tucked under his arm. It's definitely the same one Tyler and I saw on the rider outside Aunt Sandy's house. Which means it was Rik himself who was watching us then.

'But how did you find me *here*?' I look around the garage. From where we're standing only two of the petrol pumps are visible. Mum, Bess and the car are out of sight round the corner.

'Your phone wasn't working, so I traced your last message, but that was from yesterday afternoon,' Rik explains. 'I was worried, so I located your mum's car using *her* mobile.'

'Oh.' My chest tightens, as the realization properly hits me. Everything Dad said about Rik was true, including his ability to track people through their phones.

'Don't look so scared,' Rik goes on, smoothly. 'I only came back because I was concerned about you. It's a risk but I need to know what happened. Why did you ditch your phone? Are you all right?'

'I'm fine.' I try to move past him but he steps sideways to block my way.

'So how was the trip to Norfolk? Did you find your dad?' Rik makes a visible effort to smile. It doesn't reach his eyes.

I think fast. How do I convince Rik that my travels were a dead end?

'Well, Cat?' A note of impatience creeps into Rik's voice as he gives me that fake smile again. 'What happened in Norfolk?'

'I was wrong, I didn't find Dad,' I lie. 'I thought he might be there, like I texted, but . . . but he wasn't.'

Rik frowns, studying my face carefully. 'You mean he wasn't in that caravan park at Saltcliff?'

My stomach lurches into my throat. 'How do you—?'

'I told you,' Rik says, impatiently. 'I traced your messages. That was the last place you contacted me from.'

'Dad wasn't there,' I say. I take another step away from him. Lightning fast, Rik grabs my forearm.

'Ow.' I try to pull away, but he keeps hold of me, my skin now pinching painfully under his fingers.

'After all the help and support I've given you, you owe me the truth,' Rik spits, his face now horribly close to mine. 'I've put my life on the line coming back to the UK to help find your dad. And I think you're lying about not seeing him.'

'No.' I gulp, trying not to show how scared I feel.

'Well, *something* must have happened. Or else why didn't you go straight home after the caravan park? Why did you switch off your phone?'

'I got lost,' I say, truthfully. 'And it was just me and my friend Tyler, and we had Bess with us and there was no signal, then we ended up having to sleep out in the open and getting trapped by the tide. We lost everything in the sea. These holidaymakers helped us, loaned us clothes.' I point to the striped top and cream shorts of Emma's that I'm still wearing. 'I mean, you've seen the dresses I post on Instagram. Do you think I'd *choose* to wear this kind of middle-aged stuff? They don't even fit me.'

Rik glances at the top and the shorts, hanging bulkily from the belt Emma gave me, then studies my face carefully. I stare back, defiant. He purses his lips, nodding slowly.

'Okay, I believe you.' He lets go of my arm and I stumble backwards. 'But there's one thing I still don't understand . . .' Rik says slowly. 'I went to that caravan park myself earlier.'

'Oh?' Dad's grim-faced suggestion that Rik would hurt Mac to get information about him slams into my head. I try to look unbothered, but inside I feel sick.

'And –' Rik goes on – 'I asked around and there was nobody there who'd ever heard of your dad.'

My heart leaps. So Mac is safe. And he didn't give Dad away.

'I told you there wasn't,' I say, trying to sound indignant that he'd doubted me.

'So my question is . . . what made you go there in the first place?'

I take a deep breath. Whatever I say, I should stick as closely as possible to the truth. That way Rik is less likely to catch me out in a lie.

'I found a brochure for it among Dad's things,' I say,

looking Rik in the eye. 'I thought maybe he'd been there, but – as you found out yourself – it was a dead end.'

Rik considers this for a moment, then says: 'There must have been a lot of stuff your dad left behind, yeah? All sorts of brochures and leaflets, financial documents . . . that sort of thing?'

I nod, feeling wary.

'Okay, then.' Rik curls his lip 'Well, it's obvious that having you looking for your dad on your own isn't working.'

'But—'

'So we're moving to plan B.' Rik motions around the corner, to where Mum is waiting for me. 'You're going to go home. Then you've got forty-eight hours to gather together everything that might help me find your father. I want to see *anything* remotely relevant. I'll meet you in Brockledore village in two days and—'

'I can't,' I protest. 'Mum's grounded me.'

'You'll have to find a way – your dad's life depends on it,' Rik says.

I stare at him. He's still pretending that gangsters are after Dad, even though *he's* the threat. I clench my jaw, determined to protect Dad by playing along.

'Okay,' I say slowly.

'Wait for me at the war memorial at 9 p.m., the day

after tomorrow. Bring anything that looks like a lead to your dad.' He curls his lip. 'And there better be something I can use in there . . .' He pauses. My heart hammers against my ribs. 'Your sister's a sweet kid. You wouldn't want the people after your dad to hurt her, would you?'

I gasp. No, not Bess.

Rik raises his eyebrows. 'Right, I'll see you in two days. Do *not* tell anyone about me.' He glares at me for a second, then shoves his red skulls helmet on, wheels his motorbike around and roars away.

I stand still for a second. My legs feel shaky, my hands are trembling. A wave of relief that Rik's gone mingles with the terror that he was here.

A horn toots around the corner. *Mum.* I hurry back to the car, where she's leaning against the door, tapping her fingers on the bonnet as she waits for me. She throws me an irritated look.

'You took your time,' she says with a harassed sigh. 'I told you I didn't want to leave Bess on her own.' Without waiting for me to reply, she hurries into the service station.

I get into the passenger seat. Bess is curled up in the back, drawing. She glances up, then makes a silly face, sticking her tongue out at me. I offer her a weak smile.

What with all my fears for Dad, I didn't think I could feel more worried. But now I have an even greater reason to find the diamond. Without it, I have nothing to use to bargain with Rik.

Without it, it's not just Dad's life that's in danger, but Bess's too.

30

'We've got two days to find the diamond,' I whisper to Tyler.

It's almost 7 p.m. and we've been home for nearly an hour. Both of us are supposed to be grounded, but we've crept out of our respective houses and are standing along the path that runs between them, out of sight of all the windows.

'I think the attic's the most likely hiding place,' I say. 'It's right up by the roof so . . . you know . . . "under the stars".'

'Okay.' Tyler nods. 'Dad thinks I'm in my room, so I've got just over sixty minutes until dinner.'

'Good,' I say. 'Mum's with a client so the coast is clear.'

We hurry up to the attic. Surely, if the diamond is here, we'll be able to find it?

Two hours later, my hope has crumbled to despair. We've searched most of the boxes and bags we didn't get to before, as well as all the attic's nooks and crannies.

We haven't found anything.

Tyler unfolds himself with a sigh. He's too tall to stand up fully except in the very middle of the attic. 'Sorry, but I need to go back now before Dad misses me. He's already furious enough.'

'It's fine,' I say. 'There's no need to apologize. In fact . . .' I hesitate, a question I've been wanting to ask since yesterday night finally making it out of my head. 'In fact, I'm the one who should be sorry. You never got a proper chance to catch up with your friends in London.' I hesitate. 'Was . . . *is* there anyone special . . . anyone you really wanted to see?'

Tyler looks confused, his cheeks reddening. 'Er, no, not really,' he says. I stare at him. Why does he look so flustered? Is it because there is somebody and he doesn't want to talk about them? He clears his throat. 'Er, see you tomorrow.'

He heads for the stairs, leaving me alone.

The following day, Mum keeps me hard at work all morning, ordering me to send emails and type up her scrawled notes for another speech she's giving. As soon as she sets me free, I rush up to the attic again. Tyler has spent the day working on the mosaic renovation with his dad, but he joins me as soon as he's finished – and Mum is out of the way with another client.

'I don't think it's here,' Tyler says after an hour. 'We've looked through everything.'

'It *has* to be here,' I groan. 'What will I say to Rik if I don't find it?'

'He's not expecting the diamond,' Tyler points out. 'Just a good lead on your dad. Maybe you could make one up?'

'I guess, but all that does is buy us a tiny bit more time,' I groan. 'Once Rik realizes the lead is fake, he'll do something to Bess. I know he will. The only way to keep her safe is to find the diamond and give it back to him.'

Tyler has to leave at 8 p.m., to have dinner with his dad. I carry on searching for a bit longer, but it feels hopeless. I'm certain now I was wrong that 'under the stars' meant 'in the attic'. But, as yet, I have no idea what it *did* mean. If only Dad had told me where the diamond was. I know he was just trying to protect me and Bess, so I can't feel angry with him, but by keeping it secret he's actually put us in greater danger.

When, driven by hunger, I finally pad downstairs, it's obvious Mum made supper for her and Bess ages ago. She's left a plate of food for me, but she didn't call me downstairs for the meal like she normally would. Clearly, she's still super-mad at me for running off to Norfolk and – as she sees it – making up stories about Dad.

Knowing she doesn't believe me leaves an empty, aching hole in my chest. If only Tyler had actually seen Dad, he'd be able to back me up.

As it is, I feel completely alone.

I eat my food, then wash, dry and put away my plate and cutlery. I don't want to give Mum any more reasons to hate me. I go up to my room and sit on the bed. I don't know how much time passes. Mum has confiscated my laptop and, of course, I'm still without a phone. Outside on the landing, I hear Mum's heavy tread. I wait a second, wondering if she'll call out a 'goodnight', but the only sound is her bedroom door shutting. I lie back on my bed, still fully dressed.

Time passes. And passes. My insides are tied up like a row of reef knots. There's no way I can sleep. If I can't find the Blue Fire diamond by tomorrow evening, I'll have no choice but to tell Rik where Dad is.

It's the only way to keep Bess safe.

My dad's life. Or my sister's.

The choice makes me feel sick.

I get up, fetch a jumper and creep downstairs. The house is silent; it's past midnight. There's a clear sky and a cool breeze. The moon is almost full, a bright globe in the middle of the darkness.

I hug my arms to my chest and look up at the stars.

There are fewer of them than on the night Tyler and I lay outside, gazing at the twinkling sky. My throat swells with misery. Tyler was right. 'Under the stars' could mean literally anywhere on the entire planet. Dad only said those words to make me leave. He didn't want me to find the diamond. He didn't want me to have anything to do with it.

I find myself wandering along the path to the Barn. The lights are off – Tyler and his dad must be sleeping – but the moon casts a silvery glow across the courtyard.

The mosaic renovation has come on a lot in the past few days. The whole of the outer rim is in position, and most of the small gaps and chips have been repaired too. Even the three missing horoscope signs are taking shape: the two fishes of Pisces are still missing, but the Leo lion is virtually complete. It glints under the moonlight, its head lifted, as if scenting the air. Next to it the Cancer crab is almost done as well, just the claws and the background to finish off.

With a jolt it strikes me that once the mosaic is fully renovated, Tyler and his dad will be returning to London. From the look of it, they'll probably only be here for another week. Ten days at the most.

The thought sinks inside me like a stone in water: on top of everything else, I'm going to lose my only friend. I've never felt so alone in my life.

'Cat?' his voice calls out softly from the shadows.

I spin round to see Tyler emerging from the orchard, at the back of the Barn. He smiles, his eyes gleaming in the moonlight.

'I couldn't sleep,' he whispers. 'Then I thought I heard someone moving out here.'

I stare at him, feeling overwhelmed with emotion. He stands in front of me and opens his mouth, like he wants to say something.

'The mosaic is nearly done,' I say quietly, trying not to cry. 'It looks amazing.'

'Yeah.' Tyler points to the brand new outer rim. 'I put down most of the tiles for that, though Dad insisted on checking everything before he finished it off.'

I gaze past his outstretched finger, to the tiny glittering chips that fill the newly formed outer circle of the mosaic.

We stand in silence for a moment. My gaze drifts to the stone sundial in the centre.

This section of the courtyard is exactly as it always was. Original and untouched. The moon glints off the mosaic circle that surrounds the base of the sundial. It's a ring of tiles in the shape of stars, each one roughly the size of my hand.

My heart skips a beat as I stare at them. 'Look!' I gasp. 'Stars!'

Tyler's jaw drops as he follows my pointing finger to the star-shaped tiles. He turns to me, eyes gleaming with excitement.

'Do you think that's where your dad buried the diamond?' he breathes.

'It *has* to be.' I grin, then the smile slides off my face as I stare at the way the star tiles are firmly embedded in the surrounding mosaic. 'But how are we going to dig them up?' I whisper.

'Dig them up?' Tyler frowns. 'My dad will be mad as hell if we do that.'

'And my dad will be dead if we don't.' I glare at him.

'Okay, okay.' Tyler holds up his hands. 'Maybe there's a way. Just wait a sec, I'll get a chisel.' He hurries away.

Hope flutters nervously in my stomach as I examine the tiles more closely. The area next to the star by the Aries ram design looks paler than the others. I stare at it, as Tyler hurries back, a tool in his hand.

'Look.' I crouch down, pointing to the paler area. 'Does that look different to you?'

Tyler shines his torch on the tiles and I shift sideways to get out of his light. He peers thoughtfully at the star tile and the area around it.

'Well?' I ask, unable to contain my impatience.

'It *is* different,' he says at last.

'Like someone already took up the tile then put it back again and repaired the area around it?'

Tyler grins. 'Exactly like that,' he says.

I look up at him. 'Aries is my dad's sun sign,' I say.

'Okay, then.' Tyler positions his chisel at the edge of the star tile.

I sit beside him, watching intently. Tyler levers the tool under the star, then twists and presses. He moves, patiently, along each edge of the tile, tapping gently.

He's making as little noise as possible, but the sound still echoes into the cool night air. I hold my breath, praying Mr Tuesday doesn't hear us.

'Moment of truth.' Tyler frowns with concentration, then fits his chisel as deep against the tile as he can. He digs, twists and levers in one fluid movement, grunting with the effort.

One side of the star pops up. Tyler takes it carefully between his finger and thumb and lifts it out.

I shine my torch into the darkness of the gap beneath. The light glances off a small plastic package. I reach inside and lift it out. My fingers tremble as I unwrap the plastic. A small velvet pouch is inside.

Tyler and I glance at each other then, very gently, I tip the pouch against my palm.

'Oh!' I gasp, as a silver chain wound tightly around

something the size of a large grape tumbles into my hand. My hands are shaking as I unwind the chain, letting the jewel it contains dangle free.

'*Wow*,' I breathe.

There, glinting brilliantly in the moonlight, is the Blue Fire diamond.

31

Tyler and I examine the oval diamond in an awed silence: its mass of blue sparkles catch in the torchlight like tiny flames. After talking about it for so long, it's weird seeing the jewel for real.

'I can see why they called it Blue Fire,' I say softly.

'Is it really worth all those millions?' Tyler whispers.

I nod. 'Millions that people would kill each other over.'

'Yeah . . .' Tyler pauses, giving me a worried look. 'I was thinking, when it comes to seeing Rik tomorrow, maybe you should just *tell* him you have this. Don't hand it over right away. You need to be sure he'll leave you and your dad alone before you give up the only bit of power that you have.'

'How do I make sure of that?' I frown. 'I mean, you're right, but—'

Tyler hesitates. 'Or maybe we should just give it to the police after all,' he suggests. 'It seems wrong to just hand it over to Rik – and it puts you in danger.'

'I hate the idea of Rik having it too,' I say with a sigh, 'but

I don't see another option. Whatever we do, *someone* is in danger. And it's Dad that Rik is really mad with. Not me. '

'I guess.' Tyler nods slowly. He replaces the mosaic star that the diamond was hidden underneath and pats the area around it flat, shoving the disturbed bits of ground back into the grooves around the star.

'Good as new,' I say, trying to sound cheerful.

Tyler glances sideways at me. 'I hope so,' he says. 'I don't need my dad having a go at me for digging up his courtyard on top of everything else.' He pauses. 'I want to come with you when you meet up with Rik. It's too risky going by yourself.'

'No,' I say. 'You've already got into enough trouble because of me. I'll be fine. Anyway Rik insisted I come alone.'

'Then I'll watch from the trees,' Tyler insists. 'Rik's meeting you at the war memorial. I'll be able to see you there from the wood. Rik won't know. And if he does anything, I'll be able to get help.'

'Okay,' I agree, reluctantly. 'But you have to stay out of sight.'

The next day, I'm already nervous – and then Mum drops a bombshell. She's busy with one of her client groups until 2 p.m., at which point she emerges irritably from her Astrology Room and calls me downstairs.

'I have to go to a function, tonight,' she says. 'Drinks and dinner. I'll be back about eleven.'

I nod, relieved that she'll be out of the way when I need to sneak out to meet Rik. And then another thought strikes me.

'What about Bess?' I ask.

Mum stares at me as if I've lost my mind.

'You will babysit her, of course,' she says slowly, as if I'm a total idiot.

'No.' The last thing I want is to take Bess to my meeting and drag her into more danger. 'Can't she stay with Mr Tuesday?'

'Don't be ridiculous, he's an artisan mosaic restorer not a childminder,' Mum snaps. 'Anyway, I've invited him to the dinner as an apology for all the upset you caused with your ridiculous Norfolk trip.' She sighs. 'It's your Leo in the eighth house . . . makes you selfish and egotistical. I've known it from the moment I did your chart. Horoscopes are always right.'

'No, they're not,' I snap.

Mum stares at me, shocked.

I glare back. 'Horoscopes and astrology are full of unscientific and meaningless non-facts that you can twist into saying whatever you want. My life isn't decided by the planets and their positions. I *choose* who I am. Every day.'

My breath is coming in angry heaves. I've never spoken to Mum like that before. As I say the words out loud, it strikes me how much I believe them. For a second a look of deep hurt registers in Mum's eyes, then she lets out a heavy sigh, as if the effort of being patient with me is wearing her out.

'I'm not going to argue with you, Cat,' she says. 'You will look after your sister this evening and that's the end of it.' She stalks off.

I meet up with Tyler in the garden that afternoon.

'It worked!' he says.

'What?' I ask.

'Dad walked past that star tile we took up and put back at least ten times today. He was so fixated on those fishes he's working on, he didn't even notice that the grout around the tile had been disturbed.'

I stare for a second, transfixed by the way Tyler's brown-gold eyes gleam with pride.

'That's great,' I say. 'But there's a problem about the meeting with Rik tonight.' I explain that, because of Mum's party, I need Tyler to stay home and look after Bess for me.

He agrees, reluctantly. 'I still don't like you meeting Rik without me being there,' he says. 'Especially when neither of us have phones at the moment.'

I shrug. 'I know,' I say, 'but there's no way I'm letting Bess anywhere near Rik.'

The afternoon drags on. I move the Blue Fire diamond around three different hiding places in my bedroom, finally tucking it under the skeins of silk thread at the bottom of my sewing box. I glance at the dress I was making before Tyler and his dad arrived in Brockledore. It's strange to remember how focused I was on that dress less than two weeks ago, how important sewing was to me. Will it ever feel like that again?

For a second, I try to imagine a world with Dad at home and me happily making clothes again. Then I shrug off the thought. I can't let myself think about any of that.

Not now. Not yet.

First, I have to get Rik out of our lives.

Mum and Mr Tuesday leave for the party just before seven. It's a beautiful evening, the sun a perfect orange disc against a clear blue sky. It's been scorching hot today, but now there's just the hint of a breeze that brushes, soft, against our faces. I fetch the diamond from my sewing box and slip it deep into my pocket. Tyler and I take Bess into Brockledore to buy a bag of chips from the cafe. Tyler has promised to take Bess back to the house well before my meeting with Rik at nine, but there's still plenty of time to kill.

We walk to the playground on the other side of the village and eat our chips, while Bess plays happily on the swing. It's almost eight now and the air is still warm. I try to focus on enjoying the food, but my mouth is dry and I keep checking my pocket to make sure the diamond is still there.

Tyler finishes his chips and springs up. 'Hey, Bess, cartwheel time!' he announces.

'What about *you* doing one?' I suggest.

Bess slides off the swing and claps her hands together. *Yes!*

Tyler makes a fake-modest face. 'Oh no,' he says, pretending to protest. 'I couldn't.'

'Go on!' I encourage.

Bess nods enthusiastically.

'If you insist, then.' Tyler sweeps down into a low bow, then walks over to a clear patch of tarmac. He steadies himself, then flips himself over – and up again.

It's a perfect cartwheel, as good as the one I saw him do the day after he arrived here. He stands up grinning.

Bess and I applaud.

'Your turn, Bess,' Tyler says.

He sits down on the bench next to me and we watch as Bess gets into position. For some reason I feel nervous, watching the concentration on her face.

'You can do it!' Tyler calls out.

I hold my breath as Bess lifts one leg, points her toe and, focusing intently, flips herself over. Her legs are completely straight as they fly over her body then land, lightly and neatly, on the other side.

'Amazing!' I jump up, clapping. 'Brilliant, Bess!'

'Awesome!' Tyler calls. 'The best one yet.'

Bess beams.

At 8:15 p.m., we make our way back through Brockledore village. I want Tyler to get Bess home well before I'm due to meet Rik at the war memorial. Bess skips along happily at Tyler's side. She seems to have completely got over our ordeal in Norfolk. It's not just that she's stopped being withdrawn. There's a real openness about her now. It's hard to put my finger on, but it's as if she's less fearful than she used to be.

Or perhaps I'm just anxious enough for both of us. I shove my hand in my pocket for what must be the hundredth time. The Blue Fire is still there, tightly wrapped in its velvet pouch. The air is still warm but, as we get near to the memorial, I shiver.

'You okay?' Tyler asks quietly.

I shrug. 'I just hope this works, that I can convince Rik to leave Dad alone.'

'It will,' Tyler says. 'I bet when he hears about the diamond he'll agree to anything to get his hands on it'.

I smile at him, feeling more confident. Tyler is right. I just have to be strong and insistent with Rik.

We cross the road to the war memorial. The sun has set so low now that the bottom part of the monument is in total shade. I lean against it and the stone feels cold against my back.

'It's not right, leaving you here alone,' Tyler says, a worried look on his face.

Bess looks up at me, enquiringly.

'I won't be long,' I say.

Tyler gives me a reluctant nod, then takes Bess's hand. I watch them cross the road and disappear into the woods that lead up to our house. A few moments pass and then a low voice sounds behind me.

'Hello, Cat.'

That's not Rik. I spin round, my breath catching in my throat.

'You!' I gasp.

32

Rik's Aunt Sandy is standing in front of me, a mean smile on her lips.

I stare at her, my jaw dropping. 'What are you doing here?' I demand. 'Where's Rik? He said nine p.m., it's only—'

'It's just a small change of plan,' Sandy interrupts. 'Rik decided I should meet you instead, and I like to be early.' Her mouth stretches into a thin sneer. 'Get over it.'

I gulp. Sandy is wearing a zipped-up grey tracksuit top that hangs long over her hips and silver trainers that match her hair. She seems far livelier than when Tyler and I visited her flat.

I glance around. From where we're standing, I can see the high street ahead and the woods to our right. There's no sign of Rik. At least Tyler and Bess are out of sight; they should be halfway through the woods by now. Sandy watches me, her eyes cold and hard. Dad's words about her killing Pirate flash into my head.

'You murdered our dog!' The words shoot out of me.

Sandy smirks. 'If you say so,' she says lightly.

I grit my teeth. How could I ever have thought she was just a harmless old lady? She's been in league with Rik from the start.

'I'm here on Rik's behalf.' Sandy stares at my empty hands. 'Where's the papers and stuff on your dad?' she demands. 'Rik said—'

'I don't have any of that,' I interrupt. My thoughts fly to the diamond. I fold my arms to stop my hands unconsciously reaching for my pocket. Sandy's face flushes with annoyance. 'I've got something better than paperwork,' I add quickly.

'Oh, really?' Sandy snaps. 'What's that, then?'

'The diamond,' I say. 'I found the Blue Fire diamond.'

Sandy blinks with surprise. 'You little liar.' She glares at me. 'Rik warned you about—'

'I'm not lying,' I say desperately.

'But your father is the only person who knows where the diamond is.' Sandy spits. 'Are you telling me you've talked to him? Has he told you where it is?'

I hesitate. 'It doesn't matter how I found it,' I say. 'What counts is that I have the diamond and I'll give it to Rik provided he promises to leave my family alone.'

Sandy gives a hollow laugh. 'I suppose you're imagining that if Rik backs off, you'll get your daddy back?' she says scornfully. 'Well, let me tell you, I've met your father and for all his cheery ways he's as selfish as they come.' She pauses. 'Whatever happens, he won't come back here.'

'Yes, he will,' I insist. 'So long as he's safe . . . so long as we're all safe.'

'So where is this diamond, then?' Sandy purses her lips, doubtfully. 'If you've really got the thing, *show* me.' She holds out her hand.

'I don't have it with me.' I can feel my cheeks reddening and pray that Sandy will put this down to the stress of the situation rather than the fact that I'm lying. 'Like I said, I need Rik to promise he'll leave my family alone before I give it to him.'

Sandy hesitates a second. I'm expecting her to argue with me again, but instead she takes out a mobile and hands it to me. 'Wait here,' she says. 'Rik will call you in a moment on this.'

'Why?' I ask. 'What are—?'

But Sandy has already bustled away, along the high street. A second later she's out of sight.

I stand, waiting. Tyler and Bess should be through the trees now. Almost home. I wait for another minute, my anxiety rising. The phone Sandy gave me doesn't ring. I try to open it, but it's locked. Something doesn't feel right. Why didn't Sandy call Rik for me to talk to there and then? Why did she leave her phone with me?

Why didn't she insist on staying with me until she had the diamond?

My heart beats harder and faster.

Into the silence, the phone blasts. A loud, insistent ring.

I snatch it to my ear. 'Hello?'

'You've got the diamond?' Rik sounds incredulous.

'Yes.' My heart is thumping in my ears now. I look all around. The village is empty, nobody in sight. 'You can have it,' I go on. 'But only on condition you stay away from Dad.'

'What?' Rik starts, 'but—'

'I know the truth,' I interrupt. 'I know there aren't any gangsters. It's you. *You're* the one after Dad. You want revenge on him whether or not you get the diamond back.'

Silence on the other end of the phone. 'I see,' Rik says, flatly. 'Well, aren't you clever for working it all out.' He sniffs. 'What you also need to know is that you're in no position to be making demands.' He sucks in his breath. 'Your dad double-crossed me, and he has to pay. Period.'

Panic swirls inside me. 'But—'

'Now, do exactly what I tell you. Get the diamond and take it to three, Cave Street in Coombehaven. That's less than an hour's walk from where you are now. Talk to no one on the way.'

Fury surges up through my fear. 'No,' I protest. 'I'm

done with you telling me what to do,' I go on. 'If you won't leave Dad alone, you can't have the diamond.'

There's a stunned silence on the other end of the line. I cross the empty road to the line of trees that mark the start of the wood. From here I can see all the way along the road that leads out of Brockledore. Apart from some distant traffic, the place is deserted.

'Never mind your pathetic excuse for a dad,' Rik says scornfully, at last. 'You should be more worried about your sister.'

My blood turns to ice. 'What do you mean?'

'I have Bess,' he says.

'*What?*' My guts seem to fall away as I spin round. I stare into the wood. The light has faded so much now that the trees are wreathed in darkness. 'No . . . you *can't,* how—?'

Rik sighs, impatiently. 'I followed you. The three of you.'

I gasp, hurrying into the wood.

'How *dare* you?' I say, breathless, into the phone. 'She's just a—'

'Quiet!' Rik's voice cuts over mine. 'I've told you where to go. Get the diamond and go straight there. Now. Or you'll never see your sister again.'

33

The phone goes dead.

Bess. I stare wildly around. The branches of the dark trees around me hiss in the breeze. Rik has taken Bess.

What about Tyler? He didn't mention Tyler.

Panic rising, I dart between the trees, crashing over the twigs and leaves.

'Tyler!' I yell.

A thudding, thumping noise echoes through the woods. I race towards it, fear spiralling through my head. I stumble over a large root, almost falling.

'Tyler!'

The sound gets louder. I round the next tree and he's there: lying on the stony ground beside a fallen log. His hands and feet are tied with rope. His mouth is gagged.

I hurry over and tear the cloth from his face.

'Rik took Bess,' he gasps. 'He was following us.'

I nod, too shocked to speak. I sink to my knees and tug at the rope round his wrists. Tyler has already frayed some of the threads against a stone. I wrench it looser, then pull it off his hands.

'He came up behind me,' Tyler says, his voice fast and frightened. 'There was nothing I could do.' He touches my arm. 'Bess tried to run but . . . but Rik caught her. I'm so sorry, Cat, I couldn't stop him.'

'It's not your fault,' I say, numbly.

Tyler is already unknotting the rope around his ankles. He frees himself and jumps up.

'We need to call the police. And your mum,' he says.

'No.' I explain what Rik has told me to do.

'He's offering an exchange?' Tyler's voice is strained. 'Bess for the Blue Fire?'

'Yes.' We stare at each other. The full horror of the situation is reflected in Tyler's eyes. I look away, unable to bear it. Unable to cope with the idea of Bess, bound and terrified.

'Maybe we could still go to the cops,' Tyler suggests. 'Is there anything on that phone Sandy gave you? Something we could show them?'

'No, it's locked. The only number I can call on it is nine-nine-nine.' I hesitate, fear coursing through me. 'But we mustn't contact the police. Rik's already guilty of kidnapping. We know how dangerous he is. If the police show up instead of me and the diamond . . .' I trail off, unable to put the depth of my fears for Bess into words.

Tyler nods.

'Let's go,' I say, tersely.

We follow the main road out of Brockledore for half a mile, then take the turning for Coombehaven. It's properly dark now. My shoes rub against my heels as I push myself on, my heart thudding against my ribs. It's irrational to think it, but it feels like the diamond is visible through my pocket. I keep my hand over it the whole time, turning over and over its soft velvet wrap.

Coombehaven is a tiny, rundown village near the beach. It's too dark to see the sea, but we can hear it as we walk along the main street, lined with boarded-up shops. Cave Street is the last turning before the shore. The road is dimly lit – just one street lamp flickers on and off. The houses are piles of crumbling brick and cracked windows. None of them have any lights on.

'It's like a ghost town,' Tyler says.

I nod, my anxiety rising.

Number 3 turns out to be a house at the end of the row. Its windows are nailed over with wooden planks.

'How do we get inside?' I ask.

'I don't think it's locked.' Tyler gives the front door a push and, sure enough, it creaks open.

I light our way with the phone Sandy gave me. The place is empty and bleak, all concrete floors and paint-scraped walls. It's spookily silent. Together, we search both the downstairs rooms and the three upstairs. There's nothing here but litter and a couple of old, stained mattresses.

'Why isn't Rik here?' Tyler asks. The shadows from the phone's light cast a spooky glow over his face.

'And where's Bess?' My heart sinks.

We stand on the landing, uncertain what to do. And then a sound echoes up to us. The front door is creaking open.

34

Tyler's eyes widen with fear. I peer down the stairs.

A man dressed in jacket and boots with a torch in his hand quietly shuts the front door behind him. He looks up and my heart skips a beat as I catch sight of his face.

'Dad?' I gasp.

Dad frowns and shines his light up at me. 'Cat?' I can't see his expression properly now, but I can hear the shock in his voice. 'What are you doing here?'

Shielding my eyes from the glare of his torch, I hurry down the stairs, Tyler behind me. Dad and I stare at each other, open-mouthed, in the gloomy hallway of the deserted building. Thoughts run through my head at a million miles an hour.

Does he know about Bess?

Has he come to help rescue her?

Dad peers at Tyler. He frowns. 'Who's this?'

'This is my friend Tyler,' I explain quickly.

'Hello,' Tyler says.

Dad nods at Tyler. 'Hi.' His torch casts shadows across

the walls around us. His tanned, weather-beaten skin looks ghostly pale in the dim light. 'You two can't stay here,' he insists, his voice urgent. 'This is one of Rik's old hangouts. I came here to find him. I . . . I think he's got the Blue Fire.'

I feel for the jewel in my pocket. 'No—' I start, but Dad interrupts me again.

'I went to the house to get the diamond, but it was gone,' Dad explains. 'I've already been to Sandy's but there's no one there and I think—'

'Dad, listen!' I interrupt. 'Rik's got Bess. I'm waiting for them right now.'

Dad blinks, shocked. 'What? What do you mean?'

'He's kidnapped her. He wants to swap her for the Blue Fire.' My voice cracks, my terror surging up. Tyler moves closer; I can sense his presence right beside me, but I keep my eyes on Dad.

Dad lowers his torch so that it pools with the light from my phone, washing the walls with an eerie brightness. 'Rik has Bess?' He says the words slowly, like he can't believe them. 'But why? *Why*, if he already has the diamond?'

'He doesn't.' I dig into my pocket and hold out the velvet pouch. 'I've got it. Tyler and I found it, where you said, "under the stars" . . .' I open the pouch. The diamond glitters in my hand.

Dad swallows, peering at the Blue Fire. He reaches for it, then hesitates, drawing back his hand. He looks up at me. 'Clever Cat,' he murmurs. I can't read his expression.

'I think you owe Cat a proper explanation for why you're here,' Tyler says. There's a quiet fury in his voice. I glance up at him in surprise.

Why is he so angry?

I look back at Dad, still gazing at the diamond. 'It's more beautiful than I remember,' he says softly.

'I hope you enjoy it.' Tyler's voice still has that furious edge. 'I hope it was worth everything you've given up for it.'

I raise my eyebrows at him. *What is he talking about?* My thoughts flit, impatiently, to Bess. We need to be focusing on her right now. Then I look at Dad, at the shame in his eyes. And his earlier words echo in my head.

I went to the house to get the diamond.

Suddenly, everything falls into place.

To get the diamond.

Dad has risked exposure and a showdown with the man who wants to kill him. But not to 'deal with Rik', like he said. Or to be with his family.

'You came back because of that?' I point to the diamond. 'Not because of us.'

There's a long silence.

'Dad?' My voice cracks.

'It's not that simple.' Dad hesitates. 'I *am* here because of you . . . to *protect* you. Don't you see? I've already lost so much because of this thing, I can't let it be for nothing.'

I frown. 'What do you mean?'

'I . . . I didn't tell you the whole truth before,' he stammers. 'About how I ended up with the diamond.'

I stare at him. 'You said Rik stole it.'

'It was you, wasn't it?' Tyler says accusingly. '*You* stole it.'

Dad chews on his lip. 'It's a long story,' he says.

'Oh, Dad.' There's a lump in my throat.

My fingers close over the diamond. Suddenly, I can't bear to look at it. I shove it back into my pocket.

'I don't expect you to understand,' Dad says, 'but in that moment when I realized we had a priceless gem on our hands, it seemed like a victimless crime. We couldn't trace the diamond to a living owner. It didn't belong to anyone.'

'You said before that it "belonged to the world".' The misery I felt a moment ago is hardening and sharpening into a bitter fury. 'I guess that was another lie?'

'No,' Dad protests, 'it was more . . . more that nobody else was going to claim it, so . . . so why shouldn't we?'

'Because it didn't belong to you,' Tyler says.

'We didn't think about it like that,' Dad says. 'The truth is, Cat, that I was . . . in trouble. Debts.' He gives an awkward cough. 'Some bets I'd made that I thought were sure fire . . . they hadn't paid off. Plus, well, I already told you . . . your mother and I were in a bad place. She was angry with me over it.'

'Gambling debts?' I frown. Mum has never mentioned any of this.

Dad sighs. 'Rik and I made a plan to sell the Blue Fire on the black market. I knew about diamonds and Rik had all sorts of dodgy contacts. It was win-win. I was going to use my share to pay off my debts, then with the money left over buy us a second home right by the sea, get a proper yacht, maybe set up a boat design business . . . and of course spoil you girls rotten.'

I stare at him, bewildered. 'So what happened?'

There's another awkward pause. Dad's eyes glisten in the soft light. 'I came to realize that Rik was not the sort of person who should have access to the kind of money we were going to make. God knows what he'd have used it for . . . he was already a criminal, so I tipped the police off about a few things Rik had done. Like I told you before. They went to his house, found stolen goods and arrested him.'

My jaw drops. 'You mean you had Rik sent to prison

so you could take the diamond for yourself?' I gasp. 'You *double-crossed* him?' I can't believe it. All this time I've thought that Dad was the victim of a crime Rik had committed, but now . . . My body tenses as the realization settles over me like a dark cloud.

Dad – my lovable, smiling dad – is a thief.

Everything that has happened, including Rik snatching Bess, started with him.

His greed. His selfishness.

'I didn't exactly take the diamond for myself. The first step was just to get it away from Rik. I hadn't thought any further than that.' A deep frown creases Dad's forehead. 'But before I could decide what to do, everything went wrong. Rik knew I was the one who'd ratted on him. He threatened me from jail. He demanded the diamond back but he also made it clear that he was going to make me pay for grassing him up. That was when he had Pirate killed. And threatened to kill you girls too. I wasn't lying about any of that: he said I'd taken what was most precious to him – his freedom. And that he was going to take what was most precious to me, to make me suffer.' Dad gives a miserable shake of his head. 'I couldn't see how to make it stop. Rik was in prison awaiting sentencing and I had no idea how long he'd go away for. I was desperate, Cat. The last thing I wanted to do was fake my own death, but

Rik's men were after me, after *all* of us and it was the only thing I could think of that would stop them. I staged the drowning so that Rik would think I'd ended up at the bottom of the sea and taken the diamond with me.'

'But why didn't you tell us? Mum and me and Bess?' The mention of Bess's name gives me a fresh stab of anxiety. 'You could have explained . . .' My voice rises on a sob.

'I know it was selfish of me to put you through all that, but I was so full of self-loathing by then I honestly thought it was the best thing for everyone for me to be out of the picture,' Dad says miserably. 'I was in a mess, not thinking straight. I just wanted to keep you safe, don't you see? I always thought I'd come back at some point but . . . but the more time I spent away, the harder it became to find a way back when that meant disrupting your lives all over again.' He pauses, shadows flickering across his face. 'It broke my heart. I can't tell you how much I've regretted leaving like I did, how there were months when I thought I'd never feel a moment's happiness again.'

My thoughts turn to the home I found in Hallerton East.

'So Julie . . . and the baby . . . ?'

Dad nods, his expression full of shame. 'Julie was kind when I was at my lowest ebb, helped me start again.

We've been together ever since and she's great. Honestly, you'd really like her. As for little Finn, he wasn't planned, but . . .' He trails off, eyes glistening with tears.

My jaw drops. 'He *is* yours?'

Beside me, Tyler blows out his breath.

Dad nods again. 'I'm so sorry, Kitterbug. I've really screwed up.'

I lean against the wall of the rundown house, my head spinning. Dad lied before. He has a whole new family with Julie. Finn is my brother. Bess and I have a little brother. I say the words in my head but it doesn't feel real.

'I wasn't lying about missing you *desperately*,' Dad goes on. 'I look at this every single day . . .' He pulls a crumpled photo out of his pocket. It's the same print that I found in the box of his things: of him with me and Bess and Pirate. 'Like I told you, it was missing you so much that led me on to your social media.' Dad grimaces. 'I'm kicking myself about that. If I hadn't, Rik would think I was dead and you wouldn't have been dragged into all this.' He pauses. 'And I wouldn't be here now, trying to put everything right.'

'How are you going to do that?' I ask, my insides hollow.

'By taking the diamond and running away again?' Tyler's voice is knife-sharp.

'No,' Dad insists, glancing briefly at him, then turning back to me. 'That *was* my plan. After we spoke, Cat, I thought leaving the country was the only option . . .'

'You mean you were going to go abroad with Julie and . . . and Finn?' I stare at him, feeling numb. 'Start a new life with the money you'd get from the diamond?'

Dad nods.

Tyler's hand rests on my shoulder, but I shake it off. I don't want his pity.

'I'm not going to do that now,' Dad says quickly. 'Now I've seen you again, now I know Rik has Bess . . . it's made me realize that I can't just take the diamond and leave.'

I bite my lip. Does he really mean that? There's no way I can be sure. 'So, what—?'

Before I can finish my question, the phone Sandy gave me utters a piercing ring. I lift it to my ear, fear for Bess flooding through me like poison.

'Have you got the diamond?' Rik demands.

'Yes,' I snap, instantly focused on my sister. 'But where's Bess? You were supposed to be here with her? What have you done w—?'

'She's perfectly safe,' Rik says smoothly. 'I've given her something to make her sleep, she's completely unaw—'

'You've *sedated* her?'

Dad reaches for the phone, but I back away. Rik knowing that Dad's here isn't going to help us save Bess.

'Tell me where my sister is *right now*,' I order. 'I'm done waiting.'

'Fine.' Rik chuckles. 'We're on the beach just down the road. A few minutes' walk. The old jetty. I'll be waiting. That's where we'll do the trade: Bess for the diamond. Provided you come alone, she won't get hurt.'

He rings off.

'Is Bess okay?' Tyler asks.

'What's he doing with her?' Dad urges.

'He still wants to trade her for the diamond.' I turn towards the door.

'Wait,' Dad says.

I look back at him. 'Dad, it's the diamond or Bess. I have to do this.'

Dad hesitates. For a terrible second I think he's going to insist that I give him the diamond, so he can run away with it after all.

'I don't want you to have to deal with Rik,' Dad says at last. 'It should be me.'

'That's not what Rik's expecting,' I say. 'Come on, Tyler.'

'Listen to me,' Dad persists. 'I told you, I've made my choice. I'm not taking the diamond. And I'm not leaving you until I know that you and your sister are safe.'

I stare at him. *Is he serious?*

'If we do this my way,' Dad goes on, 'Bess will be rescued and the diamond *and* Rik will be handed over to the police . . .' He pauses, straightening up. The shame lifts from his face. 'I'll give myself up to them too.'

'How are we going to make all that happen?' Tyler asks suspiciously.

'*I'll* be the one to approach Rik. I'll show him the Blue Fire, then offer to trade myself *and* the diamond for Bess,' Dad says.

I stare at him. I still can't be sure he really means anything he's saying. 'Then what?' I demand.

'Once Bess is safe, I'll overpower Rik while you two call the police.' Dad peers anxiously at me. 'It's simple. Do you see?'

'What if Rik refuses to let Bess go?' I ask. 'Remember he's not expecting you to be there.'

'And what if you *can't* overpower him?' asks Tyler. 'What if he's got a knife . . . or a gun?'

'He won't have,' Dad says.

'You don't know that,' I say.

We stand in silence for a moment, then I take a deep breath.

'Actually,' I say. 'I've got a better idea . . .'

35

I go over the plan one last time.

Tyler nods, slowly. 'It's going to work.'

Dad looks at me, clearly less sure. 'I don't know, Cat, it puts you at more risk than I'd like . . .'

'Only a little.' I meet his gaze. 'Anyway, I think given everything you've done, you've lost your right to tell me what to do.'

Dad's lips give a tiny tremble, then he nods. 'Okay,' he says.

'All that matters is saving Bess,' I go on.

'Plus, Cat's idea means *she* keeps hold of the diamond,' Tyler adds icily.

It's clear what he's implying: if Dad has the diamond, the temptation to run off with it might be too great for him to resist.

'Okay,' Dad says again. He glances at me. My guts twist. Dad has made mistakes, sure, but I can see in his eyes how sorry he is and hear in his voice that he's determined to make amends.

At least I think I can.

'That's sorted, then,' I say.

Long, deserted Coombehaven beach is just a minute's walk from the house where Rik called me. The wooden jetty is about a hundred metres away, dimly visible against the navy night sky. We walk along the hard-packed sand towards it in silence. It feels like we're at the edge of the world. We're certainly too far away from the few residents of Coombehaven for anyone to hear or see us. The moon gives off a soft glow and we're careful to keep to the cover of the sand dunes. It's vital that Rik doesn't realize Dad is here.

My plan depends on it.

We get closer to the jetty. It's damaged – with gaps in the boards and half the wooden posts missing – and stretches deep into the blackness of the sea.

The three of us crouch down behind a sand dune. The only sound is the gentle whoosh of the waves.

'I can see Rik,' Tyler whispers. 'And there's Bess.'

My stomach lurches into my mouth. I peer along the length of the jetty. I can't make out anyone.

'Where?' I whisper.

Tyler points to the very end of the jetty. I squint, screwing up my eyes.

'It's Rik's boat,' Dad says softly.

As he speaks, I see it: a small white-hulled sailing boat, bobbing on the waves. The top of its little cabin reflects the moonlight on to the deck below, where Rik is standing.

Next to him, slumped against the wall of the cabin, is Bess. My heart skips a beat. I can only see her outline from here, but it's obvious from the way she's sitting that she's still unconscious.

'Ready?' Dad whispers.

I nod.

'Be careful.' Dad squeezes my hand, then disappears into the dark of the beach. He's heading for the sea, keeping low against the sand to avoid being seen.

'Are you sure about this?' Tyler asks, suddenly sounding doubtful. Even in the dim light I can see the anxiety in his eyes.

'It's going to work,' I say, trying to sound more confident than I feel. I set off. My legs are shaking as I reach the jetty and step into the rays of moonlight that stretch along its half-broken boards. The damaged wood creaks as I walk.

Rik spots me. His boat rocks from side to side as he leaps on to the jetty. I shuffle a little way towards him, careful to avoid the gaps in the wooden boards. Rik picks his way carefully towards me, then stops, his hands on his hips, about twenty metres away.

'Do you have it?' he calls out.

For an answer, I take the diamond out of my pocket and hold it up to the moonlight. It sparkles like the fire it's named after. I stare, mesmerized. I've never seen anything so beautiful in my life.

Rik paces towards me. I glance along the jetty, towards his boat moored at the end. Waves slap against the white hull. Bess is still slumped against the cabin wall. I'm still not close enough to see her face, but there's no mistaking her fair hair, fraying from its plaits. Where is Dad? He should have swum to her by now, to rescue her, get her to safety . . .

I can't see him.

I take a step back.

'Stay there!' Rik orders. He strides towards me, nimbly picking his way across the boards. I hold my breath, willing him to land on a piece of broken wood so damaged that it will collapse underneath him.

Why hasn't Dad reached Bess yet? Has he changed his mind about helping to save her? My guts give a painful twist. If I give Rik the diamond now, he'll just take it back to his boat and then he'll have Bess *and* the Blue Fire.

I glance around, looking back at the beach. I can't

see him, but I know Tyler is there, watching from the shadows with the phone Sandy gave me. As soon as he sees Dad swimming away from the boat with Bess, he's supposed to call the police.

So where is Dad?

Rik jumps lightly over another broken board. He's just a couple of metres away. I have to stall him. There isn't another choice. I draw back my arm, ready to hurl the Blue Fire, still dangling on its chain, as far as I can behind me.

With a roar, Rik closes the gap between us. He snatches the diamond out of my hand.

I gasp, horrified. Stumble backwards.

'Don't move!' Rik grips my arm. He holds me tightly as he peers down at the diamond, now sparkling in his palm. Then he looks up, a mean grin on his face. 'This is it,' he says. 'After all this time, I—'

A splash from the boat. Dad's there, at last. He hauls himself on board, water streaming from his clothes. Rik spins round, letting go of my arm. The boat rocks violently as Dad slips, sliding across the deck, desperate to get to Bess.

'*You*!' Rik yells at him.

Time seems to slow down as Rik pelts away from me, back to the boat.

The diamond is still in his hand.

36

I race after Rik, leaping over the jetty's broken boards. My heart is in my mouth, all my energy focused on Dad and Bess in the boat.

'You double-crossing *monster*!' Rik is yelling.

Dad glances round. I can see the terror on his face. He's struggling to pick up Bess. She's limp, unconscious. Her arms dangle, a dead weight.

Rik pounds along the jetty ahead of me. On the boat, Dad staggers sideways, trying to get his balance. Rik reaches the boat. He jumps on board. The boat rocks violently from side to side. Water splashes over the hull, drenching Dad. Bess slips half out of his grip.

'Help!' I yell. My cry vanishes, hopelessly, into the night air.

Rik looms over Dad, as Bess slides fully out of Dad's arms, back on to the deck.

Dad turns, looks up. Rik's fist lands with a crack on his jaw. My heart skips a beat as Dad staggers back, into the stern, the very back of the boat. He falls down, into the shadows. A loud metal clank echoes through the air.

'Dad!' I scream.

'Aaagh!' Dad yells, as Rik dives into the stern after him.

They're in darkness. All I can hear are their grunts and shouts.

'Dad!' I shriek again.

As I reach the boat, I'm suddenly aware of footsteps behind me. I spin round. Tyler is here. We scramble on board together. Now I'm close up I can see them: Dad and Rik are fighting in the stern, all fists and elbows. I turn to Bess. She's sprawled, unconscious, on the deck.

'Let's get her out of here,' Tyler urges.

We hurry over. My heart thuds against my ribs. Angry shouts and bangs from the back of the boat. We put our arms under Bess's small body. Pick her up between us.

'Get away from her!' Rik cries.

Tyler and I freeze. My head whips round.

Rik looms over Dad, pinning him down. Dad is bucking and writhing, unable to move. He's surrounded by something thick and wet that gleams in the moonlight. The smell reaches me as I spot the overturned can at Dad's head.

He is lying in petrol.

I hesitate.

'Put her down and listen to me,' Rik snarls, panting. 'Otherwise, I end your dad.'

I glance at Dad's terrified face. 'Okay,' I say.

Tyler and I ease Bess down again, letting her sink back against the deck. We straighten up. I turn to face Rik.

'Let my dad go,' I demand.

Rik lifts his foot a little way off Dad's chest, but keeps a light pressure. Dad's eyes are wild with fury, his hair glistening in the petrol surrounding his head.

'Here's the deal,' Rik says, catching his breath. 'The *new* deal. You kids take Bess and keep quiet about seeing either me or your dad.'

'But—' I start.

'I take your dad and the diamond,' Rik cuts across me. 'I'll do what your dad *pretended* to do seventeen months ago. Except, this time, there'll be no loose ends.' He gazes down at Dad, a vicious look in his eye. 'After all, Alan,' he says, 'as far as the rest of the world is concerned, you're already dead.'

My insides fall away. Rik is going to kill Dad and dump his body out at sea. Bile rises inside me. The same horror I feel is etched on Dad's face. *No.*

Even after everything he has done, I don't want to lose Dad all over again.

I *can't.*

A soft nudge, Tyler's hand on my ribs. I glance around. Tyler flicks his gaze to the petrol now spreading this way. With a jolt I realize the diamond is there, on the deck, halfway between us and Dad and Rik. Its star-cut surface glints in the moonlight.

It must have fallen out of Rik's pocket when he and Dad fought.

Thinking fast, I square up to Rik. 'Okay,' I say. 'Deal.'

I can't look at Dad. Can't bear to see the fear in his eyes.

'*I'll* get Bess,' Tyler says, his voice loaded with meaning.

I know exactly what he is leaving unsaid:

You *get the diamond.*

'Okay,' I say.

I step away from Bess, letting Tyler pick her up. Rik watches us warily. He hasn't noticed the diamond.

Tyler has Bess in his arms. He turns, takes a step towards the jetty. Then another. He lays Bess on the jetty's wooden boards, then hoists himself up after her.

Rik's eyes are on them. His foot still holding down Dad.

Dad's eyes meet mine. I want to believe he is telling me to save myself. And Bess.

But all I can see is his naked terror.

'Go on, then,' Rik urges.

I make as if I'm turning to leave then, in a single movement, I dart forward. Snatch up the diamond. It's coated in petrol, thick and gloopy.

'No!' Rik's eyes widen as he realizes.

He lunges towards me. As he moves, Dad rears up, grabbing his ankle and toppling him over. The boat lurches violently. I slip sideways, landing with a painful thud on the deck. Rik and Dad are fighting again. They're between me and the jetty. I scrabble away from them.

'Let Dad go and I'll give you the diamond,' I shout.

But Rik is fighting like a wild animal, too crazed with anger to hear me. Dad lands a punch on his chin. Rik kicks out, punching back hard.

Dad falls back into the stern again. He splutters, hauling himself up. Petrol drips from his hair. His jacket.

I watch, open-mouthed, as Rik bounds towards him. For a split second the two men stare at each other.

I hold up the diamond. But before I can yell at Rik again to let Dad go, Rik whips a lighter from his pocket. Dad's eyes widen as Rik flicks on the flame. And then everything happens at once.

Dad jumps into the sea.

Rik hurls his lighter into the petrol, which flares up into flames engulfing the whole stern of the boat . . . and the sea around it.

I'm frozen to the spot. '*Dad!*' I yell.

I stare at the sea just beyond the boat. Fire rises up, off the waves. Smoke fills the air. I can't see Dad in the water. Can't tell if he's burning. Drowning. But surely he must be. He was covered in petrol. It was all over him: his hair, his clothes.

Rik strides towards me. He holds out his hand.

'Give me the Blue Fire,' he orders.

I shake my head. 'You *killed* him,' I yell.

'No.' Rik narrows his eyes. 'He's already dead, remember?'

Behind him, the fire flares around the engine in the stern. I register – as if in a dream – that it could explode any second. That I need to move, get off the boat.

I can dimly hear Tyler shouting my name from the jetty. But all I'm aware of is the Blue Fire, hot and sticky with petrol in my palm. I stare at it for a second.

For all its beauty and value, it's brought nothing but pain and death.

As Rik lurches towards me, his hand outstretched, I hurl the diamond into the heart of the fire.

'No!' Rik roars.

He turns towards it. I catch a glimpse of his horrified face, lit by the flames. Then I turn away, flying across the deck.

'Get off the boat!' Tyler's voice rings out, now loud and clear. 'It's going to blow!'

I slip. Scramble for the jetty. Tyler's hand grabs my arm, hauling me up.

I stand, panting on the wooden boards. Rik is still on the boat, staring into the fire at the spot where I threw the diamond.

'Get ou—!' But before I can finish my warning, Rik hurls himself towards the flames, his hands reaching for the gem. And in that same moment, the engine explodes, sending the boat, and everything in it, flaring high into the sky and then down, down, into the deep, dark water below.

37

I'm knocked back by the blast, the heat flaming at my face. Bits of the boat fly into the air, landing around us on the jetty.

Tyler and I throw ourselves over Bess. I cover my head, watching as the fire flares up, licking at the air, lighting the sea all the way to the beach.

A moment passes. Shocked and trembling, I scramble to my feet, peering across the water. There's no sign of Dad . . . of his body. Just splinters of wood and the remains of the bow of the boat.

A fresh wave of misery washes over me. Dad will be sunk now, deep under the waves, along with Rik and the diamond.

'Are you all right?' Tyler's voice is hollow with shock.

I turn to him and nod. Then I crouch down beside Bess. I reach for her hand. It's like ice. Her face is unnaturally pale in the moonlight, her eyes still shut. My fingers tremble as I press them against her wrist, desperate to feel a pulse. *There*. A slow, steady beat. Relief washes over me.

She's alive.

'We should get her off the jetty,' Tyler says, picking her up in his arms.

I nod again, then lead the way carefully along the jetty, to the shore. Tyler follows in my footsteps. As we reach the beach, Bess's eyelids start fluttering, as if she's waking up from a nightmare.

'I think she's coming round,' Tyler says. He wraps Bess in his jacket, and sets her carefully on the sand. He indicates the phone Sandy gave me. 'I've called nine-nine-nine. The ambulance won't be long.'

I caress my sister's face, smoothing the strands of hair away, trying to warm her cold cheeks. Out at sea, the boat is still burning. I go to take off my jacket to add to Bess's coverings.

Tyler puts his hand on my arm to stop me. 'No,' he says. 'You need that, you're shivering.'

I look down at my arms. He's right, though I realize it only in that moment. I am trembling from head to toe. A terrible pain sears through me. Everything I've done since Rik told me Dad was alive has been for nothing.

Because Dad is gone again. Gone for ever.

Leaving Tyler with Bess, I stand up and stumble across the beach. Away from the fire, still blazing at the end of the jetty, all is darkness and silence. The only glimpses of light come in the white curls of the waves, glinting in the moonshine. The only sound, the faint lapping of those waves against the shore.

I'm too numb to cry.

And then I catch movement at the far end of the beach. I freeze. A dark shape is rising up, out of the water, staggering on to the sand. I hold my breath, waiting for the shape to take form. A man. He lifts his hand, then starts running towards us.

Dad.

My heart leaps with joy and relief as he pounds across the sand. I run to him and hurl myself into his arms. He is wet through, his sea-sodden jacket soaking into me. For a single, fleeting moment I remember exactly how safe his hugs used to make me feel. Then Dad pulls away, shivering, his damp fingers on my face. 'Is . . . is Bess—?'

'She's fine, I think,' I say, pointing back along the beach. 'Tyler saved her.'

We race towards them.

'What about Rik?' Dad asks, panting as we run.

'He stayed on board to get the diamond from the fire,' I explain. 'He was right over the motor when it exploded.'

Dad nods, his expression dark, serious.

'The diamond is gone too,' I say.

'Good.' He sounds like he means it.

We reach the others. Dad drops to his knees and reaches for Bess's hand. 'Butterbug?' he breathes.

It's his old name for Bess.

Bess gazes up at him, with wide round eyes. I'm about to explain that she doesn't speak, that she hasn't said a word since he disappeared seventeen months ago, when Bess herself opens her mouth.

'Daddy?' she lisps.

My heart jolts into my throat.

'Oh, Butterbug,' Dad says. He looks up at me, holding out his hand for me. I take it and kneel beside him, as Bess struggles on to her elbows.

'Daddy?' she says again. Her voice is slow and rasping and uncertain.

'Bess . . . you're . . . how . . . ?' I can't even form my swirling thoughts into a question. I just stare at her, utterly bewildered.

How has her voice just switched back on like that?

Tyler fades away into the darkness, as Dad pulls Bess and me into another, huge hug. We sit on the sand together for a few silent moments. Dad holds us tight. His cheek feels damp where it presses against mine. For a second I wonder if he's hurt, if it's blood. Then I realize that he is crying.

Sirens sound in the distance.

‘That’ll be the ambulance,’ Tyler says. ‘And the police.’

Dad draws back, letting Bess and me go.

Bess gazes at him, her face lost in wonder.

‘You’re on the beach, Butterbug, you’re safe.’ Dad talks in a low, soothing voice, his hand stroking her arm.

Bess leans against him, closing her eyes. I gaze at her, my head still spinning. The sirens grow louder. I stand up, as Tyler reappears from the shadows. Without speaking he puts his arms around me and we hold each other. The warmth of his body seeps into mine. Blue lights flash along the shore in the distance.

‘We should get Bess down to the ambulance,’ Tyler says.

‘Yes.’ Dad picks her up and carries her along the sand in his arms.

Tyler and I follow.

I’m still numb, unable to process what’s just happened. As we draw closer to the blue lights, voices drift towards us. I can make out snatches of their conversation.

‘It’s a family!’

‘Did you see what happened?’

‘Looks like a boat went up.’

Tyler reaches for my hand. I grip it tightly as shadowy figures hurry towards us. Seconds later we’re surrounded. Separated. Someone asks for our names. A grey-haired police officer is frowning, talking to Dad with a serious expression. Every now and then I catch sight of Tyler, rubbing his forehead as he speaks to another police officer. A young paramedic fusses over Bess, wrapping a silver foil blanket around her shoulders.

I don't say anything.

Somehow speaking will make it all real. Images rise up in my mind: Rik hurling himself towards the diamond. The boat blowing up. Tyler carrying Bess to safety.

And Dad, on the beach. Alive.

Someone puts a blanket round me and bundles me into the same ambulance as Bess. I've lost sight of Tyler completely. I feel empty, as if all the life has drained out of me. The paramedics let me sit in silence. I hear one whisper to the other:

'It's shock,' he says. 'She's in shock.'

I sit, staring out to sea through the open ambulance door. The hubbub of voices around me fades as I listen to the rhythmic suck and spew of the waves, watching as they swallow up the beach, then spit it out again.

38

We arrive at the hospital and Bess and I are put in a cubicle together. A warm, smiley nurse checks us over, then explains that Tyler is talking to the police about what happened down at the jetty. She says they'll want to talk to me soon as well, then she asks for Mum's name. I write it down on a piece of paper for her.

I still don't speak.

After a few minutes, I peer through the cubicle curtains. There's no sign of Tyler and I haven't seen Dad since the beach.

Is he even here? Or has he slipped away, back into the night?

I go back inside the cubicle and sink into the chair beside the hospital trolley where Bess is sipping at a carton of milk. There's one for me, but I have no appetite.

More time passes, I have no idea how much. A doctor comes in and examines us both. She spends a while with Bess, then strides over and shines a light in my eyes. She asks me to follow her finger in the air and does a weird tapping thing with a small metal pencil against my knees. Then she gives a brisk nod, pronounces us both 'physically okay', and leaves.

Outside the drawn curtains, I hear Mum's agitated voice before I see her.

'I knew something dreadful would happen today,' she's saying breathlessly as she hurries along. 'A negative Saturn-Pluto conjunction in my fourth house – that's the house of home and family.'

I brace myself, ready for her to yell or cry hysterically when she sees us. A second later, she sweeps in past the curtain. She's wearing a sequinned pink-and-red dress, with a long, glittering scarf wound round her curls and hot-pink lipstick that matches her highlights and ankle boots. Of course, I remember dimly that she was at some function this evening and must have been torn away to come here. *Great.* Another reason for her to be furious with me.

Mum casts an anxious glance at me, then goes over to Bess.

'Bess?' she asks, gently.

Bess looks up and gives her a cheeky grin. 'Hello, Mummy,' she says, as if it's the most normal thing in the world for her to be talking.

Mum lets out a sob, sweeping Bess into a huge hug. I

watch Bess melt into her arms, relief expressed through her whole body.

I wish I could go back to that feeling, the one that you have when you still think your parents can protect you from everything.

When it feels like they hold up the whole world.

Mum murmurs something I can't hear into Bess's ear.

Bess looks up in surprise. 'Yes, I did,' she says. 'It all just went dark and then Daddy was there and I said "hello".'

Mum hugs her again, tears streaming down her face.

The smiley nurse appears, and says she wants to check Bess over one more time. She also explains that the police are waiting to talk to me, but she's told them I need another hour or two first.

Mum comes over to the corner of the cubicle where I'm still curled up in my chair. The scent of her perfume fills the air. The nurse chatters away to Bess, asking how she's feeling, deftly checking her pulse as she speaks.

Mum perches on the arm of the chair. She leans in to me, wiping her face. I swallow hard, ready for the onslaught.

'Cat,' she says softly.

I look up, bracing myself for her fury.

'I'm sorry,' she says.

I stare at her, my jaw dropping.

'I'm so sorry,' Mum repeats. 'For not believing you about Dad. For . . . for letting you carry all this, all alone.'

Tears prick at my eyes. We gaze at each other. 'I spoke to Tyler outside,' Mum goes on. 'He told me about Rik . . . the boat . . .' She hesitates. 'And how your father was there.'

So Dad's gone again. I look away. I can't bear Mum seeing the humiliation in my eyes.

Mum reaches for my hand and squeezes my fingers. 'Nothing that's happened is your fault, Cat, you've been really brave, trying to get to the truth, doing whatever it took to protect your sister.' She tips back her head with a long sigh and, sounding more like herself, says: 'I should have realized. I did your dad's chart the day I met him. The signs were all there that he would never be . . . well, let's just say he was never going to be the most reliable partner, but my goodness, he was charming.'

I stare at her. Lost in her memories, her eyes shine as she speaks. 'When I fell in love, it wasn't just with him. It was with the way that when he was around, my dull, grey world exploded into colour.' She smiles over at Bess, then at me and, I find, suddenly, that I'm smiling, sadly, back. 'I'll never forget our time together, because he gave me you two,' she says, 'but the truth is that there were always issues with your dad, especially over money.' She pauses.

'It must have been a huge shock to see him, to discover he was alive? Everything that meant?' She pauses. I say nothing. 'Tyler said he told you about his gambling debts?'

I nod.

'You must have a lot of questions?' Mum pauses again. She's giving me time to talk, I realize, prompting me to open up about Dad and how his reappearance makes me feel. But what's the point of talking about him? He was dead, then alive and now gone.

The whole thing might as well have not happened. I swallow down my hurt, blinking away the tears that prick at my eyes.

'He did – does – love you very much, you know.' Mum gazes at me, as if she's deciding whether or not to tell me something. 'When your dad died – as we all believed – I discovered the extent of his debts. I was forced to pay off a lot of what he owed and ended up desperate for money. I own our house, of course, but my income wasn't enough to cover the debts plus all our expenses plus Bess's therapist and her tutor . . .' She sighs. 'Anyway, I want you to understand *that's* why I started taking on so many clients, working so hard. I told myself I had to let the spiritual basis for my astrological beliefs take a backseat, that I needed to focus on making money.'

I frown. I have never heard Mum talk like this.

'But I realize now,' Mum goes on, speaking softly, 'that I got carried away and all the material things I collected – my fancy clothes and all the crystals and pictures and ornaments I've been collecting in the spare room – they became an end in themselves. I lost sight of what really mattered: you two.' She plants a kiss on my forehead, then lets out a sigh. 'I love you, Cat, and I promise, from now on things will be different.' She glances at Bess. The nurse examining her is clearly finishing up – smoothing down her apron and stepping away. 'The miracle of your sister speaking again is just the first step,' Mum whispers.

The nurse announces Bess is fine and leaves the cubicle. Mum goes back over to Bess, feeling her forehead and fussing around her in a way that she hasn't for ages. As I slip out, unnoticed, Bess asks for a puppy. It must be the hundredth time she's made this request to Mum, albeit the first in actual words.

I hesitate, just outside the cubicle. Mum said just now things would change. Was that true?

There's a tiny pause and then Mum says. 'Of course, my lovely, a puppy is just what we need.'

I smile, feeling more like myself for the first time since arriving at the hospital. I stroll along the corridor, wondering where Tyler is. Past the nurses' desk, I reach the electronic doors. They part automatically, releasing me into the cool night air. There are a few other people here, a couple smoking and an old man checking his phone. I wander over to a low wall by a lamp post and sit down, my chin propped in my hands.

'How are you doing, Kitterbug?'

It's Dad. *He's still here.* My heart swells in my chest. I jump to my feet.

'I thought you'd run away.' The words blurt out of me.

Dad gives me a sad smile. I notice, for the first time, the two police officers standing just to one side.

'They've given me five minutes to say goodbye,' Dad says.

'Oh. Are you being arrested?' I ask.

Dad nods.

'Will you go to prison?'

'I don't know.' Dad hesitates. 'Whatever happens, I want you to know . . . you and Bess . . . that I'll see you soon.'

'Will you come home then . . . after . . . ?' I can hear the yearning in my voice. 'Dad?'

His mouth trembles. 'I'm afraid there's no way back for your mum and me,' he stammers. 'But I want you to meet Julie properly. And get to know your half-brother.'

I stare at him. 'Finn.'

'Yes,' Dad says. 'Finn. He's a cute kid . . .' He reaches

down and kisses my cheek. 'I love you, Cat.' He draws away, offers me a final smile, then he turns and lets the two police officers lead him away.

I watch, a dull ache in my stomach as he disappears into the trees. Having him back isn't what I thought it would be at all. He's changed too much: Dad 2.0, still the sun, just not burning quite so brightly.

Or maybe it's me that's changed.

'Hey, you,' Tyler says softly.

I look up. He's come right up beside me without me noticing. He smiles, the curve of his cheek lit by the lamplight.

'Would you rather be alone?' he asks. 'Cos I can—'

'I'd like to sit here with you.' The words fly effortlessly out of me, straight and true. Possibly they're the most honest words I've ever said to him. I smile to myself.

We perch on the wall, side by side.

'I told the police everything,' Tyler says. 'They want to talk to you too, but I'm almost sure they'll arrest Rik's Aunt Sandy.'

'Good,' I say.

There's a short pause. 'My dad's been freaking out about everything that happened,' Tyler goes on.

'That's funny,' I say. 'Because my mum hasn't.'

Tyler hesitates. 'Are you okay?' he asks. 'Not the fire and all that . . . but your dad?'

I gaze at his face. The face of my friend. And, suddenly, I know that I'll survive without Dad back at home.

'Not really,' I say, honestly. 'But I will be.'

'I guess . . .' Tyler makes a face. 'At least your dad got Bess speaking again.'

'Nah,' I say, shaking my head. 'What happened tonight might have been like . . . a final trigger, but I've been thinking for a while that she was on the verge of talking.' I pause. 'Actually, you and your dad, this summer . . . you've really helped her.'

Tyler frowns. 'What do you mean?'

I shrug. 'Just that you paid her attention . . . in a calm way, really *listened* to her. Which maybe Mum and I haven't. And that's what she needed.'

We sit for a moment, letting the night air flow around our faces. The only sound is the low murmur of people's chatter and the distant hum of traffic.

'I used to think my dad was amazing,' I say. 'People always talk about him smiling and happy. Like, whenever he showed up life was a party. And for having fun he was amazing. But—' I frown, struggling to find the words I need. 'But what I realized tonight is that what really matters are the people who spend time with you, letting you be who you are . . . *listening*, like you do with Bess. Because . . .' I meet his gaze, 'because unless people are listening, it's easy to feel that there's no point speaking.'

Tyler nods slowly. 'Maybe now isn't a good time to talk about this, but I wanted you to know that I've told Dad I'd like to stay in Devon.'

I stare at him, my stomach turning somersaults. 'Really?' I ask.

'Not in your Barn, obviously,' he says, quickly. 'You'll get that back. But there's a flat a few miles away we could rent. Dad's had enquiries about restoring other stuff in the area. And . . .' he pauses, 'it turns out that though I'd like better Wi-Fi, I don't actually miss anything about London.'

'Really? I always thought that . . . that maybe you had a girlfriend back there?'

'Nah.' Tyler shifts a bit closer, the golden-brown of his eyes shimmering in the lamplight. 'Anyway, there's too much here that I like,' he says.

I raise my eyebrows. 'Like what?'

Tyler shakes his head. 'You know already. And don't worry – I understand how you feel. You've made it clear a million times.'

I frown. 'How I *feel*?'

'Yeah,' Tyler says. 'It's there all the time, the way you . . . you always pull back.' He sighs. 'I get it. You're just not interested. Not like *that*.'

What is he talking about?

'But, even so, I figured that if I don't say something, I'll never know for absolutely sure, so tell me. How do you feel?' He pauses, his eyes locked on mine.

I stare at him, all sounds fading away. All I see is the yearning in his eyes.

'Cat?' he whispers. 'How do you feel about us?'

'Us?' I breathe. A million memories flutter through my head. All the times I thought Tyler wasn't interested. All the times I shrank away, not wanting him to see how much I liked him. 'There's an us?' I whisper, tilting my face towards his.

A tiny smile curves around Tyler's lips. And, as he leans forward and kisses me, I feel his smile flow, easy as the sea, into mine.

39
THREE WEEKS LATER

8:25 a.m. and the bus drops me at the end of the road. I smooth down my new uniform as I get off and stroll self-consciously to the school gates. I'm trying to look calm and confident, but my stomach is a bundle of knotted rope, tightening with every step. At least I like the clothes for Buckton Stanleigh Academy. There's no special stuff with a logo you have to buy, like there was at my last school, just a navy skirt to the knee, a plain white shirt and a navy cardigan or jumper. In fact, until half an hour ago I was super-excited at the prospect of coming here . . . a new school means the chance to reinvent myself, to make friends and leave all the misery from my old school behind.

But now I'm actually here, my legs are shaking and my mouth is dry.

I reach the school gates. I'm early and there are only a few other students strolling past. None of them pay me much attention. I lean against the wall beside the gate railings, trying to build up the courage to go in. Mum offered to drop me here this morning, but didn't make a fuss when I said I'd rather come alone.

She wouldn't have done either of those things before the summer.

I'm kind of regretting not being able to hide out in her car right now, but I can't blame Mum for that. She's been great the past few weeks. Not only did she keep her promise to get a dog – a gorgeous brown crossbreed that Bess immediately named Rescue – but she's also spent hours playing with the pair of them, helping Bess find her voice again. In fact, Bess is talking more and more now, doing better every day. She even started back at primary school this week.

Mum hasn't just given Bess what she needs. She's really listening to me as well. She actually cleared out the spare room so that I could move into it. It's *so* brilliant, I love it, with plenty of space for all my sewing and a proper double bed next to a huge walk-in closet.

Mum's sold or given away most of the ornaments and crystals and stuff that were in the room before. She's cleared out the attic too. I couldn't believe she was prepared to do that, but she said all the clutter was weighing her down. She's also cut back on her posh clients and given up her plans to rent out the Barn to high-paying guests.

Instead, she's going to use it as a retreat for people who need 'somewhere safe and welcoming to heal'. It won't make anywhere near as much money as she'd originally intended, but Mum says it will help her get back to the spiritual side of her astrology.

'I left that stupid TV show all those years ago in order to reconnect with that aspect of myself,' she told me with a sigh, 'and I was so much happier as a result. But then, after your dad left, I lost the connection again. Now I've got it back. For good this time.'

I don't really understand what she means, but what I do know is that for the first time in ages she's prepared to take what *I* want into account. For instance, she let me leave the school I hated. We had a long talk about that and I told her how unhappy I'd been, how much I wanted a fresh start. She did some research and suggested I came here, to Buckton Stanleigh Academy. It's smaller than my last school, but they have a great art department that includes a Practical Creatives room with a couple of sewing machines alongside the woodworking benches and photography equipment. I'll even be able to work on my dress designs as part of my coursework.

A girl walking past squeals with laughter, bringing me back to the school gates. The pavement is crowded with people now. The girl who laughed is now grinning at the mixed group beside her. She's wearing a beautiful jade-green coat over her school uniform.

I'm planning on making a coat this autumn myself, in my beautiful new bedroom. I glance around nervously. I just hope I'll make some friends here. At least I've got Tyler now. And Dad.

In the end, the police decided not to press charges against Dad. It helped that he told them everything he knew about Rik – and Sandy, who's been arrested herself now. Once he was free, Dad visited us. He explained he's planning to move back to Devon and find a new home for him and Julie and Finn. Julie's already applying for nursing jobs and Dad says he's going to get work either as a painter and decorator or running a boat-hire business.

I'm pleased, I guess, but not in the way I imagined I would be. After everything that's happened it's going to take a while to get used to Dad being in our lives again, to trust that he won't lie or disappear again.

Last week Mum drove me and Bess all the way to Norfolk to see Dad and to meet Julie and Finn properly. I could tell Mum had to make a big effort to do all that, but it went okay. Julie was really nice. There was even a moment when Dad started crawling around making silly animal noises, with Finn and Bess on his back. We were all laughing and I saw Mum and Julie look at each other and I don't know what they were both thinking, but it was obvious that *they* knew because they smiled at each other and, after that, Mum relaxed.

Later, Dad took me out sailing. It was good, having that time with him on our own, but I was glad in the end to go back to the house so that Mum and Bess and I could get into our car and drive home.

'Hey, Cat!' A familiar voice jumpstarts me out of my memories.

I look up. The school gates are busy now, lots of girls and boys swarming past. To my astonishment, Cindy Cho is standing in front of me. She's wearing the same Buckton uniform of navy skirt and white shirt as I am – and a super-surprised expression on her face.

'Hi!' My jaw drops. 'Cindy! What are you doing here?'

Cindy smiles, creating a dimple in her cheek. I smile back, not just because I'm pleased to see her, but because that dimple reminds me of how much fun we had when we were friends.

'Oh, my days, it's so weird seeing you here,' Cindy says, still smiling. 'I begged Mum and Dad to let me switch schools at the end of last term. I know a couple of the girls here. I live just around the corner, remember?'

'Of course I remember.' The smile fades from my face. If Cindy is here, now, with a bunch of new friends, then chances are I'm going to be just as much of an outcast as I was before, in our old school.

'This is such a coincidence,' Cindy goes on, running a nervous hand through her sleek black ponytail. Her smile is faltering now, too. 'I had no idea you'd be here.'

'No, well, you wouldn't, would you?' The words shoot out of me harsher than I mean them to. I grimace, my cheeks burning.

Cindy frowns. 'I . . . I just mean that we lost touch, so . . .'

'We didn't exactly lose touch,' I point out. 'You stopped wanting to have anything to do with me. And you went out and got yourself a new bestie to go to parties with – Delilah Jenkins.'

Cindy's mouth gapes. '*What?*' she says, indignantly. '*You're* the one who stopped wanting to be friends with *me*. I tried really hard after your dad, but you didn't want to know . . . And I'm not friends with Delilah. I hated that school after we stopped being friends. And Delilah only invited me along to that stupid party so she could come to my house and hang out with my brother who, by the way, doesn't like her any more than I do.'

There's a pause. Traffic is building up by the school entrance, teenagers of all shapes and sizes swarming past. Cindy shifts her backpack from one shoulder to the other.

I stare at her. Tyler's words about me keeping my distance echo in my head. Maybe Cindy really did only back off because she thought I was pulling away myself.

Maybe I did pull away.

'Your brother always was cool,' I say, grinning at her.

Cindy glances at me, her expression wary. The corners of her lips twitch, the faintest hint of a fresh smile.

'I didn't know you were crushing on Jin?'

My eyes widen. 'No, I'm not, I wasn't,' I reply quickly. 'I mean, he's great but I . . . I'm with someone . . .' I trail off, feeling self-conscious.

'Ooh, tell me.' Cindy's smile broadens, her dimple reappearing. 'Hey, was it that gorgeous guy sitting next to you on the bus the other day? What's his name? Does he come to school here?'

'Yes, he's called Tyler,' I say, feeling the heat rise in my face as I say his name. 'And no, he goes to a school a few miles away, but we see each other at weekends and a couple of times in the week too.' I smile, filling with the warm glow that thoughts of Tyler always bring me.

'Wow,' Cindy says. We gaze at each other.

'It's really nice to see you,' I say.

'Yeah,' she says. 'You too. Shall we go in and find our form room?' She turns to face the school, a huge red-brick building.

'So how was your summer?' she asks, as we walk through the main gates. 'Mine was kind of boring.'

'As it happens,' I say with a grin, 'mine was anything but.'

'Ooh, tell me,' Cindy urges.

And, as we cross the tarmac together, with the sun on our faces and excited chatter rising in the air around us, I launch into my story.

ACKNOWLEDGEMENTS

With thanks to Moira Young, Gaby Halberstam, Julie Mackenzie, Melanie Edge – and, especially, Lou Kuenzler.

Turn the page for a nail-biting extract
from the multi award-winning and bestselling
Girl, Missing, the thriller everyone's reading!

'PLEASE READ THIS BOOK: IT IS BRILLIANT'
Guardian

WHO AM I?

Who am I?

I sat at the computer in Mum's office and stared at the essay heading. New form teachers always give you homework like that at the start of the year.

Who am I?

When I was younger it was easy. I'd just write down obvious stuff like: *I am Lauren Matthews. I have brown hair and blue eyes.*

But now we're supposed to write about what interests us. Likes and dislikes. Who we are 'inside'.

I needed a break.

I texted my friend Jam. *hw u dng w/ stpd 'who am i' thng?*

A minute later he texted back: *We are sorry to inform you that James 'Jam' Caldwell died from boredom while working on his homework earlier tonight.*

I laughed out loud. Jam always cheers me up. Some of the girls in my class tease me about him. Make out he's my boyfriend. Which is like the stupidest thing ever. Jam and I have been friends since Primary.

Who am I?

I put my head in my hands.

How can anyone work out who they are, unless they know where they come from?

And I have no idea where I come from.

I was adopted when I was three.

A minute later and Mum was calling from downstairs. 'Lauren. Tea's ready.'

I raced down, glad to get away from the essay.

I didn't get away from it for long.

'How's the homework going?' Mum asked, prodding something in a frying pan.

'Mmmn,' I mumbled.

'For goodness' sake, Lauren,' Mum sighed. 'Why can't you speak properly?'

I looked at her. Same old Mum. Short. Bony. Thin-lipped.

I look nothing like her.

I spoke very clearly and slowly. 'Who is my real mother?'

Mum froze. For a second she looked terrified. Then her face went hard like a mask. No emotion.

'I am,' she said. 'What do you mean?'

'Nothing.' I looked away, wishing I hadn't said anything.

Mum sat down, the frying pan still in her hand.

'I thought you weren't bothered about knowing,' she said.

I rolled my eyes. 'I'm not.'

Mum ladled scrambled eggs onto my plate. 'Anyway, I can't tell you. It was a closed adoption. That means neither side knows anything about the other.' She got up, replaced the frying pan on the cooker and turned back to me. Her face was all anxious now. 'Has someone said something at school?'

'No.' I bent over my eggs. Trust Mum to assume somebody else was putting ideas in my head. It would be too much for her to imagine I might have started thinking about it for myself.

'What's for tea?' Rory pelted in from the garden, his fat cheeks red from the cold air. Rory's eight and the spit of my dad. 'My little test-tube miracle,' my mum calls him. All I can say is, a lot of unpleasant things grow in test tubes.

Rory skidded to a halt at the table, then made a face. 'Scrambled eggs stink.'

'Not as much as you,' I said.

Rory picked up his fork and prodded me with it.

'Ow. Mum, he's hitting me.'

Mum glared at us both. 'Sit, Rory.' Sometimes I wonder if she thinks he's a dog. I heard her say once to a friend, 'Boys are like puppies. All they need is affection and fresh air. Girls are much harder work.'

So why choose me – a girl – in the first place? I remembered all the times when I was little that Mum talked to me about being adopted – about how they picked me out of some catalogue. It used to make me feel special. Wanted. Now it made me feel like a mail-order dress. A dress that didn't fit but that was too much trouble to send back.

'Can Jam come round later?' I asked.

'When you've done your homework – if it isn't too late,' came Mum's predictable reply.

'These eggs look like your puke,' Rory said.

Sometimes I really, really hate him.

I emailed Jam as soon as I went back upstairs.

C u l8r?

His reply came back in seconds: *ill b thr @ 7.*

I checked the time on the corner of the screen: 6.15. I was never going to finish my essay in forty-five minutes.

Who am I?

Adopted. Lost. I typed the words into the search engine box.

I'd been thinking about it a lot recently. Last week I'd even checked out some of the adoption information websites. You'd have laughed if you'd seen me: heart thumping, palms sweating, stomach screwed up into a knot.

I mean, it's not as if there's going to be some site that says: *Lauren Matthews – click here for your adoption details.*

Anyway. D'you know what I found out?

That if I wanted to know anything about my life before I was three, I needed Mum and Dad's permission.

How unbelievable is that?

My life. My identity. My past.

But their decision.

Even if I asked, there's no way Mum would say yes. Well, you've seen how she is about the subject. Gets a face on her like a smashed plate.

It would serve her right if I went ahead and did it anyway.

I clicked on the search icon.

Adopted. Lost. Nearly a million hits.

My heart thudded. I could feel my stomach clenching again.

I sat back in my chair. Enough.

I was just wasting time. Putting off the homework. I reached over to close the search. And that's when I caught sight of it: *Missing-Children.com.* An international site for lost or missing children. I frowned. I mean, how do you lose a child and them not turn up? I can see how you might lose one for five minutes. Or even an hour. And I know sometimes children go missing 'cause some psycho's murdered them. But Mum's always saying that only happens like once or twice a year.

I clicked through to the homepage. It was a flickering mass of faces. Each face the size of a stamp; each stamp turning into a new face after a few seconds.

My jaw dropped. Did all these faces belong to missing children? I saw a search field. I hesitated. Then I tapped in my name. *Lauren.* I wasn't really thinking about what I was doing. Just messing about – seeing how many missing Laurens there were out there.

It turned out there were one hundred and seventy-two. Jeez. The computer was flashing at me to refine my search.

Part of me wanted to stop. But I told myself not to be stupid. The flickering faces on the screen weren't adopted children like me – with no past. They were missing kids. Kids with *only* a past.

I just wanted to see who was there.

I added my birth month to the search criteria, then watched as three Laurens appeared on the screen. One was black, missing since she was two weeks old.

One was white with blonde hair – she looked about nine or ten. Yeah – she'd only been missing five years.

I stared at the third child.

Martha Lauren Purditt
Case type: lost, injured, missing
Date of birth: March 12
Age now: 14
Birth place: Evanport, Connecticut, USA
Hair: brown *Eyes: blue*

I looked at the face above the words. A chubby, smiling little girl's face. Then at the date she'd gone missing: *September 8.*

Less than two months before I was adopted.

My heart seemed to stop beating.

The birth date was a couple of days out. And I was British, not from America like the missing girl.

So it wasn't possible.

Was it?

The question seeped like a drug through my head, turning me upside down and inside out, filling me up.

Could I be her?

ABOUT THE AUTHOR

Sophie McKenzie is the multi award-winning original queen of teen thrillers, whose debut, *Girl, Missing*, is still a top-ten YA bestseller sixteen years after first publication. She has followed its success with two further books in the Missing series: *Sister, Missing* and *Missing Me*, as well as many other teen thriller and romance novels, including The Medusa Project series, *Blood Ties* and *Blood Ransom*. Sophie's first adult novel, *Close My Eyes*, was selected for the Richard and Judy Book Club. Sophie's books have sold more than a million copies in the UK alone and are translated and sold all over the world. She lives in North London.

www.sophiemckenziebooks.com
Twitter: @sophiemckenzie_